REBEL
JEWEL

NATALINA REIS

--------------HOT TREE PUBLISHING--------------

Rebel Jewel © 2019 by Natalina Reis

Rebel Jewel is a work of fiction. All names, characters, events and places found therein are either from the author's imagination or used fictitiously. Any similarity to persons alive or dead, actual events, locations, or organizations is entirely coincidental and not intended by the author.

For information, contact the publisher, Hot Tree Publishing.

WWW.HOTTREEPUBLISHING.COM

EDITING: HOT TREE EDITING

FORMATTING: RMGraphX

COVER DESIGNER: SOXSATIONAL COVER ART

E-book ISBN: 978-1-925853-59-9

Paperback ISBN: 978-1-925853-60-5

BOOKS

M/F STAND-ALONES
HER REAL MAN
LOVED YOU ALWAYS
BLIND MAGIC
FICTIONAL-ISH

M/M STAND-ALONES
LAVENDER FIELDS
INFINITE BLUE

THE JEWEL CHRONICLES
DESERT JEWEL
SNOW JEWEL
REBEL JEWEL

*Dedicated to all men and women who stand for what is right
and bring light to a dark world.*

GLOSSARY

buugengs - a Northern weapon in the shape of a large S with blades on both ends

duivel - devil

dyrbar en - precious one

Fjorden - native of the northern lands

gele - complex tall headdress

hema - small, primitive house

indent - slave

iqhiya – turban-like hat

iyalorixá - mother of the saints/priestress of Afro-Brazilian religions

kanga - African print fabric

kidojo moja - little one

kupigana - fight

malaika - angel

matangazos - neck and shoulder markings of the Nyota people

min lilla kärlek - my little love

mjumbe - holy messenger

msichana - girl

mtoto - child

msuti - jungle lizard

mtoto wangu tamu - my sweet baby

ndege mdogo - little bird

nguba – wedding blanket

nzuri ya kufa - pretty mortal

orisa - demigods of African-Brazilian mythology

upanga - sword

wimbo wa moyo - my heart's song

wyverns - dragons

CHAPTER ONE

The Call Home

The smell of blood suffocated him. There was no running from it. It surrounded him, tightening its nauseating grip on Jaali's senses, clinging to his nostrils, not letting him go.

Where is Milenda? Jaali scanned the area around him, his glance bouncing off objects and undefined shapes, straining through the red fog closing in on him. Even the mist was tinted with blood, snaking over the wet ground, the exhale of a hidden monster. Milenda was nowhere to be seen. His heart pumped harder, the drumming echoing in his ears, deafening and frantic.

He tried to move, but invisible hands held him steadfast, feet rooted to the dirt-covered ground, unseen shackles around his ankles, breaking through skin and digging into his flesh.

No, not again.

With all the strength he had left, Jaali pulled and pushed against whatever held him in place, the sting of wounded flesh shooting up his legs, a feeling all too familiar to him.

He was enslaved again. He thrashed harder, blood now running down to his bare feet, warm and frightening.

A shadow emerged from the fog. *Milenda!* But, no, it couldn't be. Its frame was too tall and broad. Jaali opened his mouth to yell for help, but the word never left his lips. Panic rose inside of him, insidious and overwhelming. Why had they returned to Afrika? He had warned his wife it was too dangerous. Too many people wanted them dead.

The shadowy figure took shape as it approached him—brown legs the size of tree trunks and long arms to match.

No, no, no.

The sight of an impressive bald head choked him. It couldn't be. The *duivel* was dead. And yet, there he was, striding toward him like an out-of-control transport. Jaali yelled out, his voice freed from whatever was muting it, and pulled harder on the invisible chains holding his ankles. To no avail. The shackles held steady as if glued to the ground.

The slaver proceeded toward him, a cruel smirk curling the corners of his lips. "I've got you now, my beautiful boy. You can't run this time." Mnyama threw his massive weight into his stride, coming closer and closer to Jaali. "It's been too long. Ready to give me some of that milky goodness?"

"You're dead," Jaali screamed, his voice absorbed by the thick fog. "It's not possible."

The large man took a few more steps, a growl-like chuckle leaving his lips. "Well, I'm not. And I missed you, little white boy. My friends missed you too."

From the thickest part of the fog, where the blood seemed to have coagulated into disgusting blobs, a few more shadows appeared, coalescing into several human bodies, both male and female—all unwelcome echoes of his past. The slaver had brought his cronies.

"No, you're dead." Jaali's voice came out as a sob, a heart-wrenching plea to whatever gods were listening. "I killed you."

The group of human shadows united in their progress toward him. "It's about time we have ourselves a good orgy." Mnyama glanced at his friends. "Any preference about who does the boy first?"

He couldn't be sure the ear-splitting scream he heard came from himself. Jaali closed his eyes tight and, like a mantra, repeated the words, "It's not possible. You're dead, *duivel*. This is only a nightmare."

"Well, you should have stayed in Isvärld," a familiar female voice said. "You wouldn't be going through this again."

Fearfully, Jaali opened his eyes. The slaver and his friends were gone, and Freya was in their place, her barely covered body resting sensually on a padded bench. What was she doing in Afrika?

"Yes, it's me, handsome." The goddess covered a yawn with a graceful hand. "You wouldn't yield to me while you could, and now you're fodder for these savages. You could have had all this." Freya ran a hand suggestively along her body. "Instead you're going to be ravished by animals."

"They're not real," Jaali said, not sure he was talking to the goddess or himself. "*You*'re not real."

"What about all this blood?" the goddess asked, sweeping

a hand in front of her. "You should have stayed in Isvärld under my protection. Now, you have no wife, no child, and spilled the blood of thousands upon this land." She pointed at the bloody fog around them.

Jaali shook his head. "No, Milenda is safe. Johari is safe. This is just a nightmare."

Freya threw her head back, the crystal-like sounds of her laughter echoing through the thick, stifling air. "I've always liked you, Jaali. I wish you had stayed." And she was gone.

"Milenda! *Msichana!*" he called, desperation taking a firmer hold on him. Where was his wife? Was Freya telling the truth? Had he lost the two people he loved more than life itself?

Out of the threatening fog, the hooded figures of the Elders emerged, their faces in shadow and hands hidden in the wide sleeves of their clothes. Jaali watched their slow procession toward him, the humming of their voices resonating inside his head—just like during the trials. He closed his eyes and opened them again, hoping they'd be gone, but they still advanced, human lava coming to destroy him.

"Contender! Listen carefully." The voices came from inside his head, not from the moving men. "Your wife doesn't belong on the throne of Natale, aberration that she is. And your daughter—she's neither Natalian or Fjorden. We don't have room for freaks of nature, tainted bloods. We've eliminated them both. We'll let you live though so you can contemplate the consequences of your ill-advised actions for the rest of your life, *indent*. You'll be sold to the highest bidder."

All his energy had been depleted. Without Milenda and Johari, he was an empty vessel. Tears rolled down his cheeks, pooling in the corners of his nose and dripping on his lips. He closed his eyes again. Maybe if he lay down face-first in the lake of blood collecting around his ankles, he'd be blessed with the oblivion of death.

"Jaali, Jaali." Someone shook him, but he didn't want to open his eyes. There was nothing left for him to see on this earth. But the voice insisted, and warm hands gripped his shoulders and shook him again. "Wake up, Jaali. You're having that nightmare again."

Reality slowly sank in and, with it, a wave of pure joy surged through his whole being. He opened his eyes to his beautiful wife, looking at him with a slight frown, her green eyes clouded with worry. It was a nightmare, nothing else. Still sobbing, he drew Milenda into his arms and hugged her tightly, his quivering lips finding shelter in the crook of her neck.

"I'm so happy you're here," he said, voice choked with emotion. His wife was alive and so was his daughter. "Mnyama was in my dream, coming for me again. The Elders had killed…." His voice halted, not able to say the words.

Milenda brushed a hand over the back of his head, smoothing his hair and his fears. "Shhh, *wimbo wa moyo*, it was just a dream. Mnyama is dead, and we're fine. We're better than fine. We're all together and happy."

His sobs turned into laughter as he pulled away from his

wife and feasted his eyes on her amber skin, her full pink lips, and the emeralds of her eyes. "I love you."

Their lips came together in a long, desperate kiss. He had been drowning in sorrow just minutes before. Now, he needed her flavor, her touch to swim back to the surface, to hold on to life.

His nightmares had returned recently, and he was all too afraid it could mean only one thing: they would be called back to Afrika soon. Jaali didn't know Milenda's feelings on the matter, as they both avoided talking about the inevitable return to her homeland for fear of bursting their happy bubble. All he knew was that *he* was not ready.

* * *

"Leave Mjusi alone, Johari. The poor *msitu* is exhausted." Milenda tried to make her voice sound stern and authoritative, but a smile crept to her lips instead. She couldn't resist the crystalline giggle of her daughter as she wobbled after the small dragon.

Spring was in full bloom, and the air had grown warm enough for Milenda to shed her restricting winter clothes and don her beloved *kanga* dresses. She and Johari had gone to the forest to gather mushrooms, but the excursion had taken a lot longer than Milenda had expected. Her daughter was a small ball of energy that never stopped. She had spent more time chasing after Johari than actually hunting for the fungi.

While chasing Mjusi, Johari's little legs gave in under her and she fell on her well-padded bottom, lifting a small cloud of dirt around her. At first surprised, the toddler soon recovered and began gathering handfuls of soil and throwing it up in the air. It fell on her curly silver hair and bare legs like a brown rain shower that made the child giggle again.

Milenda laughed, shaking her head. "Look at the mess you're making, child. Thank the gods it's not mud, or you'd look just like a little hippo calf by now."

Johari stopped for a moment and looked at her mother, her bright green eyes sparkling in the afternoon sun. "Mamma pretty," she said with a giggle. Milenda's heart melted, and bending down, she brushed the dirt off her daughter's plump little body.

"Let's go, *mdogo*. Your father probably thinks we have been eaten by a lynx." Milenda scooped her daughter from her dirt throne, and as she propped Johari on one hip, the child leaned over and placed an open-mouth kiss on her mother's lips. "Eww, sloppy kisser," Milenda said, wiping her lips with her free hand. "You're lucky I love you so much."

Milenda swooped the toddler onto her back, wrapping a large piece of *kanga* cloth around both of them. "It will be dark soon, and he'll be worried." She tied the edges of the cloth over her chest and, with a final bounce, adjusted her daughter's little body against her back. She loved feeling Johari's warmth on her own skin. It reminded the princess of when she was carrying the baby inside her.

Mjusi shook his long tail and made the funny clicking sounds he often made when he was happy. He was as patient with the toddler as he had been with Milenda when they were both little. They began their journey out of the woods and into the prairie where the river raced them like a little tyke happy to be free of winter's shackles. Her daughter's warm breath caressed the back of her neck as they walked home while Mjusi followed them half walking, half flying.

As they approached Hoppas, a small figure came scrambling toward them, tripping over its tail with every other step. "Look, it's Gavå. She missed you."

Johari wiggled on her back, uttering nonsensical words. "All right, I'll let you down." Milenda set the basket with the mushrooms down and untied the *kanga* fabric from around her, carefully depositing her daughter on the ground. The baby dragon pounced on the little girl and proceeded to lick her face with a rough, long, forked tongue. Johari's delighted laughter spilled off her like popping bubbles.

Milenda draped the cloth over her shoulder and stared at the tall shape of her husband as it cut through the early evening horizon. Her heart still skipped a beat or two every time she laid eyes on Jaali. More than two years had passed since their wedding, and yet her *matangazos* still lit up like a chandelier in his presence. She watched him come closer, the slight limp in his step a sad reminder of his time in the desert, fighting for the right to her hand in marriage.

"*Msichana*, I was worried." Jaali opened his arms, and Milenda threw herself into their shelter, wrapping hers around his neck. He bent down and gently took her lower lip between his before covering it completely with his mouth. The feeling never changed—Jaali's lips were as familiar to her as her own. His arms and his kiss felt like home no matter where they were or whatever danger they were facing.

She moaned against him, surrendering as she always did to his body and soul, the words *I love you* never too far from her lips. "Johari made me chase her all over the woods. You know how she gets, *wimbo wa moyo*."

He kissed the top of her head and laughed. "That's our little monkey, too much energy, no sense." Mjusi had wrapped his body around their legs, asking for attention. "Yes, I missed you too, Mjusi," Jaali said, bending down a bit to pet the dragon.

With Johari scampering in front of them, closely followed by the baby dragon, Milenda and Jaali made their way to their cottage hand in hand. The sun was beginning to fade in the horizon. It wouldn't totally disappear, not in the spring in Isvärld when the days became longer and the nights short-lived. Soon there would be only white nights, when the light of the candles was not necessary to guide their steps.

"Ebba brought us rabbit stew," Jaali told her, tucking her closer to him. "It smells delicious. Are you hungry?"

"I'm famished." She hadn't eaten since before they had left to the woods late morning. "Thank the gods for Ebba. If we were dependent on my cooking, we would have starved by now." Milenda was being too modest. Even though she had been brought up in a palace with servants to do her bidding, she had learned how to cook since then and was not without skill in the kitchen.

Milenda loved their little cottage by the river. It was small, but it had been the first place she had been totally happy for the first time in her life. After months of nothing but heartache and pain, she and Jaali had finally managed to set some roots and focus on each other. She knew it wouldn't last. In fact, she was surprised it had lasted this long. Knowing the goddesses who had taken her and her family under their wings, she fully expected to have been swept across the ocean by now.

I wonder how my father is doing. And Mama Neuysi. She often thought of them, not having received any news since before Joahri was born, but she was perfectly happy living her anonymous life in Jaali's homeland.

Crossing the threshold, Milenda took a deep whiff and sighed. "That smells amazing. My stomach is dancing with excitement inside of me." She turned to her daughter who was still rolling around with Gavå. "Jo, let's have some of Aunt Ebba's stew." The little girl lifted her head, momentarily distracted by her mother's voice. "Come on, *mdogo*. Let's eat."

She sat at the small table with Jaali, Joahri perched on her father's knee, and enjoyed the intimacy and comfort of their family meal. Milenda had never had anything like that growing up in Natale. Her mother was nothing but a foggy memory, and her father, the king, had been a distant father who had not shown his love for her until shortly before she left Afrika. Mama Neuysi was the closest thing she had for a mother, and even she had not shown up in her life until it was time for Milenda to choose a husband.

"Did you get many mushrooms?" Jaali asked after dinner as they sat by the hearth to take away the chill that always came with the evening.

Johari was curled up against Gavå, eyes drooping with sleep. It wouldn't be long before the toddler and her dragon companion would be fast asleep. Mjusi had curled around himself, his tail half covering his muzzle like a blanket.

"Enough." She leaned against her husband's shoulder, her *matangazos* lighting up under the wrap she had draped over her shoulders. Being close to Jaali always triggered her Nyota's birthmarks, causing a rush of furious heat to emerge through her skin in waves of pleasure. "The little ones are exhausted. Let's put them to bed."

Jaali scooped the sleeping child in his arms and took her to the little enclosed space he had built for his daughter. It was a tiny room where Johari's cot barely fit. Gavå followed him and, as it was her habit, curled under the crib and fell asleep. Milenda watched Jaali as he tenderly lowered the girl onto the bed and covered her with a soft blanket. Her heart overflowed with love for the man who had put his life on the line to be her husband. She was so fortunate to be loved by a man like him. Johari was a rare and exquisite mixture of both of them—amber skin and green eyes like her mother and silvery hair like her father, thick and curly like Milenda's.

She smiled at Jaali as he closed the door to the small room. "I'm pretty tired myself." But even as she said the words, she knew it didn't matter—she would never be too tired for Jaali.

He crossed the space between them in two strides and cocooned her within his long arms. "Are you saying there won't be any loving tonight?" He planted a kiss on her nose as she lifted her face up to his.

"What are you giving me in return?" She caught her lower lip between her teeth, a playful twinkle in her eyes.

Jaali lowered his lips to her neck and brushed them across her neck. "I may treat you like a princess and obey all your demands."

His husky voice made her shiver in delight. "I *am* a princess, *wimbo wa moyo*." It was a weak protest as his lips caused sensory havoc in her body.

"Yes, you certainly are." Brushing his fingers along the cornucopia-shaped *matangazos*, Jaali sighed. "You rule over my heart, *msichana*. You're my princess."

Milenda hated being a princess and had always wished she was a commoner like Jaali, but when her husband called her that, her heart filled with pride. Being his princess was what she wanted, what she craved, what made her happy. That title was the one thing she would never be willing to give up on.

* * *

"Will the two of you ever stop? You go at it like rabbits." The familiar voice of Freya startled them, and Jaali—now used to the Goddess's lack of respect for their privacy—rolled from his perch over his wife and groaned in frustration. What was so hard to understand that you should never burst in on a couple while they were making love? Was Freya really that disconnected with the real world or did she enjoy the shock factor of her inopportune visits? The satisfied smile on her lips suggested the latter.

"For gods' sake, Freya," Jaali exclaimed, throwing a sheet over their naked bodies. "Why don't you ever knock?"

"Because there isn't a door between my world and yours, handsome." The beautiful woman sat on the edge of the bed, flipping her sumptuous hair with her hand. "Besides, it's not like I've never seen you naked before."

The demigoddess could be infuriating, but she had helped them before, so Jaali tried his best to not get too ruffled up by her irritating quirks. "What do you want now, Freya?" Despite his resolve to stay calm, his voice came out harsher than he had intended.

"Watch your tone of voice, little one. You don't address the great Freya like that." The crooked smile in the corner of her mouth belied her words. She was enjoying this a bit too much. "I came with good news—well, news anyway."

Milenda sat up, the sheet she was holding against her chest dropping to her lap. Jaali watched her as she straightened her back, her small breasts, now exposed, bouncing ever so slightly. He wondered for a moment if the goddess would punish him too harshly if he told her to go away so he could make love to his beautiful wife but decided against it.

"What is the news, Freya?" Milenda's green eyes shone with worry. She didn't complain ever, but he knew she missed her homeland with the luxuriant jungles and the white sand beaches that winter never touched. "Did something happen to my father?"

Freya yawned, already bored with her protégées. "No, child. Your father is fine and so is his new wife." At Milenda's inquiring expression, the goddess added, "And no babies as of yet. It seems that your *iyalorixá* is doing a great job at keeping it that way. For a mere mortal, you sure have loyal subjects."

Milenda shook her head, her black wiry hair bouncing around her perfect face. "They are not my subjects. They are my family." The protest came out full-hearted. Jaali knew that nothing infuriated his wife more than bringing up her royal background.

"Don't get your knickers in a twist, princess." Freya stretched, her perfect body peeking from behind her scarce body coverings. "Yemanjá paid me a visit last night—or was it last week? I don't know. Time doesn't mean much to me anyway."

"Will you tell us the news already?" Milenda's words were uttered from between her clenched jaws. "Please?"

"Mortals have no patience whatsoever." Jaali almost snorted. She was one to talk about patience. The creature had zero tolerance for waiting. "My dark sister asked me to tell you it is time."

Silence fell in the room. He was about to ask her what she meant, but a glance at his wife told him all he needed to know. They were being summoned back to Afrika. Milenda's amber skin paled, and her lip quivered. Jaali could almost read her thoughts. They had been happy here, the happiest they had ever been. Leaving Isvärld was not something either had any wish to do. Not yet. Maybe never.

"Why now?" Milenda sounded like a young girl again, the mere idea of going back to the place where she was worth more dead than alive too unpleasant to contemplate. "Couldn't we stay here a little longer?"

For a moment Freya's face softened, the sarcastic grin fading into a sympathetic smile as her hand reached over the sheets to touch his wife's leg. "She says you must go back now. 'The time is ripe, sister,' she said. 'Milenda owes me, and she must obey.'"

Jaali reached for Milenda's shoulders in a protective move, pulling her closer to him. She trembled in his arms, her *matangazos* turning a sickly shade of red, a sure sign of how unsettling the news was. He wanted to hug her and tell her everything would be fine, but past experience told him that might not be the case.

"Johari is still so little… it will be a hard trip for her." Milenda was grasping at straws, trying to find a good excuse not to go back yet. "I'm not ready, Freya. I'm scared and have no idea what I will be able to do to help my people. I'm barely a woman, much less a savior. I will fail my nation."

The goddess stood up and straightened invisible wrinkles from her immaculate clothing with a hand. "Sorry, Princess. I'm only the messenger. But you're hardly helpless. You survived living in the mountains with the wyverns by yourself."

"And you saved me when all odds were against me." Jaali still had nightmares about his journey through the desert, his wife the only thing holding him from giving in to desperation. "You're not *just* a woman. You're a strong, beautiful, and fully capable human being. We'll be all right. Johari will be fine. She has your genes. She's a fighter just like her mom."

Milenda raised her eyes to his, and he read the fear reflected in them. He didn't want to leave either. Here he had reunited with his father after years in slavery and exile. He had a best friend in Ebba, the outcast woman who had helped him escape his own people's prejudices, and he had a home, a place he could call his own, to share and enjoy with his wife and child. But he knew Natale needed its Jewel just as much as he did. He wouldn't begrudge them their right to be rescued by the one woman who had the motivation and the strength to do it—even if she didn't think so.

"Listen to the pretty one." Jaali cringed. Freya still had the knack for making him feel small and objectified with a few simple words. She had helped them so much, and yet he still couldn't feel comfortable around her. "There's a good brain under all that handsomeness."

Milenda's lips curved into a tiny smile. She sought his hand with hers, a comforting touch to make him feel at ease. She always knew how he felt. There was a connection between them that defied explanation—distance, time even, could not stand between them. His princess could always reach him, join him in body and spirit, no matter where he was or how far.

"I'll go. Of course, I'll go." The way she squeezed his hand was telling of how much she didn't want to go. "When?"

In an uncharacteristic move, the goddess swept her hand gently over Milenda's cheeks. "The ship won't be here for another fortnight. Time enough to get everything ready."

And to say goodbye. Goodbye to friends, family, and their home. Then head straight into the mouth of the lion. Jaali couldn't help but wonder what would happen when the Elders got wind of their return. As far as he knew, they still thought both Milenda and him to be dead. Their resurrection wouldn't be welcomed by those who hungered for power, those who didn't care how many lives they destroyed to come up on top. No, the political predators in Natale wouldn't be too happy to find out they were alive and well. What he was scared of was what they would do to his family once the secret was out. Nothing good ever came out of poking a wasp's nest. And that was exactly what Yemanjá was telling them to do.

* * *

Even though spring had brought out the green grass and the flowers to the foot of the mountain, the view from the small window still brought Milenda all kinds of memories—a mixed bag of good and bad. She remembered how nervous she had been the first time Jaali and she slept in that room. And hopeful. After their ordeal in Afrika, she had been more than happy to welcome a new land, a new life. Little did she know that life in Isvärld wouldn't be an easy one for them at first.

"Gavå tired." Johari's little voice stumbled on the words, but her expression spoke volumes. She was worried about her dragon who had been less than energetic on their trip to the outpost by the harbor. Could the little dragon be sensing the sadness and anxiety in her heart?

"It's late, Jo," she said, tears dancing just behind her eyes. "Time to sleep for the two of you."

Milenda picked up her daughter and took her to the small cot Herr Karlsson had brought up to the room. Gavå ambled closer to the girl and curled up by the bed. She was getting too big to sleep with Johari, who draped her arm over the edge of the bed so she could touch the dragon's head while she slept.

The sight of her daughter sleeping always brought her a sense of peace and happiness, but that night Milenda was too jittery to feel anything but apprehension. Jaali was still in the main room talking to Captain Kifeda. Ebba and Jaali's father were in the next rooms to be close by when they left the next morning. Milenda sighed, standing by the window and looking at the land she had come to love. Why did life have to be so complicated? Why was her heart divided between the nation that birthed her and the one that had sheltered her for over two years?

"I miss you, Mama Neuysi, but I love Jaali's father too." She spoke softly, her breath clouding the glass. "Why can't you both be in the same place? And, Father, why can't you be a commoner instead of a king?"

"You should never regret who and what you are, *kidogo moja.*"

The rich, soft voice startled her, and she turned around, her heart beating too fast. Yemanjá was standing next to her, poised and beautiful. Milenda was always surprised how different the two goddesses were. Where the Mother was calm and dignified, Freya was more of a wild card—it was hard to predict what she would do next.

"Yemanjá, you're here." She had the sudden urge to run and hug the impressive dark woman in front of her. Was it acceptable to hug a divine being? She decided against it. "I didn't think you'd come."

The goddess seemed to radiate light, her warmth surrounding Milenda like a comforting embrace. "I had to come and see you off on your journey back. My sister, Freya, was kind enough to allow me the visit. She is quite taken by you and your man."

With the northern divinity, it was always hard to tell. She favored sarcasm and often vulgarity to being straightforward.

"There's no need to be scared, Jewel." Easy for her to say. She was not the one walking into the grip of power-hungry men who wanted her dead. "Your father will protect you."

"He didn't do that great of a job when I was in Natale, did he?" Milenda loved her father and she now knew that he loved her too, but after a lifetime of being treated like a stranger in her own home, bitterness still soured her heart once in a while. "He has a new wife, why would he care to protect the daughter that can bring nothing but turmoil to his life?"

Yemanjá let out a long sigh. "My sweet Jewel, your father is as anxious to start a revolution as any of us." Why did the goddess think she wanted to start anything? "Now that he has been made aware of what's going on in his land, he wants to change it. Melchior doesn't want to be referred to in history books as the one who allowed slavery and other barbarities to coexist with a civilization proud of its culture."

The goddess had hit a nerve. Milenda wanted to end slavery and the savagery of rituals like the Trials that almost killed her husband. As reluctant as she was to start a war of any kind, she knew it was necessary for much needed changes to take place. The problem was she was not alone anymore—she had a consort she loved more than life and now a daughter too. Her *matangazos* prickled, unpleasant electric-like shocks, the cold fingers of fear running up her shoulder and neck.

"*Kidogo moja,* I came to collect my dues." The tall and exquisite woman's lips were stretched into a thin line, but her eyes were soft and shiny. "I helped you save Jaali. Now you must pay for it."

Milenda shivered. She had always known she would have to pay back what Yemanjá had given her. Everyone knew the goddess didn't offer favors for free. There were horrifying stories about what she asked in return. She had almost forgotten about that, lulled by the feeling of comfort that enveloped her every time the goddess was around.

"You're not going to ask me for my firstborn, are you?"

Yemanjá laughed. "Child, those are silly stories parents tell their children. Of course I won't be taking Johari from you." She shook her head gently, the gold of her *iqhiya* emitting a kind of glow in the dim room. "My price is for you to go back to Natale and save Jaali's people and yours from the tyranny of the Elders. You're the royal princess, and you've inherited your biological father's legacy. It's been over a century since the land of Afrika has borne someone like you."

Some days Milenda thanked the gods for her Nyota legacy, which had allowed her to help and support Jaali across the desert. Other times, all she wanted to do was forget her ancestry, her special gods-given gifts that marked her as a target for the Elders and their power-hungry minions.

"Mother, please tell me because I have no idea. What am I to do once I arrive at Natale?" Milenda rubbed the back of her neck, confusion and apprehension overwhelming her. "Do I go knock at my father's door and announce to the world the dead princess is back with her equally dead husband? I am sure I wouldn't last very long after that. The Elders have people everywhere, spying and plotting for them."

The goddess was silent for a moment, her hand clutching the *kanga* fabric over her chest. When she raised her eyes to Milenda again, the softness was gone and an icy glow of determination had replaced it. "Jewel, I will come to you upon your arrival and tell you all you need to know." She lowered her voice. "Do you think I would let you be killed as soon as you leave the ship? Do you really believe me to be that cruel? I may be a goddess, but I'm also the mother of all living things, and I love my children. I only use cruelty when absolutely necessary, *kidogo moja*."

Properly chided, Milenda lowered her eyes in shame. Yemanjá was right. She had never been anything but kind and helpful to her and Jaali. Old popular myths and superstitions should not rule her perception of the Mother.

"I'm sorry, Yemanjá. I should thank you for all you've done for me and my husband. Instead, I assume the worst." Throwing caution to the wind, Milenda took a couple steps forward and reached out for the goddess's hand. "Please, forgive me."

The goddess didn't flinch at the touch or pull her hand away from Milenda's. She brought the princess's hand up to her heart and held it there, her grasp tender but firm. "As long as my heart beats in my chest, I will always be on your side. Your people were blessed by the gods way before me or my sister Freya. We have been entrusted to protect you, and so I will."

Milenda was surprised by the steady thumping against her hand. She had never thought that gods had hearts like humans did. "Thank you, Mother. I will do as you bid me, knowing that you'll be my side in the journey."

Yemanjá smiled and gently dropped her hand. "Now, go rest. You have a long journey ahead of you." And without so much as a poof, the goddess was gone.

Milenda stood rooted to that spot for a while, her heart still racing and her *matangazos* burning on her shoulder. It was indeed going to be a long journey—one that she hoped didn't end with her demise or any of her loved ones.

CHAPTER TWO

The Storm

The ship rocked up and over giant waves, sending loose items skittering across the deck. The sailors didn't seem to notice, bracing themselves on strong legs that had long been taught to handle the motion. A storm was coming. Jaali watched the dark clouds rolling toward them from a distance. The wind had picked up in the last hour, and the rumbling of thunder echoed in their ears, stronger and closer. Captain Kifeda had dismissed the squall as nothing to worry about. "The gods have thrown a lot worse our way," he had said, his weathered skin crinkling around his eyes and lips. "A good storm is a welcome diversion from the routine for the sailors." Jaali couldn't disagree more, but he was not a sailor.

Milenda was under deck with Joahri and the dragons, who were not as giddy about the approaching storm as the captain seemed to be. Gavå had been yowling nonstop for the past hour or so. Jaali came up to talk to the captain and check on the weather. Afterward, he lingered, his back against a wall, watching the frantic dance of the sailors preparing the ship for whatever force of nature was quickly approaching. It was strangely soothing, like a well-choreographed dance, every step timed and deliberate. Mesmerizing was the word for it.

Was this a metaphor, a not-so-subtle warning about what was ahead for his family? The gods had a strange way of communicating sometimes, and he wouldn't be surprised if this storm was commandeered by either Yemanjá or Freya to keep them on their toes. But they needed no reminders of what they were heading toward. Both he and Milenda were painfully aware they were jumping into a storm of another kind, one they had to navigate whether they liked it or not. A storm he hoped, for Milenda and his daughter's sake, they would be able to survive.

CHAPTER THREE

Coming Home

Mjusi was excited. The small dragon scuttled around the house, wagging his powerful tail and making loud clicking noises with his tongue. Jaali hadn't seen him this excited in a long time. They were home, causing a bittersweet feeling for Jaali, who had spent the worst times of his life there. But there were also happy memories, all related to his wife, the woman who had scared all his demons away.

"I forgot how green it is." Milenda had emerged from inside the tiny house they would be sharing for the next stage in their turbulent married life. It was indeed luscious with the thick cover of trees stretching way above them, a canopy of green that protected them from the merciless rays of the sun. "And hot."

Jaali's forehead was wet with perspiration. The years they had spent in cold Isvärld had lowered his tolerance for the tropical heat of the jungles of Afrika. He wanted to say something but found that his tongue was tied around the bad memories Natale resurrected in his mind.

Milenda wrapped her arms around him, resting her face on his back, and he immediately relaxed, as if his wife's body heat could melt all the bad thoughts away. "Are you all right?" she asked in a soft voice, her warm breath seeping through his shirt and into his skin. He couldn't talk, so he covered her hands with his. "I wish I could erase all those memories for you, *wimbo wa moyo.*"

He spun around to look at her, a hand on the back of her head, the other on her waist. "You've done enough, *msichana*. More than enough." She had singlehandedly brought light to where there had been only darkness within him. She was the sun who had broken through his night, carrying the terror and pain away. But memories didn't just vanish. They persisted, lingering in your conscience like the glare in your eyes when you looked at the sun for too long, making it hard to see clearly.

His princess rose on her tiptoes and kissed him—a gentle, butterfly kiss, and yet powerful enough to bring him down from the dark place he had gone into. "Those days are gone, and I'm going to make sure that doesn't happen to anyone else ever again." There was such determination in her voice, he never thought of doubting her. Such intensity and strength in a tiny female body used to surprise him but not anymore. Not after she had given birth to their daughter. Anyone who could have a life inside her, nurture it with her own blood, and bring it forth into this world had to be exceedingly strong and resilient.

"I love you, my rebel Jewel." He kissed her this time, a little longer and harder, delighting in her sweetness.

"You are my world, and I want to be there by your side when you crush the slavers and the Elders who allow them to exist."

Mjusi rubbed his long body against their legs. "I think he's jealous," Milenda said, laughing. "Or maybe he wants to help out with the revolution." The *wyvern* shook his tail and coughed up two small blobs of smoke. "Maybe you'll learn how to breathe fire by then and can scare all our enemies."

Dragons were imposing animals that could scare even the toughest of men, but Mjusi still had a lot to grow. In dragon years, he was still a fledgling, Milenda had discovered. He was now beginning to exhale smoke, but the fire his family in Isvärld could produce was still nonexistent.

Jaali slid his hand to her shoulders, and they walked together to their humble home. Johari was napping on the dirt floor, snuggled against Gavå, whose growl-like snore filled the empty spaces of the sparsely furnished house. Standing by the makeshift table Jaali had built as soon as they had arrived was Yemanjá, resplendent in her gold dress and matching *iqhiya*. Startled by her presence, Jaali pulled Milenda against him, protecting her with his body.

"Sorry I frightened you." Was that a ghost of a smile on the goddess's lips? "I was admiring your child and lost track of time. She's very unique and beautiful, isn't she?"

That was the understatement of the century. Jaali stuck out from the rest of the population because of his fair skin and hair. Johari would stick out even more with her amber skin, silvery white hair, and green eyes. Jaali wondered whether she would develop the *Nyota* markings—the *matangazos*—which would set her even further apart from the population.

"Yemanjá, so good to see you again." Milenda freed herself from Jaali's arms and took a step toward the goddess.

The tall woman signaled them to sit and then smiled. "I come with instructions for your next step." Jaali felt Milenda shivering as she reached for the security of his hand. "Tomorrow, you will go to the market in disguise and wait for Mama Nyeusi. She will meet you by the *kanga* cloth stall."

Milenda's *matangazos* began glowing. She was going to see Mama Nyeusi again. Jaali's heart swelled with happiness for his wife. Milenda's reunion with her guardian was possibly the only silver lining of their return. "Isn't that dangerous? For Mama Nyeusi, I mean."

"*Kidogo moja*, everyone believes you're dead," Yemanjá whispered, as if afraid of waking up the baby. "No one will think anything of your *iyalorixá* talking to another woman while shopping for cloth. She will give you instructions on how to get in the palace to see your father."

Jaali practically jumped off the chair. "No! She can't go into the palace. It's too dangerous." What was Yemanjá thinking? She couldn't possibly believe that putting his wife inside the lion's mouth was a good idea. "The Elders have spies everywhere in the palace. They will find out about her presence there right away."

The princess laid her hand on his arm. "It's all right, *wimbo wa moyo*. I'll be fine."

He peeled his eyes from the goddess to look at his wife, his whole being burning with fear for her safety. Her forest eyes were soft, reflecting none of the fear he was feeling. Again, he was reminded of how brave that tiny woman was. How he admired her strength and resilience in the face of adversity and danger, so unlike himself who still carried the emotional scars of a childhood filled with horror and pain. Her strength had carried him through the desert when he thought he couldn't go on and banished all his demons to the back of his mind, far back enough he wasn't constantly aware of them anymore.

"No, it's not safe." The conviction in his voice belied the defeat he felt inside. He knew there was no way to change Milenda's mind if she thought it was the right thing to do.

Milenda smiled and ran her hand over his arm. "We knew it was going to be dangerous, but we came back to do what needs to be done. We have the gods on our side." She stole a quick glance at Yemanjá who nodded. "I'll be fine."

He had heard those same words many times, and they weren't any comfort to him at all. After all they had gone through for the past few years, fine just didn't ring true any longer. The idea of Milenda walking into a trap was not as outlandish as it may sound. It had happened before in one form or another. They had both been betrayed, imprisoned, and hunted. Fine was not a guarantee, but a mere hope that things would turn out better than expected.

* * *

Milenda wiggled under the cloth draped over her head and

shoulders. She'd forgotten how hot it got underneath it as she gingerly avoided a merchant's fruit cart. The market was a colorful sea of people, some selling their wares, others buying them. The air was rich with aromas—cinnamon, curry, spicy peppers, and the sweet smell of fruit. She took a deep breath, wanting to inhale the scents of her childhood, one of the few things that had made her happy back then.

The *kanga* cloth stall was visible from the distance, the sunny colors of the fabric flapping away in the breeze. Milenda tightened the scarf around her face, afraid someone would recognize her, and headed to that corner of the market. Despite the fear, excitement bubbled inside her chest—she was going to see Mama Nyeusi again.

"How much for this one, *bibi*?"

That low, slightly gruff voice lit a spark of joy in Milenda's heart. She turned abruptly, almost crashing into another customer. Her old *iyalorixá* was standing just a few feet away from her, her ballooning white skirt, typical of her position within the court, crushed against the table on the stall. The old woman was busy shuffling wads of cloth, her nose twitching every time she disapproved of a certain selection.

Carefully, Milenda approached and bent over the fabric-covered table, pretending to be interested in the samples. "Do you think Yemanjá would like this pattern?" The woman who manned the stall had walked away, allowing her to speak more freely.

Mama Nyeusi lifted her eyes to the princess and smiled. "Child, Yemanjá doesn't have time to worry about *kanga* cloth."

A smile stretched across Milenda's face, and she had to refrain from throwing herself in the arms of her *iyalorixá*. "But it's so pretty," she said, never taking her eyes off the old woman. "Worthy of a princess, don't you agree?"

Mama Nyeusi lowered her voice to a whisper. "Behind the stall. The hanging fabric will hide us."

Milenda pretended to look at the fabrics for a moment or two before turning around the corner and slipping behind the curtain of cloth. She didn't give her *iyalorixá* time to say anything; she dropped her basket and flung herself into the welcoming arms of the old woman, burying her face in her blouse.

"I missed you so much, Mama," the princess whispered against the soft folds of Mama Nyeusi's voluminous shirt. She had been happy in Isvärld after the first few months of turmoil, but there were things she had missed everyday—her palace showers, the heat, the year-round freedom of *kanga* dresses and bare feet, and the imposing but comforting presence of her *iyalorixá*.

A hand came to rest on her cheek, the callused skin a balm to her nerves. "Child, I missed you too." Was the old woman's voice wavering? "But I slept better knowing you were safe."

Milenda thought of telling her all the hardships she and Jaali had gone through, but there would be time for that later. At the moment, all she wanted to do was enjoy the peace and warmth of her guardian's embrace.

Too soon, Mama Nyeusi broke the illusion of tranquility.

"I wish we could stay and talk, but it's too risky. Someone might recognize you." The woman pulled her further behind their hiding place. "Listen, child. Remember your old secret spot?" Not so secret, it seemed. Milenda nodded. "I will leave instructions for you under Mjusi's favorite tree. The place is now a shrine of sorts, and no one will suspect another worshiper coming to pay her respects."

Milenda's eyes narrowed. Shrine? Why would there be a shrine in the very spot where she used to go hide from her palace life and where she often met with Jaali? There was nothing there but trees and a hanging harbor seat that by now was probably falling apart from lack of use.

Her *iyalorixá* didn't let her talk. "Bring flowers and a candle. It will make your ruse more believable." Mama Nyeusi brushed a fleshy hand on Milenda's cheek again and smiled. Her lips curved, but there was sadness in her eyes. "Time will come for us to catch up, but for now we must not linger. Go, child, and cover your markings well."

Milenda barely had time to place a butterfly kiss on the older woman's cheek before she was gone in a flurry of white folds and lace. She stared after her guardian with longing in her heart. What she wouldn't give to be able to sit with her and talk like two regular women at the market. It was not in her stars. The Jewel would never be a regular person.

She shook herself off, tucked the cloth around her head and shoulders, and left the shelter of the hanging fabrics. Maybe there would be time later—much later—to chat, to share all that had happened for the past three years away from her homeland. Just maybe….

She once again navigated the maze of the market stalls, keeping her eyes down and her chin tucked into her chest. There were two royal guards, conspicuous in their bright red uniforms, standing at the main entrance to the market. Milenda stopped and hid behind a pile of baskets, her heart exploding in her chest. Taking two deep breaths, the princess willed herself into calmness, her *matangazos* burning so hot in her shoulder she was afraid they could be seen through the thick fabric covering her head.

Calm down. They won't recognize you because they think you're dead.

Turning around, she bought a few pieces of fruit from a nearby stall, rearranged her head covering, and rushed through the crowd directly into the path of the guards and her way back to the safety of their minuscule *hema*. Uttering a silent prayer, Milenda dropped her gaze to the ground, hugged the basket against herself, and dashed between the two men. When she was too far to be noticed, she let out the breath she'd been holding and allowed her muscles to relax.

If they had told her she would come to miss Isvärld when she first arrived at the land of snow and ice, she would have laughed hysterically. The first few months of their stay in Jaali's homeland was anything but happy or relaxing. They jumped out of a pot to end up in the fire. Milenda shook her head, trying to disperse those bad memories and replace them with the joyful ones—the birth of her daughter, the consistent warmth of her husband's love, the acquisition of new friends and family.

She quickened her step. Jaali would be worried if she was away for too long. She could already feel that familiar sensation of his reach, like a feathery caress inside her mind. She couldn't risk having him come to her. Who knew who was watching? Milenda willed Jaali's invisible fingers away and then felt guilty about it. She had never refused his call—was this what it was going to be like in Natale? Would she have to push those she loved away so she could focus on being the queen everybody but her thought she would be? The *kanga* wrap slipped off her head and almost fell when she shook her head again; no, she would never push Jaali away. She couldn't. He was just as much a part of her as her heart; one didn't live without the other—not any life she'd want to live anyway.

Their *hema* was well hidden in the jungle, away from any other villages. It was smartly built to look like just more greenery among the trees. The wooden walls were covered in ferns and vines that crawled upward toward the sunlight, and the roof seemed to be a patch of moss-covered ground. Invisible to the onlooker, it was the perfect hiding place for her family.

As she approached, she saw Jaali standing by the door, pacing the patch of land they had cleared so their daughter and the *msutis* had some space to play. He *was* worried. Milenda pressed a hand to her chest as another stab of guilt went through her heart. Nothing was going to be the same again.

"Jaali, I'm here," she yelled once she was close enough for him to hear her. His silvery head snapped up, eyes frantically searching for the body that went with her voice. Her gaze met his and, her walls lowered, she felt what he was feeling—pure relief.

Her husband ran to her, slapping ferns and other shrubs out of his way, and drew her into his arms. "By the gods, Milenda. I was so worried." Her head covering fell to the ground as Jaali buried his lips in the crook of her neck, over her glowing *matangazos*. "I had visions of you being taken by the Elders or spirited away by the Mabaya warriors just like I was. I couldn't reach you. Never do this again, *msichana*, never."

Milenda pulled him away and framed his face with her hands. "I'm sorry, *wimbo wa moyo*, I couldn't risk letting you reach me where people could see it. I didn't mean to worry you." She rose on her tiptoes and kissed him. His lips tasted salty, and she knew he had been crying. Her husband had suffered so much loss and heartache, she hated adding more pain to his life. "Please, forgive me."

Jaali bent down and took her lips in another kiss, gently at first, light as a butterfly and sweet as the nectar it sought, and then urgent with a hunger that overtook her senses and erased all control. She yielded to his kiss, molding her body to his as his hands searched for her skin, fumbling against the barrier of her dress. She didn't have to fight to brush her hands along the hard ridges of her husband's body, his simple cotton shirt no match for her exploring hands.

"By all that's sacred, *msichana*. Help me get rid of your dress."

She giggled at the frustration in his voice and began

unwrapping the *kanga* cloth from around her until she was naked, the humid hot air covering her skin in a sheen of dew. Jaali took her in, his transparent eyes scanning her from head to toe with the expression of desire that was always her undoing.

"Maybe we should take this inside," she suggested, her voice husky with yearning. "I don't care to share you with a snake."

In one smooth move, Jaali scooped her up into his arms and carried her toward their *hema*. "Johari is sleeping, and Mjusi is away hunting."

The coolness of the interior of the small house welcomed them as her man took her to the bed they shared. As soon as she was safely and comfortably situated on top of the linens, Jaali began undressing, his shirt, pants, and undergarments flying across the small space. His eyes never left his wife who watched him in awe of his beauty. She never got tired of his muscles etching his skin into hills and valleys she loved exploring, of his silky hair so different from her own, and his eyes—bottomless oceans, reflecting a pure and brave soul. She remembered when those same eyes had been filled with pain and fear. They had killed those demons together and there was nothing they couldn't face as one.

* * *

Milenda's body had the same effect on him now as it did the first time they had made love—his heart pumped extra blood to every part of his body, drumming and echoing in his ears, making him gasp in surprise and delight. His skin came alive, tingling as if tiny electric shocks were lighting it. He had been out of his mind with worry earlier, thinking that Milenda had been spotted by the Elders' men. Despite her father's support, there was no way of knowing who was loyal to the king or to the powerful Elders. When he tried to reach her and found a wall, he panicked and almost left the *hema* running toward town. Johari had been his anchor. He couldn't leave a baby alone in the jungle. All he could do was wait and hope everything was all right.

With relief running through his veins, he had swelled in the presence of his totally unharmed and beautiful wife. The urgency in his body had surprised him as he couldn't undress quickly enough. Gods, he loved that tiny, dark woman. He loved her with his heart, his soul, and his body. Milenda waited for him, reclined on top of the bed, her skin still shiny with perspiration, her small breasts rising and falling rapidly with her breath. Finally free of all his clothes, he crossed the short space between them and climbed the bed, running his hand along Milenda's thigh. He smiled at the bright glow of her *matangazos,* a sure sign she was reacting to his touch.

"Are you going to stop torturing me and love me already?" Milenda's teasing tone made him laugh. "I may just fall asleep."

Jaali trailed kisses along her belly up to her breasts where he lingered for a while. His wife whimpered, and he swelled further against her, desperate now to be inside her, sheathed within his princess.

A loud, high-pitched sound startled him, his lips still

latched around Milenda's breast, his whole body trembling in anticipation. In unison, both his and Milenda's heads turned toward the makeshift door that separated Johari's room from the rest of the house. The familiar and unwelcome sound zoomed through the thin wood door and into their ears.

Jaali hung his head with a moan of frustration. "Every time." His whispered complaint made Milenda laugh. He raised his head to look at her, his eyes unfocused and his body still begging for release. "Can we just pretend we don't hear her?"

Milenda lifted her face toward his and kissed him lightly on the lips. "You know she won't stop, and soon Gavå will join her." She had just uttered the last word when a long, deeper yowl joined the child's crying. Milenda rolled her eyes. "And there it goes."

With a groan, Jaali rolled off his wife and lay on his back, a hand on his chest and gaze on the rustic ceiling. "Children should come with warning signs," he said, a rogue chuckle escaping his lips. "You shall never be able to make love to your wife again."

Milenda rose, supported on an elbow, and scanned Jaali's body with her eyes. "I miss Ebba already." Ebba, the Fjorden outcast who had helped Jaali escape, had become their close friend and only neighbor, who had often watched over their daughter so they could have some time alone. Milenda sighed, brushed a hand slowly over Jaali's body, lingering on the raised lines of his scars, and rolled out of bed. "Maybe later?" She winked, an expression on her face that held annoyance and amusement mixed in equal parts.

Jaali couldn't move for fear of exploding. That last caress had him hanging so over the edge, he had gone harder than the rock that held the door closed. He muttered, biting his lip and willing his body to get under control. This parenting thing was harder than he'd thought, but also wondrous. To know that walking and laughing tiny human had been made of his and Milenda's genes was amazing. It filled him with a sense of awe he had never experienced before.

From the enclosure that held the child's crib, Milenda's soft cooing sounds and comforting words wafted over to his ears. He smiled, swinging his legs over and sitting on the edge of the bed. Resigned to the fact there would be no lovemaking, he slowly slipped into his discarded pants, neglecting to put on a shirt. His body was still burning from desire, and even his loose pants felt too restrictive against his tingling skin.

His mind wandered to his house in the prairie back home. Funny how he now thought of Isvärld as home. Before, his memories of his homeland were fuzzy at best, distorted by years of separation and pain. Being a father himself now, he couldn't imagine the loss his parents had felt when they lost not one but two children to slavery. His other taken sibling had been born after his kidnapping, so Jaali did not have a single memory of this sister, but he hoped she had not ended up in the same horrific situation as him. He hoped with all the passion in his heart that she was bought by a business or to watch over the children of some wealthy Natalian. *Please, gods. Let it not be a sexual predator like his master, the* duivel.

Finding his sister was one of Milenda's main goals. "As soon as I can, I'll have people looking for her, I promise." Of course, he knew she was far from being in a position to make that happen yet, but a seedling of hope grew in his heart nevertheless. His wife was not the kind to allow their situation to get in her way, and neither was he—not anymore, not since meeting his Jewel. After a life of pain and desperation, Jaali had learned that nothing was impossible. They would find his sister.

Needing a distraction, Jaali went outside and sat underneath the only marula tree hardy enough to survive the lack of sunlight, blocked by the closed canopy of the jungle. He felt a strange affinity to the beautiful tree that produced the fruit that was often the only source of sustenance for his family. Mjusi was a great hunter, but even he had trouble spotting prey through the thick cover. Like him, the tree was alone in a world that set it apart, different from all the other trees. He leaned against the rough trunk and closed his eyes.

"Since the princess is too busy to attend to your needs, maybe I can be of service." Freya's voice nearly made him jump out of his skin. She was standing before him, half naked as usual, her thick blonde hair falling in waves over her shoulders and barely covered breasts. "I can see you're still craving release." She looked at his crotch and lifted an eyebrow to drive her point home.

Jaali's face was assailed by a wave of heat that started at his chest and spiraled out of control up his neck and all the way to his ears. As usual, Freya could bring back, with just a few words, feelings he much rather leave in the past.

"What are you doing here?" he asked, fighting to keep a modicum of composure. "Isn't it a breach of divine etiquette to show up in another goddess's territory unannounced?"

"And who says I'm here unannounced?" The goddess moved her flawless body slowly and sensually closer to him. He flinched, instinctively pulling his legs to his chest and away from her. "I have special permission to come and see you and your wife."

Ashamed of the sudden fear that made him hug his legs protectively, Jaali scowled. "Why?" The beautiful goddess had been helpful to them in Isvärld, but she still made him feel like the helpless boy he had been in the hands of his master.

"I bring you news of your father and Ebba." Her voice lost the teasing tone, and her eyes softened. "Your father wanted you to know he's doing fine and that Ebba decided to take care of him even though he really doesn't need her help." She giggled. "Ebba is a determined young woman, isn't she?"

Jaali's muscles, tightened into knots, relaxed. "They are not—you know—together?" He emphasized the final word, not sure how else to ask the question.

Freya burst out laughing. "Gods, no. She thinks it's her duty as the new town shaman to take care of those she deems need help."

Confused, Jaali stretched his legs in front of him. "Why would she think that? My father is perfectly capable of taking care of himself."

"Yes, but he's broken inside." The statement took him by surprise. In the two years he had been with his father, Jaali had never thought of him as broken. "He lost two children to the slavers, another to greed, and the wife he loved. Now, he lost his son again and his grandchild. He may take care of the people in his town, but inside he's vulnerable and in pain. Ebba sees this and wants to help him heal."

Freya never ceased to amaze and surprise him. The goddess hid layers of depth under her shallow exterior. Pity she only allowed it to surface once in a while.

"Can you tell him I will look for Elin? There's a chance she's alive." And hopefully still whole, both in body and spirit.

"What am I? Your lackey?" The shallowness was back. Jaali sighed, frustrated. "Don't get your breeches all tied up in a knot, handsome. I will give him your message."

Jaali's face lit up. "Thank you, Freya."

Freya turned her back to him, and Jaali wondered whether she was hiding a pleased smile. "I must go now, but tell the *wyverns* I miss them." Before Jaali could reply, she was gone, leaving nothing behind but a wisp of mist.

CHAPTER FOUR

R EUNITED

She sneezed, the forced air from her nose and mouth blowing some of the petals away. "My nose doesn't like the smell of these flowers, Mjusi." The *msitu* clicked his tongue in a funny imitation of laughter. Milenda chuckled. They were both heading toward her old "secret" spot. There was really nothing secret about it since everybody in the palace knew she used to take refuge there. But back then there was nothing personal about her life, being the crown princess about to take a consort. Having that space where no one but her was allowed had been the closest she had to privacy— even if her guards were never too far.

"Mama Nyeusi told me to bring these smelly flowers," she told Mjusi as they walked along the narrow path between the trees. "Something about my secret place being a shrine." She shook her head, and the *msitu* mirrored her movement. "Sometimes I wonder whether my *iyalorixá* is going a little...." She made tiny circles around her temple, and Mjusi nodded his head emphatically.

Milenda stopped as soon as she saw the edge of the jungle and she could hear the sound of people talking. "This is the end of the journey for you, my friend." She turned to pat the dragon's scaly head. "Wait here and don't be seen."

Gathering courage and willing her heart to stop panicking inside her chest, Milenda adjusted the cloth over her head, held the flowers in front of her face, and stepped into the clearing. She wanted to look around and check if anyone had noticed her, but she kept on walking, her eyes focusing ahead, praying she wouldn't trip and fall.

When she finally allowed herself to breathe again, Milenda risked a side glance. The place that was once quiet and lonely was now crawling with people—men and women, carrying flowers or plates of food, flowed toward the spot she had once shared with Jaali before the Trials. The harbor seat was still there, precariously hanging from the branches of the giant tree, but it was all different now. Around it, in a large circle, flowers lined the grassy ground interrupted here and there by platters packed with food. With a pang, she recognized the practice—an ancient ritual of paying respects and asking for favors from the dead. Popular belief held the idea that the dead had been elevated to a higher form, that their souls had ascended to a place of power and wisdom. According to lore, the dead could grant wishes and favors if properly bribed with flowers and food. But who exactly were they honoring? And why here?

Letting curiosity win over caution, Milenda approached an older woman. "Do you come here often?" She couldn't possibly ask her directly.

The woman's paper-thin face opened in a smile, and her dark brown eyes filled with the kind of awe and hope Milenda had not seen in a long time. "Every week, child. If someone can help us, it is the Jewel."

Milenda almost dropped the flowers she was carrying. "The Jewel?" Her voice didn't sound like her own, choked and squeaky.

"The Jewel was the princess of the people, and now that she is with the gods, she will grant our humble wishes, won't she?" The woman raised her hands into the sky and then brought them down to her chest, clutching at the fabric of her dress. "What did you come to ask of the Jewel today, my child?"

Speechless, Milenda stared at the woman, lifting the flowers closer to her face. Thankful she had had the sense of placing her back to the sun, she squinted. What if the old woman could see her green eyes, one of the things that marked her as a Nyota?

"That's all right, child. You don't have to tell me," the woman said with a chuckle. She patted Milenda's arm and winked. "I wish you luck with your young man."

Milenda's heart must have stopped for a moment, because she couldn't breathe. Had she been recognized? How did the woman know about Jaali? It took Milenda a moment, as she watched her walk away, to fully grasp what the old woman meant—she thought Milenda was there to ask for a love favor like many of the other young women obviously were doing. She let out a long sigh of relief and checked her head covering, pulling the edges of the cloth further over her face.

"Why aren't you here, Yemanjá?" she whispered, her chin tucked in and eyes semi-closed. "This is when I need you the most."

Inside her head, a voice whispered back, "You are stronger than you think. You can do it."

Startled, Milenda stopped in her tracks. *Yemanjá?* The goddess had made herself scarce since they arrived in Afrika, allowing her slightly psychotic sister from the north visit them instead.

"I'll do the best I can, Mother. But I'm only a human." Milenda felt she had to drive that point home since both goddesses seemed to think she was some sort of divine being at times.

The female voice echoed in her brain again. "You're a queen and a Nyota. Strength runs in the veins of Nyota women. You are Natale's hope, Jewel. Don't ever doubt it."

Feeling chastised, Milenda resumed her track to the tree where Mama Nyeusi had left her instructions for whatever it was she was supposed to do next. Studying the shrine, she noticed people placing their offerings around the suspended seat and on the bottom of different trees, snuggled between the protruding roots of the green giants. Taking another deep breath, she sped up her steps toward the tree Mjusi loved to perch on back when they were still just the two. There were no flowers there, maybe because it grew further into the wooded area, which made her nervous. What if people got suspicious that she was the only one targeting that one tree? She shook her doubts off—there were other trees with just one offering underneath them.

Feigning great reverence to her own spirit, Milenda dropped to her knees, her back to the crowd, and placed the offering by the roots. Without moving, she scanned the base of the tree, and her gaze soon snagged on a piece of paper sticking out from the ground below the arch of one of the large roots. She leaned forward, pretending to arrange the flowers, and pulled the edge of the paper, which came free easily enough. Milenda stole a glance around her and, when she was satisfied no one was watching, tucked the note inside the bodice of her dress.

She lingered a little longer to pray. Milenda had so many things to be thankful for: Jaali, her daughter, Mjusi and Gavå, her new family and friends in the northern lands. Most of all, she was thankful that even after all she and her husband had gone through, they were both still alive and in love. Bowing her head, she uttered an old prayer of thanks to Yemanjá and whatever other gods had been protecting them for the past three years.

As she was bracing herself on the ground to stand up, Milenda felt a presence, a ghost of a touch. Alarmed, she whipped her head around, her head covering almost slipping from its perch on her thick hair. Knelt beside her was a woman equally covered in cloth, her hands flat on her chest as if in prayer. Milenda relaxed and pulled the ends of her covering tighter around her neck—the woman was close enough to see her *matangazos*.

She bowed her head one last time and moved to stand up. The woman next to her put a gentle hand on Milenda's arm, making her heart clench in her chest again. But there was no aggression in her touch, rather it felt like a motherly caress, an assurance. Milenda lifted her eyes to her again, no longer afraid she'd notice her forest green eyes.

"You're welcome, Jewel," the woman whispered so softly Milenda was not sure she had heard correctly. Her face was still hidden by the *kanga* covering, but the voice sounded oddly familiar. "You deserve every second of happiness the world and the gods are willing to offer you. Never fear because you are never alone."

Milenda opened her mouth to ask her who she was and why she was talking like that, but the women got to her feet in a fluid move. "Tell Johari her grandmother loves her."

Stunned into silence, Milenda watched as the woman moved away, her step so light it looked as if her feet didn't quite touch the ground, and when she blinked, the stranger was gone. Nothing was left as witness of her presence, and no one seemed to have noticed her. Milenda's *matangazos* prickled, a feeling of great peace washing over her. Whoever that woman was—a human or a ghost—her touch had brought a special kind of joy to Milenda's anxious heart, and for that she was grateful.

* * *

"Was it like when I reach to you?" Jaali was leaning on his bent arm, stretched on the bed beside her. Her encounter with the mysterious woman at the shrine still bothered his wife. Milenda was sure she had wished her no harm. Her presence felt far from maleficent, that pleasant sense of serenity she had left behind still glowing inside her, she had told him. But the incident worried Jaali, whose protective instincts had immediately kicked in full force.

"No, not that way. It was more like…." His jewel bit her bottom lip, deep in thought.

The sudden urge to replace her teeth with his made him shiver as he imagined his lips gently pulling on hers, her sweetness making him want so much more. Jaali shook his head, trying to focus on what his wife was saying.

"It was more like the touch of a feather or the warm feeling of an exhale against my skin." Satisfied with her description, Milenda smiled, a mischievous glint in her eyes. "Nice. Here I am telling you about a momentous event in my life, and your mind is on something totally different."

Jaali smiled. Of course she would know what was going through his head. Milenda had no need to read his mind since his lower body was sending the message loud and clear. "Sorry. But it's your fault, you know. Stop being so breathtakingly beautiful, and I'll stop reacting to you this way."

His wife arched her back, laughing. With a wiggle, she turned to face him, their legs entwined like the vines that hugged their marula tree. She placed a hand over his chest, and his heart thumped against it, enchanted and excited all at once.

"Flatterer." Her teasing voice made him want to kiss her even more. "You know you can't bribe the Jewel with your pretty words."

Thirsty for her love, Jaali draped an arm over her and

cupped the back of her neck. He felt the heat of her markings and smiled wider—she was as hungry for him as he was for her. "So, how exactly can I bribe the princess?"

Milenda ran a finger over his bare shoulder and up his neck, covering his skin in goose bumps. A soft groan escaped him.

"With your soft, exploring fingers and your lips, of course." As if to demonstrate, she leaned over and took his mouth with hers, her tongue flickering along his inner lip, turning him into liquid. She moaned against his mouth and pulled away, his body shaking in protest. "But not now. We have to discuss the message from Mama Nyeusi."

For a moment, Jaali wished her *iyalorixá* would stop intruding in their lives. Their intimacy always seemed to be dependent on others—the demigoddesses, their daughter, and one time even the king's men. He inhaled deeply and let out a long, calming breath. "So, what did she write?"

Milenda twisted around to pick up the note from the rudimentary chair that doubled as a nightstand. The rustling of the paper as she unfolded it resonated too loudly in his ears where the beating of his heart had taken over. Jaali focused his eyes on the Jewel, a smile popping onto his lips as he watched her squint to read it in the semidarkness of their *hema*.

"She says she'll make sure the service door in the back that is never used is open tomorrow as the sun rises." She squished the paper into a ball and stared at him. "I'm to sneak into one of the storage rooms and wait for her to come get me. My father wants to see me."

Jaali shook his head vehemently. "No, that's too dangerous. Has Mama Nyeusi lost her mind?"

Milenda laid her tiny hand on his cheek, familiar and comforting. "It will be fine, *wimbo wa moyo*. Nobody ever goes through that door or uses that storage room. I used to hide there as a child when I didn't want to be found by my tutors and guards." She giggled. "They could never find me."

That was reassuring, but the part of him that had learned not to trust anyone or anything was still protesting. "You've been away for three years. Things may have changed." He covered her hand with his, soaking in her heat. "For all we know, that storage may be the most popular room in the palace now."

With a clicking of the tongue, Milenda leaned over and placed a brief kiss on his lips. "Mama Nyeusi would never tell me to meet her there if she didn't know it would be empty. It will be all right." Jaali didn't know whether she said that to soothe his trepidation or her own doubts. She kissed him again, this time longer and deeper.

His heart quickened. "Your kisses are not going to distract me from thinking both you and your *iyalorixá* are reckless." But it was working. As her tongue explored his mouth, the palace, the Elders, and all dangers they implied moved to the back of his mind, blurring around the edges like a wet painting. Seconds later, they had vanished completely and all he could think of was his wife—her kisses, the way she felt under his touch, how much his heart spilled over with love and yearning for her.

For once Johari slept peacefully through their lovemaking, and Mjusi, who often got restless at dawn, never once raised his head. Jaali, winded and sated, lay on his back, Milenda's head resting on his chest. The thick kinks of her hair and the heat from her *matangazos* caressed his skin. He loved this part of their lovemaking the best—the afterward, when they were both still glowing from their connection, flying high on their love for each other. At moments like this everything felt possible. It was as if the world took on a different hue, one full of hope and promise.

He kissed the top of Milenda's head, her hair tickling his lips, and heard the soft sounds of her breath slowing as she fell asleep. "I love you, *msichana*," he whispered, unwilling to wake her up. "I'm so lucky to have you in my life, even if I don't deserve you."

Believing her asleep, Jaali was startled when he heard her voice. "If you say that again, I'll feed you to the lions myself." He chuckled. "I love you too, *wimbo wa moyo*, and don't you ever forget it."

Jaali kissed her again and closed his eyes. He would never dare to doubt his tiny firecracker of a wife. As he drifted off to sleep, he wondered why everyone knew how strong she was except herself.

***

It was strange to be inside the royal palace again. It didn't feel like home to Milenda—not that it ever did. Growing up in the spacious mansion had not made her love it. She had grown up alone, in the hands of nannies and other palace staff, her father always distant, always emotionally unavailable. Mama Nyeusi had given her precise instructions on what to do once inside, and Milenda was now waiting in a storage room close to the service door that had been left unlocked for her. Nervously, she chewed on the *kanga* headcover's loose end.

Jaali had been more nervous than her, if that was even possible. He had tossed and turned all night, jumping out of bed to pace the dirt floors of their *hema* in a frenzy of anxiety. By morning they were both tired and no closer to being calm. She had fed Johari and Gavå before hugging Jaali with all her might, absorbing some of his heat and love.

"Please, be careful, *msichana*," Jaali whispered against her neck, and she felt re-energized. "This is a terrible idea. We might as well hand you over to the Elders with a bow on your head."

She chuckled, holding him tighter. "I'll be fine. Unlike in Isvärld where I stuck out like a red flag in the snow, I actually blend in with the people here."

"Nevertheless, be on your toes." Jaali pulled away and stared into her eyes. She could always see the skies and the oceans in his. "For me, for our daughter, please be safe."

Mjusi had accompanied her most of the way, clicking his tongue and rubbing his head against her legs every so often, as if telling her he was worried too. Milenda patted him one last time before leaving the shelter of the jungle and venturing into the outskirts of town.

Now, standing alone in that storage space, she was fidgety and anxious to get things done. When the door suddenly opened, she hid behind a storage bin and watched as a voluminous shape entered the room, closing the door behind her.

"Child, are you here?" Mama Nyeusi's voice was a welcome sound. Milenda sighed deeply and left her hiding spot. "There you are. What are you doing behind that? We have to do this quickly."

The princess threw her arms around the older woman's neck and gave her a hug. "So good to see you again, Mama."

The *iyalorixá* clucked and held her close for a brief hug before pulling her away. "No time for being sentimental," she said, her soft eyes belying her words. "We don't have much time. Come, child."

With a hand planted firmly on Milenda's back, Mama Nyeusi escorted her out the door and into the wide, stone-lined hallways of the palace. The air was so much cooler here than in her *hema*, that her thoughts immediately veered toward the terrible injustices being perpetuated by her own government. The powerful lived in comfort while the poor who worked long, hard days had to put up with the uncomfortable, humid hot air of the Afrikan weather. Something had to be done and, like it or not, she was the only one available to do it.

"Your father is waiting for you in his private chambers," the *iyalorixá* whispered. "Queen Amare is out with her women servants on a shopping trip. You have King Melchior all to yourself for a while."

Milenda hadn't thought much about her new stepmother. She had never met her, and all she knew about the woman was that Mama Nyeusi had been feeding her a contraceptive without her knowledge. "How's she? Amare?"

The old woman glanced around her before speaking again. "She's young and energetic." Was she being purposely reticent? "But we'll talk about that later."

They had stopped in front of the king's chambers, the same rooms where he had hidden from his daughter for most of her life. Milenda had stood before those same doors many times as a child, craving for her father's attention but rarely gaining access to his room or his heart. Her eyes misted as her *iyalorixá* rapped her knuckles on the thick wooden door, and she wiped them with the back of her hand. The door opened slowly and the imposing figure of her father filled the empty space between.

Milenda didn't have time to say anything. Mama Nyeusi pushed her inside the room and closed the door behind them. The king backed away from them as if he had lost his balance, his hands half stretched toward her. Milenda stared at his hands, shocked to find they were shaking, and then looked in her father's brown eyes, her chest inflating and deflating quickly with her breath.

"Milenda." It was something between a question and a statement of fact. Unsure of what to do or how to behave, Milenda stood still, her hands and legs trembling. "My sweet Jewel. Will you allow me to hug you?"

She didn't need any more encouragement. In a single move, Milenda threw herself into her father's open arms, her face squished against his robes. She had forgotten how tall he was, her head barely reaching his chest. His long arms wrapped around her, hesitant at first as if afraid of breaking her, but then more fiercely, fired by the long years of separation—before and after her departure for Isvärld.

They stood in the middle of the room for a while, holding each other in silence, too overcome by emotion to talk. It was Mama Nyeusi who broke the spell. "We don't have much time, Your Majesty. It's too dangerous for Milenda to stay long."

The king reluctantly let his daughter step away from him. "Are you well, daughter?" His eyes searched her as if he expected her to be hurt in some way. "Is your husband well?"

Milenda turned to the old woman, a question in her eyes. "He doesn't know yet," the *iyalorixá* told her, stealing a glance at the king.

"I don't know what?" The monarch's eyes bounced between the two women. "Is something wrong?"

With a smile, Milenda reached for his hand. "No, Father, nothing's wrong. Much the opposite actually." The king looked so confused, she started laughing. "It's just that you are now a grandfather."

There was silence for a moment as Melchior seemed to process the news. Then, he loosened a loud hoot, dropped Milenda's hands and clapped his. "A grandchild?" His laughter soon turned into a half sob, tears emerging in his eyes and rolling down his cheeks. He held her hands again. "Daughter, you made me the happiest man in Afrika."

"It's a girl, Father. Johari is almost two years old, and

she is—" She paused, looking for the right words. "—she's different." A concern since Milenda would like her to blend in with the rest of the population, camouflaged against recognition by the Elders or their men. "She won't go unnoticed, Father."

The king laughed, gripping her hand tighter. "As it should be. A future queen should distinguish herself from the rest. Like you and your green eyes and Nyota markings."

Her father's words touched her. After a lifetime of reclusing himself from her life, her existence and physical appearance a constant reminder of his wife's betrayal, he seemed finally ready to fully accept her as his daughter. Milenda may wear the markings her biological Nyota father had passed on, but she had not known him. Despite King Melchior's infertility that had forced him to use a surrogate, he was still her father, the only one she had ever known.

"We have to hurry, child." Mama Nyeusi had her ear to the door.

Milenda looked at her *iyalorixá* and then turned to her father again. "Father, I need something from you." The king squinted and nodded. "I need you to find Jaali's sister."

Melchior straightened himself up, his head tilted to the side. "Jaali has a sister? Here in Natale?"

"She was born after he was kidnapped at a very young age." Milenda kept throwing Mama Nyeusi glances as the old woman kept her focus on the door and whatever might be happening outside. "She's here somewhere, and we need to find her. I promised Jaali's father."

Her father sighed deeply. "I'll do what I can. What's her name?"

"Elin, but she was so young they may have changed her name. I don't know whether she would know her last name." Her heart sank as she realized how difficult it was to track down a slave who had been kidnapped so young. There weren't many records on the children brought in the country since the trade was technically illegal, even if secretly endorsed by those in power.

"We'll find her sooner or later, you have my word." King Melchior held Milenda by her shoulders and looked her in the eye. "I'll come to you soon. It's too dangerous for you at the palace. I'll send instructions as soon as we know what our next steps should be. You stay hidden in your *hema* with your family until it's safe."

They said their goodbyes, and Milenda left with Mama Nyeusi, covering her face and walking along the deserted hallways of the palace. When they finally arrived at the door where she had entered the building, Milenda turned to her *iyalorixá* and hugged her. "Mama, the king is right, but the thing is we aren't safe anywhere. We have to start doing something because if we are waiting for the right time, we'll never accomplish anything."

Mama Nyeusi nodded and cupped Milenda's cheeks with her hands. "I know, child. Your father wants to keep you safe, but I know you won't stand still."

Milenda left, weaving through the trees and thinking of all the happy days they had left behind in Jaali's Isvärld and the dangerous times they had ahead of them. As long as they were together, they would weather any storm, face any peril. It didn't mean it would be easy.

CHAPTER FIVE

Johari was running in the grass, spiraling as she chased butterflies, closely followed by Gavå, who whipped her long tail, knocking over whatever stood in her way. Jaali leaned against the tree, his legs stretched and crossed in front of him, watching his daughter, a smile dancing on his lips. The jungle was alive with the sounds of animals that made their home there, a cacophony of growls, hisses, and buzzing. If he ever had to define happiness, this would be it. The only thing missing was Milenda in his arms. His princess was inside, plotting—not that she had told him that, but he recognized that furrowed brow, the lip biting, and the glazed eyes. She was plotting. It should have made him nervous, but he knew his wife was a force to be reckoned with, one that no man or nature could curb. That's the woman he had fallen in love with, and he wouldn't change a thing.

It had been a few days since her visit to the palace, and Milenda didn't seem to be able to relax. She was fidgety and absentminded as if her mind was somewhere else. The king's instructions hadn't sat well with her—she didn't believe she should just wait for the right time. While they were waiting, Fjorden children were being taken from their beds and brought into slavery in Natale. Jaali knew she saw herself as the one person who could make a difference in these children's lives—children who like him had been robbed of their childhood and innocence. Milenda also thought she wasn't strong or brave enough to actually do anything about it. It always puzzled him that his wife didn't believe in her strength when everyone else could see it loud and clear, which made him admire her even more. In spite of what she saw as her flaws, she was willing to risk her life to save others.

"Pappa." Johari plopped herself on his lap, startling him out of his reverie. She threw her short, chubby arms around his neck and went in for one of her sloppy kisses. Jaali laughed and tickled her, kissing her cheeks several times. "Pappa silly."

"Pappa loves you, *min lilla kärlek.*" Jaali lifted his little love high in the air, delighting in her giggles, tiny bubbles of joy, and innocence—the kind the Mabaya warriors were denying the children of the north. He lowered her until her face was leveled with his and kissed her cheeks again. "And Pappa will never, ever let the bad people hurt you." At least not without a fight. No one was going to touch his little girl—he and Milenda would see to it.

Milenda appeared at the doorway, her gaze still distant, twisting locks of her hair around one finger. He loved her wild hair, not very long but puffy like an explosion of black wool on top of her head. She had told him that without Asha, her patient young maid in the palace, she had long given up on trying to tame her hair into a resemblance of a hairdo. She sooner cover it up with a *iqhiya* than attempt coaxing it into braids.

Silently, she wandered up and sat next to him, her head resting on his shoulder. "We have to start with the people." He was not sure she was talking to him or herself. "If we start by building up their confidence, they will be more willing to fight the system."

Bored by the conversation, Johari slid off her father's lap and began another crazed circular race with the young dragon. "What are you thinking? Do you have a plan?"

"Maybe." The whispered word held a promise, and Jaali waited for her to say more, but she didn't. Instead, she kept her head on his shoulder, one hand on his thigh, and sat quietly watching their child play.

He didn't ask. She would tell him when she was ready. He was in no hurry to put his wife and child in danger and perfectly content with the simple life they were living.

A loud swoosh of a giant wing lifted dirt and leaves up in the air around them. Mjusi was back, a dead animal hanging from his mouth and hot steam coming out of his nostrils. He dropped the carcass with great aplomb and shook his head from side to side in greeting. He had brought them dinner. They hadn't had meat in over a week. This was a welcomed change of pace.

"Thank you, my friend." Milenda got up to pet the dragon, and Jaali picked up the animal to take it to the back of the house where he would skin and prepare it to be cooked. Mjusi had been invaluable as a source of food for the family, here and in Isvärld.

When he went back to the front of the house, Johari was crouched by her mother, intently watching Milenda draw letters and shapes on the dirt. With her head down, her gaze following the movement of the stick, she didn't notice him at first. *What is she drawing?* He came closer, and she lifted her eyes to him. A smile slowly stretched her full lips and sparkled in her eyes.

"What's that?" he asked, tilting his head to get a better view of the drawing. Johari, still crouched in that way only children can, looked at him and giggled as if saying, "You don't know?" *Cheeky like her mother already.*

Milenda got to her feet and opened her arms in a grand gesture. "A plan. My plan to bring down the Elders and their tyranny."

Jaali didn't know whether to laugh or panic. It was one thing to know something eventually had to be done but another to actually have a plan of action. "You have a plan?" He choked on his own words, his heart suddenly clenching in his chest.

As he stood paralyzed by apprehension, his wife stepped closer and hooked her fingers on his, pulling him closer to what could be the topography of their future. "It may not make much sense to you, but I had to sketch it in order to understand how it would work," she explained. "Johari helped. Right, *kidojo moja?*"

The little girl hooted and clapped her hands. Jaali stared

speechless and confused—the scribbles on the floor made absolutely no sense to him.

"I'll explain later, but basically I will start with what we have in place already and go from there."

"We have something in place?" Jaali asked, pressing his eyebrows together. "What are you talking about?"

Milenda dropped his hand and slid her arm around Jaali's waist. Whatever confusion and fear he had instantly melted at her touch. Little witch she was. The invisible wires connecting and sustaining them never ceased to amaze him.

"The shrine." She looked up at him as if that word explained everything. It didn't. Unconsciously, Jaali reached out to her and told her without uttering a word. Milenda's eyes opened like small orbs of light. It had been a while since they'd communicated that way. "The Elders use the people's superstitions to keep them tamed and under their control. It's time we turn that into our advantage."

He still didn't understand what she meant. "How is that going to help us or the people of Natale?"

"The Elders allowed the worshiping of my soul to keep the people distracted and hopeful." Milenda bit her upper lip. "They even built the shrine and encouraged people in their belief that I'd listen to their prayers and keep them safe. What they didn't take into account is that if there is a thread of hope, there is a gateway to rebellion."

Milenda's plan was slowly becoming clearer in his mind—not the details but the overall concept. She was going to feed the people's hope and faith in her in order to create the perfect growing ground for a revolution. The idea was just as exciting as it was frightening. Revolution was careening toward them, and he was afraid they would be crushed under its weight.

* * *

Sleep hadn't come easy to her for the past few days. Revolution was not a word she relished. Its scared her to think there could be a war because of her, that people might be thrown in jail or killed in her name. It frightened her that she might have brought her daughter into something no one should ever have to go through. Mjusi, always well tuned-in with her emotional state, wouldn't leave her side, wrapping his tail around her legs when she sat and stumbling over the low vegetation and rocks instead of flying so he could be close. He had grown a lot bigger than he was when they had left for the Northern Lands—still not full adult size but almost double of what he was before. It would not be as easy to hide him now, his green scales taking on an iridescent glow that refracted sunlight in all directions like diamonds.

"Mjusi, I'm fine. You don't have to protect me all the time." The flying lizard cocked his head in a bird-like movement. "Really. Nobody knows I'm alive and here. You need to go fly and hunt." Her friend shook his head with a growl. He had also taken the responsibility of watching over little Gavå who was now slightly bigger than a dog but much bulkier and stronger.

Jaali had emphatically protested against what she was about to do, but she stood her ground. Milenda wished she could have talked to Mama Nyeusi or Yemanjá beforehand, but she was sure it was the right move—at least she hoped it was. Her stomach flip-flopped as she approached the shrine site, Mjusi still by her feet, obviously not too happy about the plan either.

"I have to do it, my friend," she said, more to herself than the dragon. "I owe it to Jaali who suffered for years in the hands of the slavers, and I owe it to my people who have long languished under the control of the Elders. I have to do this."

This was a visitation. The plan was that she would reveal herself to the people visiting the shrine. They would assume she was a spirit coming to help them and listen to her commands—well, suggestions or requests, she didn't think she could bring herself to give her future subjects any orders. Milenda was going to sneak into the shrine in disguise like she had done before and then at the right time drop her coverings and…. She shuddered at the thought. She had been so sure of herself that morning as she sat with her husband by the marula tree, but as she approached the site, her confidence began wavering. What if this was a terrible idea? *Oh, gods. I should have consulted Yemanjá first.* Just as she thought it, she knew exactly what the *orisa* would have told her: "You're a future queen and perfectly capable of coming up with a workable plan. Trust in yourself, child."

The edge of the jungle, where the trees stood further apart and the ground was easier to navigate, materialized in front of her. She had been so buried in her own thoughts, she hadn't realized they had gone that far already. Milenda took a deep breath, made a face at Mjusi to soothe his nerves, and took a tremulous step into the clearing.

The place was a lot like it had been the last time she was there—peppered with worshipers and a couple guards. It wasn't exactly a huge crowd, but there were enough of them to spread the word. In her superstitious nation, it didn't take much for a rumor to spread like wildfire. In fact, she was counting on it.

She lowered her eyes, and her body curved into the submissive stance she remembered Asha often assuming when addressing her. A pang in her chest made her gasp—she wondered where the young girl was and if she had been given a proper position at the palace after she left or if she had been thrown out in the streets. Milenda hoped her father saw to it that her faithful girl-servant was well taken care of in her absence.

A beautiful woman who seemed to radiate light from underneath her nondescript *kanga* dress walked by and glanced at her. Afraid she would notice her green irises, Milenda took a quick look from the corner of her eyes and stumbled—the woman was looking straight at her, a smile stretched lazily on her well-shaped lips and a glint of recognition in her eyes.

Her green eyes!

Milenda turned to take a better look, but the woman had somehow vanished from sight. Who could that be? Only Nyotas had green eyes, and there weren't that many of them around anymore, not in Natale anyway. With her heart in a frenzy, Milenda pulled the head-covering over her forehead and quickened her step toward the harbor seat she had so often shared with her husband. Better do what she had come here to do and leave as quickly as she could.

Once in place, a quick look around told her no one was paying attention to her, everybody busy with their own prayers. As fast as she could, she removed all her coverings to expose her *kanga*-covered body and the *matangazos* on her neck and shoulder. Her anxiety had them already lit up like stars in a midnight sky, exactly what she was hoping for. It was a rare occasion when she wanted to be noticed. She swallowed the bile that had risen to her mouth, raised her arms in the air, and began singing, her voice gaining tread and power with each verse. Two women, who were close by, looked up suddenly at the singing woman and gasped as their gaze met the shining markings in Milenda's skin.

"It's the Jewel." Their scream of recognition echoed through the clearing, triggering a chain reaction from all who were present. One by one, the worshipers lifted their eyes to Milenda, who was now illuminated by a single ray of sunlight as if the gods themselves wanted her to be seen. Shortly after the first outcry of surprise, people began falling to their knees, their foreheads meeting the dirt on the ground, and their voices rising in prayer.

"Sisi tunakushukuru, tunakuomba kwa ulinzi wako na msaada wako. Jewel, tunakupenda na kukuuliza kwa uongozi wako."

Their chant caught the guards' attention, and they ran to where everyone else had gathered, too shocked by the sight to react. Like everyone else, their jaws fell opened, and they forgot to act as they watched Milenda finish her song, her voice tremulous but determined. As soon as the last note had left her lips, a soft but heavy blanket of silence fell over the shrine. Milenda swallowed the lump that had gathered in her throat and blinked her eyes to clear the dots that spotted her vision.

"People of Natale," she shouted, her voice somehow echoing around her. "Your Jewel hasn't left you. When I promised to fight for you, to give you better lives, I meant it. The Jewel does not promise idly. I'm here to keep my word, but I need your help."

The crowd murmured, their hushed voices growing in a crescendo around Milenda, suffocating her with their urgency. She raised her hands in front of her to stop them, and silence returned, every eye in the shrine focused on her, devoted and in awe.

Milenda squelched a gasp of anxiety, licked her dry lips, and continued her speech. "I need you to spread the word. I need my people to tell the rest of the world their princess is here and she's going to make it right. But you need to release your anger, your frustration with the way things are in Natale. You need to question the slavers and those who sponsor them. You, the people of Natale, are the ones who can win this fight. Get ready, because the day has come for the people to rise up."

More whispers and sighs moved through the crowd like a wave in the ocean. For a moment, Milenda panicked. She had everything planned except her exit. How was she going to leave the shrine in a way that made her look like the spirit her worshipers thought she was? Just as the thought began to choke her, a great clamor arose on the other side of the shrine, a great confusion of voices and unidentifiable sounds. Everyone turned toward it, and Milenda saw her chance. With a whisper of thanks to whoever had sent her this boon, she grabbed the discarded coverings from the floor and hastily covered herself, stepping out of the circle of gifts to join the distracted crowd. By the time they turned toward her again, she was gone—anonymous again among them all.

As she moved slowly but purposely to the edge of the jungle, she overheard words of wonder. As hard as it was for her to believe, her countrymen thought her to be godsent, a divine instrument to liberate them, to end their centuries-long misery. Every man and women in the clearing that day thought her to be their savior. That thought made Milenda feel as inadequate as when she was just a young princess roaming the hallways of the palace with no one to play with and nobody to love her. What if she let them down?

CHAPTER SIX

Eshu

It was not exactly the shower he had built for his princess in Isvärld, but the water was cool and refreshing as it splashed on his shoulders and ran down his back and chest. Jaali had found this spot just a five-minute walk behind their *hema* as he was chasing Johari and Gavå one day. The great river Miungu stormed through the jungle, racing the beetles and roaring like a lion, but it forked through several smaller rivers before joining again further into the jungle. One of its tributaries ran behind their home, a pale version of Miungu, much tamer and narrower, and dropped in waterfalls here and there as it made its journey to meet the wilder parts of itself. One of the spots where the river fell in a cascade of bubbling freshness into a small lagoon had quickly became Jaali's favorite spot to bathe and swim. Selfishly, he had kept its existence a secret for a few days before surprising his wife. Milenda had been delighted. Jaali knew she missed the amazing showers of the palace where she had often found refuge from a life she hadn't asked or cared for.

Even though they often bathed together, today Milenda had gone to meet with her *iyalorixá* again. The old woman was keeping them informed of the rumors and whispers of the populace. These meetings were a source of great anxiety for him—he had visions of his jewel being caught by palace guards and taken before the Elders. A dip in the lagoon kept him calmer. Mjusi was watching over the little ones while they napped so he could enjoy a few moments of peace. When he dipped underneath the water, the silence enveloped him like a protective sheath, the embrace of a mother. Holding his breath for as long as he could, Jaali said a silent prayer of thanks. He wasn't sure who he was thanking exactly, but he needed to credit his happiness to someone or something. Even now with that same happiness threatened by the circumstances of Milenda's royal status, he still felt that bubbling of joy inside his heart.

As he broke the surface of the water, an odd feeling assailed him—a prickling of the skin on the back of his neck. *I'm being watched*. The revelation turned his body to ice, cold and hard with tension. Swiveling on his toes, Jaali scanned the area around the lagoon but saw nothing. In fact, everything was eerily quiet—the leaves were still, and the animals had gone quiet. A shiver ran through his body. It couldn't be the Elders' men. They would have spooked the jungle into a frenzy of movement. Something supernatural then. The question was, was it friend or foe?

Slowly, he made his way to the bank, the sloshing of cool water separating for his body and uniting again behind him the only sound he could hear. With his hair dripping, Jaali walked out of the water and into the grass-covered earth, the greenery tickling the soles of his feet. He grabbed his long tunic and slid it over his head to cover his nakedness, never once stopping his careful survey of the jungle around him. Strange how he didn't see anything special about being visited by a deity anymore. The past three years had taught him that the spirit world was not as unreachable or perfect as he'd thought. It had also taught him that when it came to otherworldly creatures, there was no point in trying to make them do something. They did it when they so desired and not a minute earlier.

Jaali sat on a large rock not far from the swooshing waters of the lagoon and waited, poised for any eventuality. The jungle was still muted, the silence grating on his nerves more than anything else. He didn't have to wait long.

"Are you Jaali, the slave who wedded our one and only Jewel?" The booming voice seemed to come from everywhere and nowhere in particular.

The use of the word slave smarted. He hadn't been called that in a long time, but now that simple term brought a gush of bad memories to his mind. Jaali shook his head, trying to shake the thoughts off. "I'm no longer a slave, but, yes, I am Jaali. Who are you?"

"Silence!" It was more of an explosion rather than a voice, that of a male for sure, not any of the goddesses he had met so far. "How dare you correct me, mere mortal that you are?"

Chided, Jaali reluctantly lowered his eyes in a sign of respect and submission, even as his soul was rebelling against it. "Forgive me. I spoke out of place."

There was silence for a moment. Then another explosion, but this time there were no words as laughter filled every inch of that little corner of the jungle. Perplexed, Jaali scanned the area again but came up empty. Where was this spirit? Was it another *orisa*?

The laughter continued for a while, the sound popping in Jaali's ears like the beating of a drum, somewhere between amusement and mockery. Knowing how unwise it would be to protest, he bit his lip and waited.

The laughter stopped as abruptly as it had started. "I knew I would like you the moment Yemanjá told me about you." Without the previous boom, the voice sounded ordinary and almost feminine. "Spunky and just a tad reckless."

Jaali had never thought of himself as reckless, but then again, his life hadn't allowed for much introspection—he'd spent his days wishing he was invisible and praying his master had no unsavory appetites that day. "May I ask who you are?"

"I'm the great Eshu, the *orisa* of crossroads and your shadow from now on." The air seemed to blur and blink as the shape of a man appeared just a few steps ahead of him. The demigod was tall and lanky, giving the illusion that he never quite ended, with well-defined muscles rippling through his chest, abs, and arms like ocean waves on a windy day. The vastness of his brown skin seemed to reflect the sunlight as he stood, legs spread apart and arms crossed over his chest. A ghost of a smile pulled at the corners of his lips as Jaali studied him, not sure yet of what to think or feel. The *orisa* was obviously enjoying Jaali's scrutiny. "Just let me know when you're done with your perusal."

A wave of heat crawled up Jaali's neck into his face. Why were all these deities so hell-bent at making him feel uncomfortable? Was that how gods amused themselves, by making mortals squirm? "What do you want from me?" The familiar anger at being made to feel less than clean made him careless.

The *orisa* moved then, the long strap of *kanga* cloth that hung from his waist all the way to the ground swaying along. He wore nothing else, leaving the rest of his body exposed to the air and light. "I bring you a message from Yemanjá."

That was a new development. The goddess had never spoken to him, choosing to communicate only with Milenda. "Why me? Milenda is the Jewel."

"The Mother wants you to do something for her." Eshu uncrossed his arms and waved one hand over his head. "She knows the Jewel will not ask you herself." Which could only mean it was something dangerous.

His wife was still protecting him, sheltering him from harm. "What could that be?" His voice betrayed the fact he was still annoyed by the *orisa*'s insinuation. "Yemanjá has never asked anything from me."

"The Mother favors females." Eshu's voice had dropped to a whisper as if he didn't want anyone to hear his words. Was that a note of anger in his voice? If it was, it dissipated quickly. The god shook his head and raised his voice. "She needs you to help the Jewel address the slaves."

Jaali's heart skipped a beat. The word alone brought him memories he didn't want to think about. He certainly didn't want to face what was once his daily reality. "And how exactly does she want me to do that? It's not like *indents* are allowed to move about freely." Bitterness colored his words. He could almost feel the tartness on his tongue.

"The *indents*—why not call them what they really are, slaves?—will gather if Yemanjá so desires." Jaali cringed at the word. He wondered if he would ever be able to hear the word slave without a sudden flood of anger and fear. "She'll let you know when she's ready for you to talk to them and where."

"Don't I get even a chance to think about it?" Jaali's annoyance at being told what to do showed in his tone.

The *orisa* laughed again, throwing his bald head backward and showing a row of sparkling white teeth. "Have you met my sisters? When one of them gives an order, she expects obedience."

Of course he was not surprised, but it still bothered him. "Milenda won't be happy," he said, more to himself than the god.

The laughter died suddenly, and a frown replaced the smile. "Milenda must not know of this, you understand? Not until it's a done deal."

The seed of a suspicion lodged itself in his mind. "How do I know you really speak for the Mother? What if its all a ploy from the Elders to trap us?" The one thing his years of slavery had taught him was never to trust anyone at face value.

Eshu seemed offended, a hand flying to his chest. "Now I'm hurt. Why would I be lying? Only a fool would provoke Yemanjá's wrath, and I am no fool." The *orisa* swatted an invisible insect off his arm. "I grow tired of this conversation. What do I care if you obey the Mother's orders or not? It's your life on the line. Do as you please. I did my job."

The god turned around as if to leave but looked back at Jaali one more time. "And you haven't seen the last of me either, pretty mortal." Unlike Freya who would just dissolve like a mirage, Eshu made a show out of his departure. A great eruption of smoke blocked Jaali's view of the jungle beyond as Eshu walked into the cloud and disappeared.

Jaali dropped to his knees, his legs suddenly weak and wobbly. How was he going to hide this from his wife, the woman who could sense his feelings and read his mind? Between them there were no secrets, no lies. Until now.

* * *

"They think I'm some kind of goddess, Mama Nyeusi." Milenda was still finding it hard to accept that she was being revered by her people as a savior. "I'm just a woman, not the heroine they think I am."

The *iyalorixá* sighed. "Child, when are you going to accept the fact that you are extraordinary?" The old woman hummed a note of disapproval and sat down on one of the rickety chairs in the *hema*.

Tempted to stomp her feet like a little girl, Milenda sat next to her *iyalorixá* instead. "But I'm not extraordinary, Mama. Being a princess doesn't make me any more important or special than anyone else."

Mama Nyeusi held the princess's hands in hers. The touch of her papery skin against her own soothed her even if the words didn't. "Milenda, you're the Jewel, the crown princess and a Nyota. The gods were on your side even when you went against tradition and married an ex-slave. You have the power to project not only your image but your physical form across great distances. Accept it. It's part of who you are. And you are indeed extraordinary."

She didn't want to be anything but regular, ordinary, just one of the girls. Why did everyone else seem determined to elevate her to heights she didn't care for? All she wanted was to spend the rest of her life loving her husband and child, but however simple, that was the one thing the gods wouldn't grant her.

"What do I do next?" she asked, resigned to go along with whatever fate had written for her life. "I'm afraid for Johari and Jaali."

"Jaali is perfectly capable of taking care of himself and his daughter. Besides, Yemanjá wouldn't let anything bad happen to you or your family."

Milenda bristled, pulling her hands away from her *iyalorixá*. "You're the one who told me the gods are fickle. What if the Mother decides she is tired of the whole thing and stops protecting me?"

Mama Nyeusi crossed her arms over her generous bosom and pinched her lips. "Stop fretting so much, girl. There's no point in fighting your destiny."

Throwing her hands up in the air, Milenda hmphed. "See? You also told me that destiny is always in our hands, that we can change it."

A roar-like sound escaped the old woman's lips. She wrapped her arms around her waist and bent over in laughter. "I'm happy you remember some of the things I taught you."

"Glad I'm amusing you, Mama, because I'm not in the very least enjoying this." Her lips twitched at the corners, belying her words and tone of voice. She had always had trouble resisting her *iyalorixá*. As soon as the old woman stood up and opened her arms, Milenda fell into the hug, grateful for the familiar warmth. "I'm scared, Mama Nyeusi. I'm so scared."

The *iyalorixá* tightened her arms around Milenda. "I know, child. I know."

A great racket of screams and clicking noises interrupted their moment. They both dropped their arms and looked toward the door where a running, laughing Johari was being chased by an equally active Gavå. The toddler ran directly to her mother's legs and hugged them with such enthusiasm Milenda almost lost her balance.

Mama Nyeusi bent down and scooped the child off the ground and held her in her arms. "What's this wild thing?" Johari laughed and dropped a kiss on the old woman's nose. "And it kisses too. What are you?"

The child giggled and bookended the *iyalorixá*'s face. "Am Johari. Pappa's *lilla kärlek*."

"Oh, yes? And what does that mean? Wild thing? Little monkey?" Mama Nyeusi bounced the girl in her arms.

Johari looked at Milenda, suddenly out of words. The Jewel laughed and came to her rescue. "It means little love, Mama."

Johari nodded emphatically. "Lit lurve," she repeated, a serious expression in her amber face. As soon as she was done talking, the toddler began squirming in the old woman's arms, and she put her down. Not missing a breath, Johari ran out the door, chasing the baby dragon just as Jaali was coming in.

"That child has more energy than the sun," he said, following his daughter with his eyes. "And is just as bright." Jaali crossed the space between him and his wife and enveloped her with his arms. "What are you doing here, Mama?" Milenda knew he worried every time the woman came to visit, afraid that someone followed her.

The *iyalorixá* waved her hands in front of her. "What a worrier you are, Jaali. No one followed me."

"How can you be so sure? It's easy enough to hide in the jungle." Milenda stretched on her tiptoes and kissed his chin, trying to assure him everything was well. "I'm glad to see you, but considering the danger—"

With another shake of her hands, Mama Nyeusi dismissed his concern. "I understand, but I'm an old hen who has learned quite a few tricks through the years. Besides, nobody pays much attention to an old *iyalorixá* and her quirks." Milenda doubted that very much. Her surrogate mother was not one to go unnoticed; she had scared everyone off the idea of following her anywhere most likely. "Well, it's time to go back. Amare will be looking for her daily medicine."

She winked, and Milenda felt guilty all over again. She didn't like the fact they were preventing her stepmother from having a baby.

After the old woman left, Jaali chased his daughter down and took her to her crib for a nap, closely followed by the baby dragon who had bonded with the child much like Mjusi had with her. "Sleep, *min lilla kärlek*," the Fjorden whispered as he placed a gentle kiss on his daughter's forehead.

Milenda snorted. "So she can recharge that unharnessed energy of hers." Jaali turned his head to her and shushed her with a finger before joining her just outside the tiny makeshift room. "She'll be running circles around us as soon as she wakes up."

Jaali draped an arm over her shoulders and guided her to the bed they shared. "I have something to tell you." Milenda sobered instantly. Those words always seemed to bring something unwelcomed. "Let's sit down for a bit and talk."

Suddenly assailed by an irrational fear, Milenda wanted to wrap her legs around her husband and do every and anything to avoid the conversation. Jaali looked serious, a cloud dulling his lake blue eyes. Her stomach clenched. "What's wrong?"

Sitting on the edge of their bed, his legs stretched in front of him, Jaali held her hand in his and bit his lip. "Nothing's wrong. I've been keeping a secret from you for a few days, and it's killing me. I was told not to say anything to you, but I have to."

Her heart was beating so hard, she could hear and feel its

echoes in her ears. "What is it? What secret are you talking about?"

He told her then, spilling the information along with his heart, his eyes never leaving his wife's. Milenda was too stunned to be angry. Yet. She listened patiently—not her best quality—her hands holding his tightly as if afraid he'd float away. Instinctively, their minds connected, and she could feel what he felt, see what he had seen, hear what Eshu had told him.

"Who's this Eshu?" she asked, curiosity winning over the anger and fear that was beginning to bubble inside of her.

Jaali shrugged. "Another demigod. But I got the feeling he was somehow less than Yemanjá or Freya. He referred to himself as a messenger from the Mother, as if he served her." Jaali was worried that she was angry at him, she knew. She wasn't. How could she ever be angry at the man she loved more than life, the man who had gone through hell to be with her? "I had to tell you, *msichana*."

Milenda brushed her fingers on her husband's ivory cheek, trying to smooth out the wrinkles of worry creasing his skin. "Eshu should have never asked you to hide it from me—or whoever gave the order. What gives them the rights to rule over our own free will?"

The corner of Jaali's lips curled up. "Because they're gods and us mere mortals?" Milenda frowned, and he dropped a kiss on her nose. "I feel better now that I've told you, even though I may be in for a rough ride once Yemanjá finds out I went against her wishes."

"Are you going to do it?" Jaali raised his eyebrows. "What she asked. Are you going to talk to the *indents*?"

Jaali bit the corner of his lip before answering. "Yes, I think I will. Isn't that what we are here for? To help those who can't help themselves?"

Milenda nodded and laid her head on his shoulder. "I don't like it, but Yemanjá is right. No one better to talk to them than someone who's been in their position before." Jaali flattened his hand on her back and kissed the top of her head. The man had survived the Trials, he could survive this as well. "Just promise me, *wimbo wa moyo*, that you'll be careful and come back to us, safe and sound."

"Nothing and nobody will ever keep me from coming back home to you and Johari. Nothing."

* * *

A nest of wasps had settled in Jaali's stomach, tickling and stinging until he felt it would explode. He sat behind a giant bush, waiting for Eshu's signal to reveal himself to the small crowd that had gathered there. Jaali had no idea how Yemanjá had done it, but a group of slaves had somehow evaded their overseers to assemble in this clearing, not far from where he had been taken to prepare for the Trials three years ago.

"They're mostly house slaves—domestics and such." The demigod's voice came from behind without warning. Jaali jumped to his feet, losing his balance and almost falling. "I don't know why the Mother is trusting you with this. You're as clumsy as a hippopotamus and twice as squeamish."

Jaali regained his balance and wiped his hands on his pants. He wondered what would happen if he punched a god. Whatever the consequences, he was tempted. "When you're done insulting me, maybe you can explain what I'm supposed to do exactly."

The god wrinkled his nose as if he was smelling something bad. "Calm down, human. Just because you're easy on the eye doesn't mean you're exempt from being smitten." Eshu was practically naked, just like the last time, a long sash of *kanga* cloth covering his loincloth on both sides. His dark skin glittered as if covered in microscopic diamonds from head to toe.

"Do you have to be so rude?" Jaali knew he was pushing it, but between the anxiety about his situation and the growing exasperation with the divine beings who played them as pawns in a game, he had lost his fear—or maybe common sense.

"It is not rude when you're stating a fact." The wish to punch Eshu came back full force. "In a few minutes, you'll walk into the clearing and reveal yourself as the prince consort. They're going to ooh and ahh for a while, but then you must go back to the reason you're here."

His patience was stretched to the maximum. "Which is what exactly?"

"Give them hope." The demigod's voice had lost the sarcastic bite and had grown quiet and somber. "Tell them that there is hope. You were a slave once, and now you're the Jewel's husband. Ask them to spread the word among the other slaves and make sure the news doesn't reach their masters' ears. Speak from the heart, Fjorden."

Jaali took a deep breath and stepped into the clearing. At first nobody noticed him, just another man coming to the gathering, but then the talking hushed and silence dropped like a heavy curtain, all eyes turning to him. Despite the quickening of the blood flowing through his veins, Jaali didn't stall. Head held up high and eyes scanning the crowd for familiar faces, he strode to the middle of the small ocean of people.

He lowered his eyes for a moment so that nobody would see him taking in a breath of air as if he was drowning. No one was talking, the silence unnerving, clawing at his heart and soul. These people had been silent for far too long.

"Brothers and sisters, do you know who I am?" It was clear by the expressions on their faces that they had recognized him, but he had to begin somewhere, and establishing their commonalities first seemed the right way to go.

Nobody answered. After a long pause, one woman stood, her arms stretched along her sides, her gaze glued to him. "You're Jaali Asker. We thought you were dead."

Jaali cleared his throat. "As you can see, I'm very much alive." An undulating whisper broke the oppressing silence, reminding him of his wedding day when he was presented to the populace. "I came back to help you, to free you."

The sounds grew around him—sounds of surprise, disbelief, even anger. The woman who had spoken was still standing, her head turned to the crowd as they talked to each other in a frenzy of whispers. Then, she looked at him again.

"Nobody can help us. Why would you? You're the husband of a princess. You married one of *them*. What do you care about us?"

The words lacerated his heart. Is that what they thought of him? That he was now one of the people who condoned *indenture*, who supported slavery.

"I'm one of you." His voice escaped him louder than intended. "Not that long ago, I was where you are—a slave, a thing my master could use as he pleased. I just came from Isvärld, where your mothers and fathers cry themselves to sleep every night missing you."

A sob interrupted his speech, and he tried to slow down his breathing, but his heart ached too much—for his people, for his mother who had lost two children to slavery before dying herself, and for Milenda whose life was in constant peril.

"My wife and I promised your families we'd come back and fight for you," he continued in a strangled voice. "We keep our promises." There was silence for a moment as the slaves exchanged surreptitious glances. A young man, not much older than he was when he freed himself from the cruel hands of the *duivel* who owned him, stepped forward. His blond hair reflected the light of the sun, and Jaali felt that pang of anger and sorrow he had grown so familiar with as he was reminded of himself years before he had met his wife—blue eyes clouded by despair and the ever-defeating sense of hopelessness that filled his heart every time he woke up to the harsh reality of slavery.

"What can you do to help us? The Jewel is not around

anymore, and the king is weak and powerless against the Elders." The young man opened both hands in front of him, palms up, in a gesture that was half defeat, half prayer.

Jaali swallowed hard and clenched his jaws so tightly together, a stab of pain shot across his cheek all the way to his ear. He unclenched his teeth and took a deep breath. "The king is on our side and the Jewel is alive." The statement caused a string of whispers to run through the crowd. "The Jewel and I are working with him and Yemanjá to come up with a plan to free all slaves. I know I'm asking a lot, but you must be patient for a while longer." The whispering grew angry. "For now, I ask you to spread the news among our people and keep it away from the slavers. The Elders must not know we are alive. As long as they think us dead and gone, we have some wiggle room to put our plan into action."

Guilt tasted bitter on his tongue—they didn't have a plan yet, but giving his people a thread of hope was important. Hopelessness did not inspire the will to fight.

"I've been a slave since I was seven," the young man said. "Not once has anyone tried to help me. Why should I—all of us—believe you will?"

In his mind, Jaali heard Eshu's words. *"Speak from the heart."* He stepped forward and offered the man his hand. "What's your name?"

Confusion eclipsed the anger in the young man's face. Hesitantly, he took Jaali's hand and shook it. "Bjorn. My name is Bjorn Nilsson."

"I'm Jaali Asker." They all knew his name, but saying

it out loud was a good reminder that he was one of them, a Fjorden who had been yanked from his country and family by slavers. "I was snatched off my bed when I was twelve while my parents slept next door. They packed me with a number of other Fjorden children into the cargo hull of a ship bound to the cultured and wealthy kingdom of Natale. Wretched and hungry, we slept piled up on hard, mold-covered wooden floors with hardly any space to move our legs and told to relieve ourselves where we lay."

The crowd had grown silent, their eyes fixed on him and lips twisted into frowns. The story he told was familiar to all of them, he was sure.

"Some of us jumped overboard, preferring the darkness of death to the one expecting us at our destination. We were children, but we knew—we had heard the stories and watched as parents lost their spark and will to live when their children didn't come back. We knew these men and women taking us across an ocean did not plan on treating us like humans at all. We were less than animals to them, and they made sure to remind us of that every day of that harrowing voyage. We knew we would never see our families or be loved and taken care of again. We were cattle for the slaughter."

Chancing a glance at the quiet group of slaves, Jaali was not surprised to see tears in most eyes. He knew he was reaching them, stirring them up into being willing to risk their lives for freedom, the one thing that had so savagely been taken away from them.

"I was luckier than most at first, working for a kind

owner who had me and the other Fjordens use our skills for woodworking but fed us and treated us decently." Jaali swallowed hard. He had never told this story to anyone but his wife and had hoped never to tell it again. But he would do whatever it took to help free his brothers and sisters still in captivity. "Unfortunately, my luck didn't last, and I was sold to a cruel, sadistic slaver who took a shining for my body and used me to pleasure himself and his friends for years. Do you know how many times I wished I was dead? How many times I tried to kill myself to escape the nightmare my life had become? How many times I dreamed about the chance to one day be able to wake up in the morning and not fear being raped and beaten?"

There was a collective inhale, and it took all he had not to lower his eyes in shame. Yes, he still felt shame every time he thought of his past. Even though he knew he had nothing to be ashamed of for what others had done to him, his slaver's voice still rang inside his head, taunting him, brainwashing him into thinking he was the one "asking for it." His stomach twisted inside of him, threatening to empty its contents.

"Yes, I was—I am one of you, and I know that if I had been given the chance the Jewel and I are giving you now, I would gladly take it, to hell with the risk. Nothing can be worse than what my life was from the moment I was taken from my home. Nothing."

"I know those of you who are here have less cruel situations and more freedom than most, but heed my warning, so did I at first. There is no guarantee you won't be sold to another master who will treat you like mine did. Do you want to run that risk?" Jaali cleared his throat and looked directly at the young man who had addressed him earlier. "Pleased to meet you, Bjorn. Are you willing to fight for your freedom, or do you prefer to live the rest of your life in captivity?"

The young man looked around, searching for an answer to some question only he knew before replying, "I choose freedom. I will do whatever it takes to be free."

Jaali smiled for the first time, and a weight lifted from his shoulders, quickly replaced by the lightness of hope. The corners of Bjorn's lips stretched slowly upward, and Jaali knew then that he had won this battle.

CHAPTER SEVEN

The Kidnapping

Milenda's foot snagged on a loose tile, and she fell, her knee hitting the hard floor with a loud thump. Muffling a cry of pain, she braced herself on the wall next to her and stood up, a furious burning flaring around her knee and radiating up and down her leg.

"Clumsy idiot," she whispered, rubbing the joint and glancing around her. No one seemed to have heard her. She had sneaked into the palace one more time to talk to her father, but this time it hadn't been as easy. Guards were around the whole perimeter of the palace as if they expected an attack. She had to wait in the shelter of the jungle for a long while, Mjusi by her side as always, before she ventured through the back door.

Her time was short, so she limped her way down the hallway toward her father's chambers. Mama Nyeusi had brought her a servant's dress so she could blend in easily with the rest of the people roaming in between the palace's walls. Her eyes kept faithfully on the floor, she walked along the wide corridors, her side covered by the markings of her people as close to the wall as she could manage.

Jaali had been successful at lifting the slaves' spirits and they were a step closer to starting a revolution from the inside out. She had made a few more appearances at the shrine where a growing crowd converged daily, but the progress was painfully slow, and she couldn't be sure of how effective their ruse was. With a loud sigh, she turned a corner and walked straight into a palace guard.

"Girl, watch where you're going." The man towered over her and rattled her to the bones with his gruff, low voice. "Where are you heading?"

Milenda could have sworn her heart had climbed to her mouth and taken residence there. She fixed her eyes on the floor and instinctively pulled the cloth further over her head and shoulders. "To the servants' quarter." She kept her voice meek and soft even as panic rose inside of her and the urge to take off running overwhelmed her.

The guard waved his hand, dismissing her and resumed his walking, grumbling under his breath, "These servant girls. No brain at all."

Fighting the wish to tell him exactly how brainless the royal servants were not, Milenda turned on her heels and dashed down the hallway. Her heart had not dropped to its proper place yet, and she felt weak in the legs, a feeling further aggravated by the fact that her knee throbbed as if it had a life of its own. Turning another corner, she saw a cluster of guards just a few feet ahead. *What am I going to do?* If she ducked into one of the rooms along the hallway, she risked walking into an even more dangerous situation since she had no idea what they held inside. Silently she chided herself for never having taken the time to explore the rooms on that side of the palace when she still lived there.

Her breathing was shallow, as if she had been running. She closed her eyes and walked forth, begging the gods the guards wouldn't stop her. As she passed yet another room, she heard the unmistakable sound of a door opening and barely had time to blink before a hand shot through the gap and pulled her inside. The door closed behind her and darkness filled the room. Milenda prepared herself to fight, the smooth moves of Fjorden martial art quickly flashing through her mind. Jaali had been teaching her for a couple years, but she was not good at it. Not good enough. It didn't mean she wouldn't put up a fight.

"Stop squirming. You'll alert the guards." It was a female voice, too close to her ear for comfort. The mystery woman had her pinned between her and the wall. She was strong, her arms holding her like a vise, and her legs braced against the back of Milenda's so she couldn't move.

"Let me go," Milenda whispered, not wanting to make her situation any worse. "Who are you? What do you want?"

Again, she felt the warm breath on her ear. "If you stop trying to get away and promise not to do anything, I'll let you go. I mean you no harm, I promise."

Reluctantly, Milenda nodded and stopped moving. The woman loosened her hold enough for Milenda to free herself. She turned around to face her attacker, but the room was too dark to discern any details. The woman was just slightly taller than her and was wearing a *gele*, the silhouette of its typical edges sticking out from the top of her head.

Milenda heard a scratching sound and then a wavering flame appeared between them. Her attacker was a young woman with smooth, amber skin and large, round brown eyes. Milenda didn't recognize her, but a quick look at the royal loops she wore around her neck told her everything she needed to know.

"Amare?" In her surprise, she forgot where she was and spoke loudly.

"Are you crazy? Do you want to be caught?" Amare—for it was indeed the new queen, there was no doubt—lit a small oil lamp and looked at her in a way reminiscent of Mama Nyeusi's looks when she wasn't pleased with her charge. "Your father is away visiting the new hospital. You really should be more careful."

"How did you know I'd be here? And why are *you* here?" Her stepmother didn't look threatening, hardly older than herself, but Milenda couldn't help being suspicious. This woman had a lot to lose if the Jewel showed up to claim her throne.

"You wouldn't believe me if I told you." Milenda very much doubted that. After all Jaali and she had gone through, she was ready to believe almost anything. She nodded, encouraging Amare to tell her more. The woman licked her lips and rubbed her chin, blinking her eyes rapidly. "I was told in a dream."

If she told her this four years ago, Milenda would have laughed, but after encounters with demigoddesses, *wyverns*, and her own special gifts, she didn't even blink. Her stepmother was telling the truth. "When?"

Amare hesitated, obviously surprised by her quick acceptance of such a wild statement. "Last night. Nothing like that had ever happened to me," Amare explained. "I had to come and check to see if it was true or just a figment of my imagination."

"Why would you want to meet me? My existence prevents your children from inheriting the crown." Milenda doubted Amare's seemingly earnest motivations.

"Do you think I want to be a queen?" Her eyes widened, and her lips formed an almost perfect circle. "I don't want my future children exposed to what you had to go through. I didn't ask to be picked as your father's wife. The Elders made that decision for me." Bitterness colored her words, and Milenda realized this woman hated the Elders almost as much as she did.

"But that doesn't explain why you came to meet me."

Amare sighed. "I had to find out whether the dream was a true premonition, and if it was, I needed to make sure you didn't get caught." Her stepmother pressed a closed fist to her chest. "This palace is crawling with guards, and it'd be just a matter of time for them to capture you."

Milenda's heart fluttered—not in a good way, but rather with the feeling of dread. "I noticed. Why is that?"

"The Elders know you're alive."

Milenda stumbled. How was that possible? Nobody knew, nobody had seen her other than the people at the shrine. She gasped. "The guards at the shrine! Why didn't I think of that? Of course they would run and tell the Elders. How stupid can I be?"

The other woman reached for her stepdaughter's hand. "Don't beat yourself up. They would find out one way or another. The Elders have spies everywhere, even among the populace." Milenda allowed her hand to relax within the cocoon of Amare's. "Besides, that's not important right now. I have to get you out of this palace safe and sound. The Elders also know where you've been hiding."

Her legs gave out beneath her, her wounded knee hitting the stone floor again. Milenda didn't notice the pain or care that she had accidentally pushed a small ceramic jug crashing onto the floor as she fell. The Elders knew about her *hema*. Her *hema* where she had left Jaali and Johari still asleep, unprotected and oblivious of the danger that was about to descend upon them.

*****

Gavå had followed him to the stream to get water. He carried the large cylindrical container over his right shoulder. "I told you to stay with Johari," he told the baby dragon who immediately ran to rub herself on Jaali's legs. "Gods give me patience," he exclaimed, trying not to trip over the creature.

Johari was still asleep when he left, and he wanted to make the short trip to the water a quick one. It made him nervous to know his daughter was alone, even if he wouldn't be that far. It was a five-minute trip at the most. Gavå was only complicating things, circling around him, her long, thick tail whipping against his legs. With Milenda gone to the palace, he didn't have much choice. They needed water, and there was no running water at the *hema*.

As soon as he reached the stream, he filled the container, splashed some water on his face to cool himself off, and hoisted the large container onto his shoulder again. One of the very few advantages to the tough life he had led was well developed muscles and strength that belied his slim frame. He dashed through the thick greenery, ignoring the pressure on his upper body and legs from the heavy load. A sigh of relief escaped his lips when he finally set eyes on his humble home. Setting the water container down by the wall, he walked in the house to check on his daughter.

"*Min lilla kärlek*, time to wake up."

His singsong voice died on his lips as he laid eyes on Johari's door—or what should have been her door. In its place there was the gaping hole left by the fallen wooden panel. Jaali propelled himself inside the little room, only to find what he feared—nothing. His daughter was gone. He stood by the crib, covering his mouth with a hand, panic setting his heart on a race and rendering him paralyzed. Where was Johari? She couldn't have left by herself, being too small to push the door down. That left him with one frightening conclusion. Someone had kidnapped her.

Without hesitation or much thought, Jaali reached out to Milenda, who by now should be on her way back from the palace. He closed his eyes to get a better focus, but he didn't need it. His wife was already reaching to him.

"*Wimbo wa moyo*, are you all right?" Her voice came

in gasps as if she was running. The sounds and the feelings were clear, but the image was coming in not as clear as it normally did.

He shook his head and pulled his own reach to allow Milenda to fully have access to his mind. Immediately, the long fingers of her thoughts wrapped around the cells of his brain, and he was with her. She was running, her *kanga* dress gathered up on her hips to free her legs, a wild glint in her eye. Mjusi followed closely behind. With the reach now complete, Jaali set out running to catch up with her, be by her side.

"They know," she said, never slowing down. Jaali didn't have to ask who they were. The Elders. "They know. It was my fault."

"*Msichana*, they got Johari." Saying it out loud made it terrifyingly real. The Elders had their daughter, and it was all his fault. He had left her to go fetch water. He could have waited a few more minutes. Thirst would not kill them that quickly. Why had he decided to go to the stream?

Milenda stopped so abruptly, he still kept going for a moment. "What? They have our baby?"

Backtracking a few steps, Jaali tried to catch his breath. "I didn't see who it was, but she's gone, *msichana*. Gone." Tears were burning their way to his eyes as the nightmare became more coalescent. Remembering what had been done to him after his own kidnapping brought a red-hot anger mixed with paralyzing fear. Would they do the same to her? Or would they just kill her?

Mjusi landed beside them with a roar. Jaali had never

heard the *msitu* roar, and for a moment he saw a reflection of the magnificent *wyverns* in the much smaller body of their flying friend. Milenda had fallen silent, her eyes lost in some distant horizon he could not see, her *matangazos* shining like angry stars.

"Milenda," Jaali whispered, suddenly worried about her. His wife was a strong woman, but this was her child, the fruit of her womb. "*Msichana*, are you all right?"

The princess turned her eyes to him, as if seeing him for the first time, and threw herself into his arms, crying. He didn't remember ever seeing her weep. Mama Nyeusi had told him she had cried inconsolably when she thought he had died in the desert, but he had not been there to see it. Not quite sure what to do, Jaali tightened his hold on her, one arm around her waist and the other on the back of her head. "It'll be all right," he whispered, knowing all along it might not be. Johari was a baby, innocent and helpless, in the hands of ruthless men.

His princess raised her tear-streaked face to him, her bright green eyes hard. "They will pay for this," she said, a growl escaping with the words. "I'm going to destroy them."

Jaali shivered. This was not a Milenda he was familiar with—most likely one she herself did not recognize. It scared him a bit to see her usual kind, soft demeanor turned into that of what he was before he met her—haunted and angry. "We'll find her. There is nothing we can't do together." He believed his words. They had faced all kinds of dangers and hardships and always came out on top. Together they could win this battle too.

They held each other a moment longer, sharing their pain but also their strength, their determination to find their baby daughter. Milenda was the first to break the bond. "We better go. Grab our things and hide further in the jungle. They'll come back for us, and we can't help Johari if we are both in their hands."

The *hema* soon was in sight, beautiful in its humble structure. Jaali sighed. Why could they never have a home for long? As soon as they let down their guard, someone or something always took it away—the comfort, the sense of peace and familiarity that came with a home. He was tired—tired of running, of hiding, of fearing for his and his family's life.

Without a word, they started collecting basic articles for survival: a couple pots, blankets, the meager stash of clothing they had brought with them from the northern lands, whatever could be used as a weapon. Jaali opened the trunk that doubled as a seating area and removed his *buugengs*. He had made himself a new one while in Isvärld since he had left his first one in the desert after being shot by the headhunters. Milenda favored the bow and arrow he had taught her how to use shortly after they had settled in Hoppas.

Mjusi watched them as they moved silently about the space, his head following Milenda's every move. Jaali often wondered whether his wife and the *msuti* were mentally connected, because the flying creature always seemed attuned with her moods. On the other hand, Gavå was strangely agitated, whimpering as she stood upon her short legs only to lay down again.

He closed the large bag he had been filling with items from the house and crouched by her. "What's wrong, *lilla* Gavå? Does something hurt?" The young dragon whimpered again, rubbing her large head against his hand. "I miss her too. We'll get her back. Soon." He was not sure if he was comforting the dragon or himself.

Milenda, who had not made a sound since arriving at the *hema*, kneeled beside him to pet the dragonling. "She's scared," she said, a catch in her voice. "She's very scared."

Jaali turned to her and brushed his fingers along her cheek. "Gavå is strong. She'll be all right."

His wife lifted her wet eyes to his and shook her head. "Not Gavå. It's Johari. That's why Gavå is acting like this. She can feel it too. Our daughter is scared and all alone."

The weight that had been hovering over him since he had found Johari gone, dropped and crushed him with all its might. Throwing his arms around Milenda, Jaali held her tight, her heart beating against his chest, their tears blending together into a rivulet of pain and sorrow. Their little girl was gone.

* * *

The whispering of the trees grew the deeper they burrowed into the jungle, putting as much space as they could between them and their *hema*. Milenda hadn't said a word since they left, her chin tucked into her chest, an occasional sob escaping her lips. Jaali, weighed down by several bags, refused to let go of her hand even when she pointed out they would make better time if he was unburdened from her lagging body. She couldn't gather enough energy to walk fast, moving as a brainless slug through the thick greenery, her mind so far away she couldn't tell where it was exactly. Her husband's touch did not bring the usual comfort as she slogged forward, numb in body and spirit.

Her baby was gone, taken by the same evil men who had tried to kill her and Jaali—the same men who would keep a people poor and superstitious to serve their hunger for power. Milenda couldn't hold a coherent thought in her mind, overwhelmed with strains of feelings and fears all vying for her attention. She hadn't felt this helpless since she was a young child wandering the corridors of the palace hungry for love and with no one to offer it to her. Her usual skill to come up with solutions to every problem seemed to be buried somewhere under the worry and the sorrow.

Jaali pulled her behind him, turning every so often to check on her, but she couldn't muster the smile he was hoping to see on her lips. Anger had yet to erupt as her heart was bursting to the seams with the pain of loss. Another sob bubbled to the surface. She didn't bother to hide it from her husband—she knew he was every bit as broken inside. Jaali was used to dealing with loss, dealing with pain. His life had been a string of horrible events, and yet he had come out victorious at the other end. She was not so sure she could do the same. Losing her mother before she was old enough to remember her was a pain of a different kind—it had a remoteness to it, a sort of fogginess that disguised its intensity. The pain of losing her daughter was as clear and as close to her as the bags she carried, only heavier.

Distracted by her own thoughts, Milenda crashed into Jaali's back when he stopped abruptly. "This is a good place," he announced, his voice tremulous and thick with emotion. "We can rest here."

Milenda dropped her bags and looked around, not out of interest but out of the need to do something. It was a small clearing by a Miungu tributary that ran the opposite way they did, in a hurry to meet its mother. She dropped to her knees and cried, the tears she had been holding back the whole way freely rolling down her face. Johari would be running to meet her if she could, but she was but a baby in the hands of ruthless men.

Jaali squatted by her and wrapped his long arms around her shoulders, his hand tenderly cradling her head and pulling it to his shoulder. "We'll find her, *msichana*. I won't rest until we do."

She wanted to believe him, but her fear wouldn't let her. What could a powerless princess and an ex-slave do against the power of the Elders? Milenda shook her head. "What can we do, Jaali? We're nobody."

"Don't ever say that." Jaali's voice was firm. "You are the Jewel, the same princess who defied the Elders and the natural laws to help a worthless freed slave. The same woman who banished his demons and made him hopeful and happy again. You, *msichana*, are as bright and as strong as the sun. You're my love and the hope of a whole nation."

Milenda didn't feel like she was any of those things.

She felt like a little girl, like the loveless child she had been in the past. "I'm nobody, *wimbo wa moyo*. I'm nobody."

"Shush, child. We've had this conversation before. You are no such thing." The voice startled both of them. Milenda raised her head to confirm what she suspected. Yemanjá was back, regal in her golden *kanga* dress, not a hair out of place. "The Jewel must not doubt herself like that." Even though she spoke words of reproach, her tone of voice was soft and soothing. "Times are hard, and your heart is breaking, but not all is lost yet. You knew you had to fight for your people."

Still protected within her husband's arms, Milenda looked up at the goddess with defiance in her heart as anger was finally making its way through the mist of heartbreak. "I didn't expect my baby daughter to be one of the casualties."

The *orisa* pursed her lips. "Don't be petulant my child. Your daughter is not dead, and you will get her back just like when you got Jaali out of that hellish desert." Yemanjá took a few steps closer to them, the folds on her dress barely moving, as if she was floating instead of walking. "You must gather your wits and think of a plan."

Milenda lifted her hands toward the goddess, palms facing up, a gesture Mama Nyeusi had taught her to mean respect and willingness to accept divine grace. "But how, Mother? When I don't even know where they took her."

The beautiful woman clicked her tongue. "Think, *kidojo moja*, think. Johari is also a Nyota and is connected to you by the strongest of bonds—that of a mother and child."

Milenda and Jaali both looked at her, confusion in their eyes. "Ask her, Jewel. Ask your daughter where she is."

Before they could ask any more questions, the *orisa* vanished into thin air, leaving nothing behind to hint at her presence. What had she meant by that? Ask her daughter? How could she do such a thing if she had no idea where Johari was? Milenda turned her eyes to her husband who looked as stunned as she felt. "What do you think she meant, *wimbo wa moyo*?"

Jaali took a deep breath. "Do you think you can reach to Johari like you do with me?" His voice was a mere whisper, as if he was afraid to give her and himself a glint of hope.

Her heart fluttered. Could she? Was that what Yemanjá was telling her in the usual divine, cryptic language? A small flame of hope ignited in her. "If I could do that, how would she tell me where she is? Johari can't say much yet."

For the first time that day, a smile spread across Jaali's lips, lighting his face. "No need for words. You can figure that out yourself when you get there." Assuming that Johari's kidnappers weren't hanging around her all the time, Milenda could do some snooping once she had located her child. The flame of hope flared into a roaring fire. He smiled even wider. "And we can finally find out what happens to your body when you reach out."

Milenda jumped to her feet and pulled Jaali up with her. "We will find and rescue her," she said, throwing her arms around his neck. Rising on her tiptoes, she pulled him closer and kissed his smiling lips, intoxicated by the exhilarating taste of promise. "And then we'll show the Elders who the princess really is."

CHAPTER EIGHT

Tree branches floated down with the furious current, as if late for some encounter or running from imminent danger. Jaali sat on a rock and watched in silence. The symphony of the jungle surrounded him in a cacophony of animal sounds, the rustling of the wind rushing through the trees, the soft growling of the river, dashing, racing, never stopping. Years ago, when still an *indent*, he often wondered what it would be like to be that free, to be able to run anywhere he wanted, not followed by those who made his life a living hell. The Miungu river with all his tributaries had a personality of its own, here quiet and humble, there furious and proud, but at all times blissfully unattached from humans, their tempers and desires.

Milenda had helped him set up camp on the small spot of treeless ground by the mighty river the night before. He knew she was anxious to reach out to their daughter, but he had convinced her to wait a while. What if they were still in transit to wherever they were taking Johari? It wouldn't do them any good if she was to show up while the child was surrounded by her kidnappers. Better to wait until the kidnappers were settled somewhere, lulled by the knowledge they had not been followed, sure enough of their own invulnerability to be careless. The Elders still didn't know what Milenda could do, which worked in their favor—it was their secret weapon, the reason why he had survived the harrowing trek through the merciless desert. It didn't make them powerful but gave them an edge, a weapon against the powers that be.

When his wife had fallen sleep, Jaali left her lying by the firepit they had carved off the ground and came to the river, looking for some peace of mind. As serene as the place might be and how soothing the sound of the rushing waters was, Jaali couldn't calm down. His thoughts, faster than bullets, tripped over and entangled themselves on each other, crowding his mind while his body was filled with something akin to energy, only negative. He felt jittery and anxious for action, frustrated that there was nothing he could do to help his daughter, angry that he had to hide again. Well acquainted with the heavy sense of helplessness, Jaali cursed the gods under his breath—the same gods who had allowed him to be taken from his bed as a child and sold into slavery.

"I wouldn't curse the mighty powers of the *orisa*, pretty mortal."

Jaali jumped to his feet and took a defensive stance, expecting to see one of the Elders' men. But it was only Eshu in his usual immodest loincloth and little else.

The demigod's brown skin glistened as if covered in tiny diamonds, and Jaali wondered if it was accidental or an affectation. Eshu gave him the impression of someone very much into himself.

"Well, they haven't been generous with their graces, have they?" Jaali couldn't help feeling anger toward all gods who had it in their power to prevent things from happening and yet chose to stay back and let mortals fend for themselves. "What do you want?"

"You really need to improve your attitude toward those who are more than you, young mortal." More than him? Jaali was tired of having people elevating themselves to heights they didn't deserve. Granted, this was not just somebody—this was an *orisa*. If Eshu was offended, he hid it well. With a sigh of impatience, he continued, "Do you want to hear the news or are you going to stand there and insult those who are offering you their generous assistance?"

Jaali stood a little taller. News? He never knew whether to get excited or scared any time he heard those words. "What's wrong?" he said, deciding on going the negative way.

Eshu threw his head back in a roar of laughter. "Aren't you a ray of sunshine? Why do you assume it's bad news?"

"Do you know anything of my past life?" He couldn't help but frown at the frivolous demigod in front of him. He should be used to it after his experience with Freya, whom he never knew exactly how to interpret, but it still rubbed him the wrong way.

The laughter stopped, but the mocking tone still tinted

the *orisa*'s voice. "You need a shot of optimism, *nzuri ya kufa*."

Why did he insist on calling him pretty mortal? The nickname brought on so many bad memories, Jaali shivered. "Do you have news of my daughter?"

Eshu dismissed the idea with a snort and a wave of the hand. "The *mtoto* can take care of herself. I bring you news of your sister."

Jaali was so shocked that he didn't have time to wonder what the demigod meant by his claim that the child could take care of herself. "Elin?"

"Whatever her name is—mortal names mean nothing to me." The *orisa* spread his legs, anchoring himself to the wet ground, and crossed his arms, the muscles of his chest and biceps bulging to double their size. Jaali was certain Eshu did those things out of vanity, a need to show off his prowess—odd thing for a god to do, considering they had more power than any human could even imagine. "She's well enough for a slave but needs help."

"That's not news. Of course she needs help. She's being kept like property." Bitterness had once again sneaked out with his words. "Tell me something I don't know."

Eshu pinched his lips into an O. "Ooh, is that a challenge? Accepted." Jaali shook his head and dropped his chin to his chest. It was not easy talking to these divine beings when they so often acted like children. "Your sister is with child. There! Did I surprise you?"

Jaali's mouth fell open, and he lifted his eyes to the *orisa*. "With child? Does she have a mate?" As soon as he said those words, dread took over him. The slavers would never allow an *indent* to have a partner. This could only mean one thing. "Who's the father?" His voice dropped to a whisper as he tucked his hands into his pockets to stop the tremors.

"How would I know, *nzuri ya kufa?* One of her owners, I'd assume." Then Eshu did something Jaali was not expecting—his mocking face smoothed out into a somber expression and his voice thickened. "You have to rescue her quickly before they take the child away."

Jaali dropped to the rock he had been sitting on before the god's appearance and covered his face with trembling hands. It was the nightmare all over again, only now the victim was his sister instead of him. "Where is she?" Tears burned in his eyes. He wiped them with the back of one hand and stared up at Eshu. "What can I do?"

"The Jewel has been given instructions in her dreams. When she wakes up, she'll know what to do." Eshu lowered his voice again. "Elin will have the baby very soon. You must hurry."

His heart was ripping in two. How could he rescue his sister and his daughter at the same time? He was no god and had no special powers. "But Johari—"

"The *mtoto* is safe. She can take care of herself, trust me." And there it was again, that ridiculous assumption that a two-year-old child could defend herself from adults. Jaali didn't have time to say anything because the demigod departed as quietly and mysteriously as he had arrived.

Torn, Jaali walked the short distance from the river bank to their campsite to wake up Milenda, but she was already up, peeling and cutting fruit in chunks for their meal. As soon as their eyes locked, he knew his wife was already well aware of the news. She tried to smile, but her lips quivered. "I can't abandon Johari, *wimbo wa moyo*, not even for your sister."

Jaali crossed the distance between them and held her tight. "I know. I don't expect you to. It's an impossible choice." To choose between rescuing a sister he didn't even know existed until three years ago and his flesh and blood, the miniature version of his heart and soul. "I don't know what to do."

"I'm going to reach out to Johari and find out if she is indeed safe like the gods say she is. Then, we'll decide." Some of the Milenda he had fallen in love with had come back with her determined and strong voice. She looked up at him, eyes searching for his agreement. He nodded, unable to utter any words. "Yes, we will then decide what's best."

The question was, best for who?

* * *

Reaching out to Jaali had come naturally, out of their desire to be together. Milenda couldn't be sure whether it would work the same with her daughter who could barely articulate the wish to eat or take a nap. She hoped that their mother-daughter bond would be enough to carry her thoughts and body to wherever Johari was being kept. With Jaali sitting close by, Milenda closed her eyes and projected her mind to her daughter's. It was still strange, the sensation of thin, long fingers stretching out and searching through space.

With Jaali, there was always a sense of peace whenever her thoughts found and met his, like a comforting hug of sorts, soft and warm. With Johari, she wasn't sure what to expect.

Milenda felt a tug, a playful pull and release on the edge of her consciousness. "Johari? Is that you, my little love?" She thought she heard giggling, and her chest tightened. Was that her daughter? "Johari, say something sweetheart, so mama can find you."

Darkness replaced the white, misty light she had been navigating through, and she panicked before realizing there were two tiny hands covering her eyes. "Is that my sweet little monkey?" Milenda kept her voice as low as she could for fear of alerting the kidnappers.

"Mama here." Her daughter's voice came from behind her, and she could guess lines and shapes through the gaps in the child's fingers.

Gently, Milenda pulled the chubby little hands away from her eyes and turned around to face her beloved child. "Johari, I was so worried." She looked perfectly fine, her green eyes had the usual spark and there was a smile on her face. Milenda glanced around quickly, finding no one else there. She held Johari tight against her chest. "Are you all right? Did anybody hurt you?"

The young girl pulled away from her and shook her head with gusto, sending the white coils of her hair flying around her face. In spite of the situation, Milenda almost laughed. Johari had a lot of hair, thicker and unrulier even than her own.

"Where are the people who brought you here?"

Milenda asked, keeping her voice down and throwing glances at the only door in the room.

Johari pointed at the door just as Milenda heard the unmistakable sound of footsteps approaching. She looked around the room, searching for somewhere to hide. "Sweetheart, Mama is going to hide in the closet." She held her daughter by the shoulders and kept her eyes fixed on the child's. "You can't tell anyone that I'm here, do you understand? It's our secret and you can't tell. Mama will be very mad if you do."

As soon as Johari nodded her assent, Milenda ran to squeeze herself into the small standalone closet by the wall. If Johari said anything, she could just break the connection and vanish before being caught, but she wanted to stick around for a bit and find out what exactly was happening. Darkness fell as she closed the door and leaned against the soft clothes hanging inside.

The door squeaked open, and the heavy footsteps were in the room. Johari giggled, and the sound of her tiny feet ran away from the closet.

"*Mtoto*, let go of my legs." The voice was gruff and male, but Milenda denoted an underlayer of amusement. "What are we going to do about this little one?"

There was some shuffling and the scratchy sound of chairs being dragged on the stone floor. "I don't know," the other man—no, woman—said. "I should never had listened to you, Mukami. Now we are in serious trouble if the Elders find out."

"The Elders will never find out," the man replied in a

whisper, as if afraid the Elders were listening in. "We were careful." Inside the closet, Milenda rolled her eyes and was almost sorry for this Mukami, who was naive enough to think they could effectively hide anything from the powers in charge.

"We should have done as we were told," the female said. "We should have killed the child right away."

Milenda's heart lurched, trying to get out of her body and run to her daughter. Kill? The Elders wanted Johari dead? Why? What threat could a baby possibly pose? By the time she was old enough to rule, the Elders would have done their best to make sure she would be their puppet—like her father had been all these years.

"How could we, Naki?" the man continued, groaning quietly. Milenda chanced a peek through the thin gap between the door and the doorframe. "She's just a *ndege mdogo*." The *little bird* was now sitting on the man's lap, dwarfed by his size. Fighting the instinct to go take her daughter away from his hands, Milenda bit her tongue and watched. Mukami seemed almost gentle in the way he held her baby, a protective hand behind Johari's back as one of his fingers was being held captive by the child.

"A *ndege* who our masters want out of the way." Milenda couldn't see the woman's face as she sat facing the man, stooped back and elbows on her legs.

Mukami seemed captivated by Johari's playful fingers. "If we killed her, Yemanjá would have our skins. Look at her hair and her eyes—she's a Nyota *mjumbe*, one of a kind."

Milenda squinted and switched to her other eye. What were they talking about? *Mjumbe*? There hadn't been one in centuries. In fact, no one was really sure such a being had ever existed—probably a mere figment of people fertile imagination. She couldn't remember how the legend went, but Yemanjá had some explaining to do apparently. But for now, Milenda was happy the two kidnappers believed the myth, because obviously it was what was keeping them from killing Johari.

"We are stuck between two spears." Naki covered her face with her hands and shook her head. "We kill her, and we enrage the gods. We don't and we enrage the Elders. No matter what we do, we might as well dig our own graves."

Johari giggled again, her little face turned up to Mukami's. "Play?"

The man laughed. "We just have to keep her hidden for a while."

"Then what?"

"Then, maybe the Jewel will come and make things right in Natale." The statement hit her with the force of a speeding elephant. It was one thing that the populace thought she was their savior, but these were the Elders' minions, their soldiers, the hands at the end of their powerful and cruel arms. Shaken by this new reality, Milenda pulled her face away from the door and closed her eyes. There was nothing else she could do here.

Jaali was waiting patiently by her side, his hand griping hers as if afraid she might evaporate with the heat of the jungle. She blinked her eyes open and sat up slowly, still trying to make sense of everything she had just learned.

"Well?" Jaali's voice betrayed his worry. She reached out to caress his cheek. "Is Johari all right? Where is she?"

She smiled then, suddenly realizing that for the moment her daughter was in the safest place for her. Mukami seemed gentle and taken by Johari's childish charms. As strange as it sounded, she believed he would protect her daughter with his life if necessary—there was something in the reverent and tender way he had looked at Johari as she pulled on and pinched his fingers that spelled adoration. This was a man who truly believed Johari was a divinity of sorts and that it was in his best interest to see to her safety.

"Johari is fine, *wimbo wa moyo*," she whispered. "Let's rescue your sister."

* * *

It had been a long time since he'd hated his own skin—too white to blend in with the population of Natale. Even in disguise, Jaali stuck out like a sore thumb, and he wanted desperately, now more than ever, to be invisible, to be able to roam through the city or, inside the palace, never given a second glance. In order to save his sister, they needed the help of the king. To get it, it meant sneaking into the palace like thieves. Milenda had done it several times already, but this was his first time.

Milenda had been strongly opposed to his idea, but he argued—quite passionately—that this was his sister and that he needed to be included in every step of the plan. Unfortunately, there was the issue of his skin color, which made his determination to smuggle himself into the palace a rather unwise decision. Jaali tugged on the cloth that Milenda had wrapped around his head into a bulky top. The ends of the headdress swaddled his neck a lot closer than customary in order to hide part of his face. Jaali had spent a long time covering the whiteness of his skin in a dark layer of river mud. Anybody who chanced a closer look would know that there was no Natalian under that wrap.

"This is insane," Milenda said in a furious whisper, huddling closer to her husband to put her small body between him and curious eyes.

Jaali tripped on the edge of the long tunic that covered his full body. "It will work, you'll see." Except he was beginning to doubt it would. Already the mud was beginning to melt and drip down his neck in big, slimy globs. Soon the cloth around his neck would not be blue anymore as it absorbed the brown goo. As they turned a corner, a woman intercepted their progress, standing in front of them with her hands firmly set on her wide hips and a scowl on her face.

"What do you foolish children think you're doing?" Mama Nyeusi looked fierce in her all-white *iyalorixá* garb. "Did the icy air of the northern lands freeze your brain?" As she spoke, she reached to the side and opened a door. "Get in here quickly."

Too surprised to say anything, Milenda and Jaali obeyed. She followed them inside the room and closed the door, throwing a suspicious glance over her shoulder. Jaali grabbed his wife's hand and was shocked to find it trembling. He was not the only one who was anxious about the whole thing.

Mama Nyeusi stroke a match and lit a small oil lamp by the door. A soft, flickering light flooded the space, slightly blurring everything. "Care to explain this madness?" The old woman's voice did not hide her annoyance.

"How did you know we were here?" Milenda asked, cleverly diverting the focus away from them.

It didn't work. "No, no, my silly Jewel. Those tactics won't work with me." The *iyalorixá* crossed her arms in front of her, squeezing her bosom almost out of her dress. "If it weren't for little Aisha who saw you and immediately came to tell me, you would be caught by the next group of guards prowling just down the hallway."

"Yemanjá wants us to go rescue my sister," Jaali blurted out, annoyed in equal parts at being chided like a child and for realizing how stupid he'd been to risk coming to the palace.

Mama Nyeusi moved her big brown eyes to him, her eyebrows raised in surprise. "Your sister? Did the Mother find her?"

In as few words as they could manage, Milenda and Jaali took turns reporting on the conversation he'd had with Eshu and Milenda's visit to little Johari. The *iyalorixá* listened attentively, never interrupting or asking questions until they were finished. She kept silent for a while after they had stopped talking, her hand cupping her chin and deep in thought. Jaali exchanged glances with his wife, who shrugged.

"You two, unwise children, stay here. Do not move out

of this room." She emphasized the last command with a single raised eyebrow. "You cannot reach the king safely, so he must come to you." She turned to leave, but before she opened the door, she turned around and repeated, "Lock this door and do not do anything, you hear?" They both nodded, and she left, the door opening and allowing some light in as she did.

Jaali looked around him, his skin itching from the mud that covered it. There was not much in the room. A few chairs, some broken, were stacked by one of the walls. He pulled out a couple for them to sit on while Milenda locked the doors. They sat close together, their thighs touching, fingers entwined.

"Do you think he'll come?" Jaali whispered, scratching his neck beneath the wrapping.

Milenda smiled and helped him loosen the cloth away from his neck, her fingers soft and warm against his skin. "He will if he can."

Time seemed to crawl rather than tick away as they sat, waiting for Mama Nyeusi to return with or without the king. Their anxiety made them jump at every little noise behind the door, half expecting the guards to come barreling through the door. When a knock interrupted their quiet talking, Jaali's heart must have stopped for a moment.

"It's Mama Nyeusi. Open quickly."

Jaali got up and opened the door slowly and found the old woman's face on the other side. He stepped aside so she could come in. The king, a man he hadn't seen since he left Natale, followed her in. Jaali instinctively bowed his head, taking a step backward.

"Jaali Asker, my good man," King Melchior said, holding Jaali's hands between his. "So happy to see you again. You're looking well." Not surprising. The last time they had been together, Jaali was still gauntly thin and limping after his ordeal in the desert. "I hear you found your sister."

Even though this was Milenda's father, Jaali felt a rush of heat climb up to his neck and face—hard to believe he was in this tiny room, holding hands with the monarch. "Yemanjá did, not me." He threw a quick glance at his wife, hoping she'd get his telepathic help-me message. A mischievous smile stretched across her lips as she shrugged. Milenda was enjoying his discomfort.

Surprisingly, it was Mama Nyeusi who came to his rescue. "As you know, the Mother has located her and is very anxious to have her rescued before she gives birth." The king dropped Jaali's hands and frowned. "Her owner has a buyer already lined up for the baby."

The silence that fell over them was heavy and suffocating. Melchior must have felt it more than the others since, as the ruler of the nation, he was guilty of being an absentee king. As much as he was against the practice, he had never done anything to change it. Now it was complicated—the Elders had amassed so much power during his reign of apathy, it wouldn't be easy to go against them. Jaali wanted to feel sorry for him, but he couldn't. As a slave himself, he could forgive but not forget that Melchior's lack of initiative to stop the inhumane commerce of human beings had caused him years of abuse and pain.

Melchior finally broke the silence with a whisper. "What do you need me to do?" His sorrowful brown eyes, so different from his daughter's, roamed to Jaali again. It felt like an apology in disguise, an "I know I'll never be able to make up for your loss" admission.

"Can you buy her and the baby?" Jaali asked, stumbling over the words. What kind of world did they live in where you could own a human like you owned a chair or a table? "And then free her."

The king sighed and lowered his eyes. Was that shame Jaali read in his posture? "Unfortunately, I can't do that, my son. Officially, Natale doesn't condone slavery. If I buy your sister, it will look as if the king himself is breaking the law and incite revolt."

All the anger and frustration Jaali was holding in check exploded in his voice. "Let them revolt. Anything is better than this situation we're in. Where humans are property and treated worse than that. Beaten, isolated, stolen away from their loved ones, raped." His voice caught on the last word, terrifying memories assailing him from all angles. A sob climbed to his mouth, threatening to escape with his words. "You could have stopped this a long time ago, and instead you chose to close your eyes to reality while these horrors happened around you."

Milenda step closer to him and placed a grounding hand on the tense muscles of his arm. "Jaali—"

Jaali turned to her, a fire roaring inside of him and tears dancing in his eyes. "No, *msichana*, it's enough. You saw the heartache and misery inflicted on the parents and siblings of the taken ones. You saw the despair in their eyes, the weak hope in their hearts." His eyes softened and darkened as he lowered his voice to a whisper. "You saw what they did to me. How can the king ignore it? How can your father stand idly by and do nothing?"

The Jewel's eyes blinked at his words. The memories he had inadvertently shared with her during the Trials must still be fresh in her memory. It wasn't easy—if at all possible—to erase such images from your mind.

"You're absolutely entitled to your anger, young Jaali," the king said, his hand raised in surrender. "You're right about my weakness and guilt by omission. I'm as guilty as the slavers who yanked you out of your bed as a child and carried you into a living hell. I knew about it but chose to do nothing because my heart had died with my wife, because I had given up on life and everything that went with it. There's no excuse. I'm the king. I'm responsible for what goes on in my nation."

The heat from Milenda's hand was calming him down as it always did. Jaali took a deep breath and allowed a couple angry tears to roll down his cheeks, not bothering to hide or brush them away. "I mean no disrespect, Your Majesty, but I won't apologize for what I said. Even now you refuse to do the right thing."

Jaali expected the king to look ruffled by his comments, but instead he seemed contrite and resigned. "I said I can't buy her, not that we couldn't do anything about it." Jaali opened his eyes wide. What was his father-in-law planning? "What I can do is provide a major distraction for his owners and guards so you can go in and get her out. I understand she's being kept in the women's quarters since she is at the end of gestation. She'd be all alone during the day, while the others are out working."

The galloping of his heart had slowed to a trot. "What do you propose then?"

The king's sad eyes locked with his. "I won't ask for forgiveness because I don't deserve it, but can we at least strive to be in the same room without hate?"

Jaali's anger had ebbed away already as it usually did, his arm muscles relaxing under Milenda's gentle stroking. "I don't hate you, Your Majesty. I could never hate the father of my love." He offered his hand to the monarch who took it in his. "I trust that you'll do the right thing from now on and allow Fjordens some peace and happiness at last."

* * *

"Why didn't you tell your father about Johari?" Jaali was walking slightly ahead of her, gallantly moving branches and greenery out of her way. Milenda smiled at the small kindness, so typical of her man.

"I didn't want to distract him from rescuing your sister." Milenda had surprised herself by not panicking about her daughter's kidnapping anymore. The gentleness with which the giant guard had talked about Johari and the kindness in his eyes had soothed her heart. As long as the Elders thought her dead, her girl was probably safer in hiding with two armed guards to protect her than in the middle of the jungle, vulnerable to all kinds of danger. "Once we have your sister, I'll let him know."

Jaali winced, his lower lip caught between his teeth and a crease on his brow. "What if the guards change their minds and do what they were told to do?"

Milenda caught up with him in a couple steps and anchored her hand around his waist. "Don't worry, *wimbo wa moyo*. She's safe. Trust me." She tugged at him playfully, trying to distract him from his own thoughts. "I'll visit again today. Johari was not scared or worried when I saw her. She's a Nyota—she can sense danger just like I do."

Her husband's chest rose and fell in a deep exhale. "When are we going to be able to have a quiet, peaceful life? The three of us without worrying about being kidnapped or killed?" They had had a reprise while in Isvärld, a deceptive two-year lull that made them maybe too complacent. Their lives had been in turmoil since they were born—Jaali taken by slavers as a young boy, and her mother taken from Milenda when she was just a baby. Chances were they would always be in some kind of danger.

What could she say? "At least we have each other, Jaali. I'm so lucky I found you." She smiled up at him, and he stooped down to drop a kiss on her lips. "I love you, *wimbo wa moyo*."

Jaali cupped her cheek with his hand, and she instinctively leaned against it. "I love you, *msichana*. And you're right; I shouldn't complain. After all, we are richer than most because we have each other's love." Milenda tilted her face upward to kiss him again.

"Don't forget about me. You have me too." They both

gasped and jerked their heads back in the direction of the male voice. "Don't be so shocked. Think of me as your guardian angel."

Angel he was not, Milenda surmised by his practically naked body and smirk on his lips—a dark male version of Freya. "Eshu, I presume." She had pressed a hand to her chest to try to coax her heart into slowing.

"Could you give us some kind of warning you're coming?" Jaali's flustered cheeks had turned a pale shade of pink, jaw clenched tight. "You about scared us out of our skins."

Eshu, tall and brown like the trunks of the surrounding trees, cackled. "You pretty mortals scare so easily."

Annoyed, Milenda crossed her arms and tapped her foot in a perfect imitation of Mama Nyeusi. "These pretty mortals would like to have some privacy once in a while." Jaali chuckled quietly by her side, and she had to fight the urge to laugh like a madwoman at their ridiculous and unbelievable situation—whose life in Natale, maybe the world, was always being interrupted by gods?

The demigod brushed a big hand over his bald head and rolled his eyes like a sulky adolescent. "We gods have so little amusements. We need pretty mortals like you to keep us entertained." He yawned for effect. "It's not much to ask, is it? After all, I'm helping you."

Milenda was never quite sure whether the gods were really helping them or causing them more trouble. The divine world was too complicated for mere mortals like them to totally understand, she concluded.

"What now?" Jaali seemed out of patience with this handsome, well-toned and half-naked god. Another characteristic of gods it seemed—lack of any kind of modesty. But Yemanjá was different though—not a grownup child like Freya and Eshu seemed to be.

Eshu yawned again and stretched his arms way over his head. Milenda averted her eyes as his loin cloth moved with him to reveal way more of his perfect body than she wanted to see. "I know the king will provide a distraction of sorts, but I thought I may help with that too."

"And how will you do that?" She was forever nervous about divine help. Sometimes the so-called help caused more problems than what was worth.

The *orisa* squinted his eyes at her. "When everyone is gathered in the palace pavilion for the king's speech, I will send rain. Lots of it."

Could he really control the weather? "How will that help?" Jaali asked, his arm draped over her shoulders. "What is rain going to do exactly, other than get everyone wet?"

"Oh ye of little faith." Eshu pinched his lips and glared at them. "It will deter any heathen from sneaking out of the pavilion unannounced and catching you in the act of rescuing your sister."

Melchior had decided he would call on the slaver who owned Elin, his whole family and staff for a royal visit to the coffee plantation. He hoped that while they were all gathered inside the pavilion, Jaali and Milenda would have time to smuggle Elin out of the estate. Eshu was right though—who was to say that one of them would not slink out of the crowd and catch them in *flagrante delicto*?

"We're grateful for your help, Eshu," Milenda said, lowering her eyes in a sign of respect as she had been taught growing up. "Please forgive our impertinence." Jaali was obviously not getting the message, so she pulled on his arm until he followed her lead.

The half-naked god snorted and vanished.

"Can you explain to me why you get the nice gods and I get the crazy ones?" Jaali asked, annoyance plastered across his brow.

Milenda burst out laughing. "It's because you're so pretty," she teased, laying her hands flat on his chest and winking.

A smile peeked at the corners of his lips. "You think I'm pretty?" he teased back, hands trailing softly around her waist. She shivered in delight. Jaali's touch always took her to a wonderful place. "How pretty do you think I am?" His mouth hovered tantalizingly near hers.

She took a deep breath and swallowed, her body suddenly alive. Jaali brushed a finger up one of her arms, and electricity coursed through her veins, making her skin tingle and her *matangazos* light up. Her husband glanced at her glowing marks and bit his lip. "That pretty? I'm flattered." He lowered his lips to her ears and whispered, the heat of his breath turning her insides to goo. "I happen to think you're prettier than me, and I'd love to show you how serious I am."

Jaali's warm lips touched the edge of her ear, and she

squirmed, wrapping her hands under his arms and around to his back. They'd been so worried about Johari and being found by the Elders, they hadn't made love in a while. Milenda found that her body missed it. A lot. "Please do show me."

With a quick glance around him, Jaali scooped her into his arms and carried her away. Milenda was always amazed at how effortlessly her husband could carry her, almost as easily as when he carried their daughter. His body was deceptively slim but covered in hard-earned muscle—the fruit of years of physical abuse and the grueling track through the desert to win her hand in marriage. He traveled the rest of the way to their hiding place by the Miungu holding her tightly against him, the beating of his heart mingling with hers in a song only they could hear.

As soon as they arrived at their campsite, Jaali set her down gently on the blanket they had spread under the makeshift tent and kissed her, stretching his tall body alongside hers. "You taste like nectar, *msichana*. Are you sure you're not a goddess?"

Milenda whimpered under the pressure of his lips and touched his tongue with hers, delighting on the moan it drew from her husband. "Pretty sure," she whispered, pushing away for a moment.

Jaali pulled her back to him until their bodies were glued together, his hardness fitting perfectly into her softness, his rigid ridges into her yielding valleys. While his hands were busy coaxing the dress off her body, his lips were hard at work trailing kisses along her neck and neckline, tasting the warm skin where her *matangazos* held testimony to her arousal. Milenda yearned to feel his bare skin on hers as he slid her dress all the way down her hips and legs until she was finally naked, the warmth of the dying sun kissing her skin. Jaali sat, straddling her legs and watching her, his eyes scanning her body from top to bottom, his transparent eyes softened further by desire. She sat up, anxious to undress the man she loved, to watch him like he watched her and run her hungry fingers along his ivory skin.

The obstacle of clothes now removed, Milenda swept a hand from his neck to his chest in a caress that set her on fire instead. She followed her fingers with her lips, scooting from under Jaali to kneel before him and continuing her trek down his lovely body. Jaali groaned as the hardness of his arousal rubbed against her belly and her lips moved tantalizingly closer to it. He trembled in anticipation under her touch, fanning the fire within her. Deep, red-hot longing liquefied her as she sheathed him with her mouth. He yelled in pleasure, arching his lower body closer to the stroking of her lips, bracing his hands on the ground behind him. Milenda could feel him pulsing against her tongue, and her body mimicked his, heat and wetness spreading between her thighs.

Jaali interrupted her, pulling himself free. "Lay down, *msichana*." Her eyes never leaving his, she did as he asked and lay down on the soft blanket as her husband, swollen with desire, slid his warm hands up her thighs and then down again to pry her knees apart and settle himself between them. Even before he touched her, a wave of pleasure ran through her body. She arched toward him, inviting and welcoming, body and heart already anticipating the touch of his lips against her sensitive folds. A familiar panic of pleasure erupted inside of her—did she stay put and let him take her into that place where everything else was obliterated by sensual ecstasy or did she skip it altogether to join him as one body, one soul?

"Jaali, I love you," she managed to utter in between whimpers as, undeterred by her thoughts, Jaali tasted her fully, exploring her with his tongue, fondling the part of her that was reserved for him alone.

When she thought the power and beauty of the northern lights had taken shelter within herself, Milenda laid a hand on his silky, pearly hair and first pulled him against her and then tugged him away. She wanted—no, needed—to feel him inside her, to be one with the man who had saved her from a lonely, loveless life, the man who made her strong and ready to face a cruel world head-on. Jaali slid along her burning body until her softness yielded to his hardness. Milenda moaned and tightened her arms around Jaali as he drove himself deeper inside her. They sailed the rocking waves of pleasure until they reached sensory overload and came together, bodies shaking against each other, finally fulfilled and released.

Jaali collapsed on top of her; still flying, she relished the weight of his long, hard body on her much smaller one. As Jaali moved to roll off her, always afraid he'd crush her, she held him tight. "Don't move yet," she begged urgently, still intoxicated by the feel of his skin. "Stay a little longer." He relaxed against her, his cheek tucked into the crook of her neck, his lips brushing against the now fading *matangazos*. "Thank you, *wimbo wa moyo*."

She felt his lips moving against her skin. "What for?"

"For reminding me that no matter how bad things get, we have *us*. We have our love." And that was all that mattered.

* * *

Mjusi flapped his impressive wings as if trying to take off, and the greenery around them swayed back and forth in confusion. He was not happy about what they were doing, and Jaali couldn't blame him. It was insane. Even with the promised assistance of the gods, their mission to snag his sister from her owner was frothed with danger. So many things could go wrong. Jaali shook his head, trying to focus on the task at hand and put all his anxieties away for the moment.

Milenda was walking ahead of him, so tiny and dark he was assailed by panic every time she disappeared around a tree or bush. The usual bright *kanga* of her dresses had been replaced by a solid dark green one to camouflage her against the verdant background. Jaali's coloring made him hard to hide as usual, and he resigned himself to take shelter behind his wife and wear a hot, green head-wrapping that made him itch and sweat. He wanted to be the one in front, the scout, to protect Milenda from the looming danger. Instead, he was walking behind her like a submissive servant, protected rather than protecting. Mjusi, ever vigilant, stumbled close to her, growling quietly once in a while as if expressing his disagreement with their choices.

The wall of trees suddenly opened into a large clearing, and the bright rays of the sun, now out of the cover of the jungle, made their eyes burn and squint. They stopped on the edge of the trees, still safely sheltered by their wide, brown trunks and gnarled branches, and watched in silence as a procession of people advanced leisurely away from the buildings and disappeared around the corner. The pavilion the king would be using to communicate with the plantation owner and his family must have been behind the main building, a flashy manor that blatantly boasted their wealth.

Mama Nyeusi had shown up at their hideaway early in the morning to babysit Gavå, who was too young to help them out. The baby *wyvern* had been inconsolable since Johari had been taken a few days before, growling constantly and even howling, something neither Milenda or Jaali knew dragons could do.

As soon as the last person vanished from view, Milenda stepped out from behind the trees and, closely followed by Jaali and the *msuti*, scampered toward one of the side buildings that held the *indents,* one for the women and a second one for the men. Jaali swallowed hard, well acquainted with the setting even if he hadn't been housed in one for most of his years in slavery. He didn't work the fields or cleaned the house. He had been kept inside the main house for a different purpose, kept in a small room with no windows, close by and handy for when his master and his cruel friends felt the need to sate their unsavory appetites. A shiver ran through him and tears of fear and rage erupted in his eyes. Angry at himself for still feeling that way after all that time, Jaali wiped the tears with the back of his hand and glanced at his wife, who he was glad to find oblivious to his discomfort.

"Sorry that you have to do this, wimbo wa moyo,*"* her voice whispered inside his head, debunking the idea that she had not noticed his distress. "I hate that this brings you so many painful memories."

He couldn't lie to his wife. *"I hate that it still affects me this much."* Their silent conversation brought him a measure of comfort as it had done during the Trials and later in Isvärld. It reminded him he was not alone or helpless anymore. Milenda's love for him made him strong, gave him the motivation to continue fighting even when all seemed lost. It reminded him of how powerful her love had been against his demons.

"I don't even remember my mom, and it still hurts every time I think of her." There was a note of sadness, of melancholy in her thought. *"Life is made of good and bad moments. It seems to me that sometimes the gods try us by balancing the good ones with the bad ones, as if telling us, 'Listen, mortals. Don't get too comfortable because all this goodness can be gone in a blink of an eye. Don't be complacent.'"*

As it applied to them, complacency never quite settled in. Their lives seemed like a long string of stressful and painful moments with short peaceful semicolons in between. Jaali sighed and mentally kissed his princess. Even though he couldn't see her face, he knew she was smiling, and his lips stretched into a smile in response.

They were standing by the women's quarters, ironically marked with Yemanjá's symbols, a bundle of cowrie shells strung together and hung from a hook on the wall next to the narrow door. Jaali knew the door had been designed that narrow to prevent more than one person leaving the room, to better control the slaves inside. He also knew that beside the men's quarters there would be a single red feather, the symbol for Elegguá, the most powerful *orisa* of all—as if the demigods condoned slavery.

"What now?" Jaali asked in silence, the thin fingers of his thoughts reaching out for Milenda's.

"We wait for Eshu to drop the rivers of heaven on us," Milenda answered, her hand reaching for his as they crouched quietly by the door, semihidden by the thick trunk of a tree.

They didn't have to wait long. As promised, a thick wall of water soon fell on the beaten dirt paths of the plantation and everything else around it. In seconds, both he and his wife were drenched to the bones, their head coverings dripping water over their eyes and making it difficult to see. Jaali wiped the water away to clear his sight and opened the door.

At first, they couldn't discern anything in the darkness inside, but soon weary faces emerged, the light in their blue eyes long extinguished and their pearly blonde hair drab and lifeless. Jaali's heart dropped a few inches and lodged itself in his stomach. For a panicky moment, he thought he was going to lose all control and vomit as the stench of sweat and unwashed bodies reached his nose. It was unbearably hot and stuffy in the building, the barred windows closed and shuttered, steam immediately rising from their wet clothes. Jaali coughed, trying to keep the contents of his stomach inside, and made himself look around. He had no idea what his sister looked like. She'd been born after he was taken, and inside that hellish space, the women all looked alike in their misery.

"Look for a pregnant woman."

Milenda's message came through loud and clear, and it was all he needed to snap out of the kind of shocked stupor he had fallen into. His eyes roamed the room, registering every face and looking for a swollen belly among them. He couldn't find any. Had they moved her to another building? Had she delivered the baby already?

"Jaali, here." Milenda was standing by a bundle of leaves and cloths, bending over to help the woman lying there to stand up. "Are you Elin?" Milenda asked in a soft voice as he approached, his heart pounding in his ears.

The thin, tall woman nodded and cupped her hands around her belly, revealing a small bump, barely noticeable under the colorless dress she wore. Jaali swallowed the tears that were burning in his eyes and extended his arms to her. "Elin, I'm Jaali, your brother."

Elin's eyes displayed only confusion and fear. "Don't be afraid, *dyrbar en,*" Milenda cooed the Fjorden endearment—precious one. "We're here to take you away from this prison."

The realization that this girl—for she was barely a

woman—was his sister punched him in the stomach, and he covered his mouth with the palm of his hand, on the verge of throwing up. "Elin, you're my sister." He looked up at Milenda and met her eyes, wet from the tears that rolled freely down her cheeks. "We have to get her out of here quick."

He looked around the room and tried to close his heart to what he saw—desperation, agony, hopelessness. They couldn't rescue the others today, and that knowledge killed him. In a single move, Jaali scooped his sister off the ground and carried her out into the torrential rain, closely followed by Milenda, whose quiet sobbing he could hear both with his ears and his mind. He held back the tears that stung his eyes with the fierceness and heat of fire. He'd cry later, once Erin was in a safe place away from this hell. Jaali's hopes that she had been bought by a benevolent master had been crushed by reality—Elin was nine months pregnant and was as light as a feather.

The water stabbed them with the sharpness of tiny daggers, but it also created an almost solid wall, impenetrable to roving eyes. Eshu had done well by them. Jaali made a mental note to thank the impish god later. Mjusi was waiting just behind the first line of trees in the jungle. They didn't stop. Fueled by a sense of urgency, the four of them continued their track through the thickness of the greenery, weaving around trees, with Milenda being the one moving branches out of their path this time.

Jaali's legs threatened to give away beneath him, his feet burning from hitting the merciless ground, covered in rocks and broken branches. He would not stop, not until his sister and Milenda were safely far from the places that haunted his sleep, that brought the nightmarish memories he had hoped to never again revisit. No, he wouldn't stop running.

***

The humid heat had not relented with the arrival of the night. Milenda's body was sticky and uncomfortable, and she longed for a dip in the cool waters of the Miungu. It was unwise to bathe at night, especially alone, because the great river was not the lamb of the tributary that flowed near their *hema*. This branch was wider, deeper, and raced through the jungle as if running away from danger. She glanced over Jaali, curled into a ball by the dying fire, and considered waking him up from his fitful sleep to bathe with her under the moonlight.

After what they had seen today, she knew Jaali's heart was bleeding as much or more than hers. She yearned to touch him, soothe away his pain with her lips, envelop him in the cocoon of her loving arms and rock him until the break of dawn. But they were not alone, and she hesitated on how to act in front of her new sister, the frail young woman they had rescued from the plantation.

Milenda's heart went out to her, remembering how her own pregnancy had developed happily under the tender care of her husband and Ebba, their one and only friend in the northern lands. She had plumped up through the months, her stomach swelling with each passing week, the anticipation of motherhood filling her heart with joy and peace. How different it must be for Elin, filled with the fruit of rape, so young she should still be playing with dolls, undernourished and possibly sick. Was she looking forward to the birth of this child? Would she be able to love this baby, planted in her womb against her will the same way Milenda loved Johari?

Milenda wiped the sweat from her brow with a wet rag and leaned against a big rock, hoping to absorb some of the coolness from the stone into her skin, and closed her eyes. She couldn't sleep. Her mind kept wandering from Elin to her daughter. Milenda had been too drained the night before to attempt reaching Johari, but ironically ended up barely sleeping, her thoughts pulling her out of slumber every time she drifted off. She'd visit today after they heard from her father. Neither Jaali or her knew what exactly to do with Elin. She couldn't possibly stay with them, as close to her due date as she was, even if their hideout was a huge improvement from the living conditions at the plantation.

"Stop fretting, *kidojo moja*. Everything will be all right."

The voice came from behind her, and as she turned around to see who was talking, a dim shimmer faded into a shadow and then to nothing. Yemanjá was the only one who called her that, but the voice didn't sound like hers—female, for sure, and faintly familiar.

"Mother?" Milenda's eyes scoured the area to no avail. Whoever had said those words was gone. She shook her head, half-convinced she had dreamed it. Maybe she was hallucinating, exhausted and anxious as she was.

She didn't have time to dwell on it because Elin began

moving, a soft groan reaching Milenda's ears. She jumped to her feet and rushed to the girl's side. "What's wrong, Elin?" Elin flinched when Milenda touched her arm and stared at her with fear in her blue eyes. "It's just me, your brother's wife. You're safe." Safer anyway. Nobody would be totally safe until the Elders had been exposed as the despots they were and brought down quite a few notches.

Elin's eyes and arms seemed to relax, but she was still groaning between tightly closed lips. Milenda was not sure what to do. The girl didn't trust her enough to tell her. Maybe Jaali could reach her. He was her own blood after all, and his Fjorden coloring a lot less threatening to her.

Milenda turned to where her husband slept soundly, his lovely face free from the anxiety of the day before. She couldn't resist and brushed a hand along his cheek, running her fingers on his light stubble. "Jaali, wake up. There's something wrong with Elin." Jaali's eyes fluttered open, and Milenda watched with regret how his lips tightened in worry right away. "She doesn't trust me."

Jaali rolled over and sat up by his sister who was now holding her belly with both hands and rocking from side to side, a mournful sort of humming slipping through her lips. "Elin, *dyrbar en*, what's wrong? Does something hurt?" The girl moaned some more, not acknowledging the presence of her brother at all. Jaali reached out to touch her hand, and her head snapped to his side, her eyes opening wide. When she saw her brother's face, she relaxed, but still moaned. "Elin, tell me. What's wrong?"

"You fools!" Eshu's usual mocking voice rose from a

wisp of smoke that quickly solidified into his long frame. "Can't you see she's deaf and a mute?"

Milenda and Jaali gasped at the same time. "Deaf? But my father and sister never mentioned that when we were there." Jaali was still holding his sister's hand over her pregnancy bump.

Eshu's lips curled into a frown. "Because they didn't know," he said in a condescending tone. "The child was barely four when she was kidnapped, and your father just thought she was a late bloomer. Or simpleminded, not sure which." He circled a hand close to his head to emphasize his words.

Milenda's mouth fell open. It was bad enough to have been kidnapped and abused, but to have no way of communicating seemed to add another level of pain to the whole situation. "How can we communicate with her?"

"After all these years, I'm sure she's developed some sort of lip-reading skills." For once, Milenda thought she'd detected a note of compassion in the demigod's voice. "Make sure she's looking at you when you speak."

Tears danced in Jaali's eyes as he turned to his sister again and made an attempt at a smile. "Elin, I'm your brother. I was taken like you." His voice wavered, thick with emotion. "I want to help you. What's wrong?" He gestured toward her belly, hoping she'd understand what he was asking.

Elin glanced at her brother's hand and grunted. She pointed at her belly and made sounds as if in pain. Milenda noticed for the first time the puddle Elin was laying on. "Her water's broke," she exclaimed. "She's having the baby."

Jaali's eyes opened into almost perfect circles. "No, no. She can't have the baby before Mama Nyeusi arrives. We don't know how to do this."

"You have a daughter, don't you?" It was not a question. Eshu lifted a brow and crossed his arms.

"I didn't deliver my daughter." Milenda could hear the word idiot added silently to the end of Jaali's statement. "I don't know what to do."

Eshu turned his eyes to Milenda. "You had a child. You do it."

Milenda almost laughed at the *orisa*'s obvious ignorance in the matter of childbirth. "Giving birth to a child is very different from delivering one, Eshu. Can't you call Mama Nyeusi?"

The demigod rolled his eyes. "I'm not your footman, Princess. Even if I was willing to do it, I don't think she'd make it in time." He pointed his chin at Elin who had bent her knees and was bearing down, her hands solidly pulling her knees toward her.

Making an uncomfortable decision, Milenda settled herself by the girl's feet and pried her legs further apart. She had seen babies being born before but from a distance. The lonely child she had been would sneak around unnoticed to witness many of the servants' births in the palace. This was up close and personal. It didn't take an expert to see that the baby was crowning, the little dark-haired head peeking through Elin's stretched folds. Milenda gasped.

"What are you doing, *msichana*?" Jaali asked, laying a hand on her shoulders.

"What can I do? I'll do the best I can to help deliver this baby, but your sister will have to do most of the work." She sounded a lot calmer and sure of herself than she really was. Inside she was shaking, her stomach clinging to her back and her mouth dry as a desert. "Hold her hand. Give her something to squeeze."

Jaali didn't hesitate. He had done it when she had birthed their daughter. He crawled on his knees closer to Elin's shoulders and held her hand, which she immediately squeezed until his knuckles turned white. With his free hand, he rubbed her shoulders, his eyes following Milenda's every move. She smiled at him and then winced as Elin grunted and bore down again.

"You can do it, *dyrbar en*. You can do it." Milenda knew Elin couldn't hear her, but she hoped she could feel the vibration of her voice through her hands still holding Elin's knees steadily apart. The baby was on its way out, and Milenda coaxed her new sister to push harder by squeezing her knees and pulling her legs to the girl's chest. "Push, Elin, push."

The girl surprised her with a strength that came from nowhere. Half-starved and battered, it was a wonder she had strength enough to push her baby out. Jaali checked with Milenda constantly, silent questions flooding her mind: *"How's she doing?" "Do you see the baby?" "Is she going to be all right?"* The anxiety that oozed from him through their joined thoughts was overwhelming, muddling her thinking. She cut off the connection so she could focus on the job at hand.

The baby's head was out, and Milenda knew how crucial it was that the rest of his tiny body slid out of her as soon as possible. She prodded the girl's legs, encouraging her to give it one more strong push. Elin didn't delay, and with one deep groan, the baby's body poured out into Milenda's waiting hands.

"It's a boy." Milenda held the baby and looked for the pulsing umbilical cord to make sure it was not wrapped around the baby's neck. She let out the breath she was holding when the cord came loose in her hand, freeing the child. Drained, she sat back, the bloodied baby boy still in her arms, and remained still for a moment, her eyes closed and her breathing slowing down.

"*Msichana*, the baby," Jaali's voice snapped her out from her half trance. "Why is the baby not crying?"

The sun was breaking through the darkness of the dawn, and Milenda looked at the little body in her arms with a new sense of urgency. Jaali was right. Why wasn't the infant crying? There was a strange bluish color to the baby's lips and face and no evidence of breathing. She looked at the cord and saw it still pulsating. "There's blood going to him, why isn't he breathing?" Panic was taking over her senses.

Jaali left his sister's side and came closer to Milenda, who gave him the baby as if hoping he'd know what to do. He stared at the baby, panic burning in his eyes. Mimicking what Ebba had done when Johari was born, he stuck one finger in the boy's mouth to see if there was anything obstructing the throat and then began rubbing his hand gently over the child's chest, massaging the tiny heart in hopes of bringing it back to life.

Elin had sat up, the placenta spilled between her legs and a look on her face that betrayed the fear and pain she must be feeling inside. She did love that baby. Milenda was not sure how to feel about that sudden realization—glad because of the baby, but horribly sad if the child did not survive. Elin would be crushed. Jaali was still trying to revive the baby boy, but the infant was not breathing. The umbilical cord had ceased its pulsing, still connecting mother and child. To distract her mind from what was happening, Milenda sought a cutting tool of some kind to sever that connection that at this point was serving no purpose other than making her want to burst out crying. Selfishly she wanted to reach out to her daughter, confirm that she was all right and hold her tightly in her arms.

Jaali whispered something, and at first Milenda couldn't understand the words. With a small dagger in hand, she came back to where brother and sister were sitting and looked into her husband's teary eyes. He had stopped rubbing the boy's chest and held him close to his heart. He shook his head and continued whispering—a song. He was singing the same Fjorden lullaby he often sang to Johari.

"Like the song I sing the best, sleep, sleep, little one, sleep. Weary you are, next to my heart, sleep, little one, sleep.'" His words stumbled over his sobs, now joined by Elin's who knelt next to her brother, her hand over the tiny head of her dead son. Milenda fell on her knees and hugged herself, overcome by the knowledge than unless she and her father did something about the Elders, things like this would continue to happen. Things had to change.

* * *

Jaali squatted behind the giant elephant-ear plant, waiting for the signal to come out of hiding. Milenda was the architect of this caper. "They think I'm the spirit of the Jewel, so if they see you, they'll think you're a spirit too," she had said.

"And what purpose would that serve?"

"To show a united front. If they know we are both working to free them from the Elders, it will go a long way to boost their sense of hope." Milenda had been leaning against her favorite rock on the river bank, his head cradled on her lap. "The more hopeful they are, the more willing they'll be when the moment is ripe for a revolution." She raked her fingers through his hair, and he closed his eyes, lulled by the peace and pleasure of such simple touch. "The people of Natale have been told they are helpless for far too long. They think they aren't capable of anything, that there's no hope for them and their children. You give them hope, you earn a formidable ally."

There was wisdom and truth in her words, even if he hated to admit it. After holding his dead nephew in his arms, the product of a culture of power and entitlement that gave rapists and other deviants legitimacy, he no longer wanted to wait for the "right moment." Jaali was ready for the fight and its consequences.

"How long are you going to have me crouch here?" Jaali asked Eshu, standing tall by his side. It irritated him to no end that the *orisa* could stand there and not be seen while he had to bend his knees until he could barely feel his legs.

Eshu shrugged. "It's up to you. You can get up now, show up in the sanctuary, and get killed, or you wait for our friend to provide a distraction for the guards." The identity of their so-called friend was a mystery neither Eshu nor Yemanjá were willing to reveal. "Your choice."

Jaali grunted, annoyed that he couldn't argue with the demigod's reasoning. He switched the weight to his other leg, trying to relieve the tingling and burning all that crouching was causing.

"Now!" Eshu exclaimed suddenly, scaring him up straight. Eshu stared at him, not a hint of mockery on his face this time. "It has to be very quick. In and out. Go."

It was hard to sprint when he couldn't feel his legs, but he did it nevertheless. He came into the sanctuary from the back and emerged from behind the trees into the space where the harbor seat stood. Most of the faithful were turned the other way, curious about what may have made the guards run out so suddenly. So much the better, it gave him time to settle his heart before speaking.

"People of Natale." He hoped his voice sounded deep and solemn, but feared it came out more like a squeak— his throat constricted by nerves. Heads turned abruptly in his direction. He gulped, facing the small crowd gathered there, a small sea of colorful dresses and *iqhiyas*. "My wife, the Jewel, spoke to you already, but I wanted to come and let you know I'm as committed to helping you as she is. Like you, I have suffered at the hands of the ruthless men who call themselves the Elders. I want to help you free yourselves from the noose they've tied around your necks, and I want to save my people from slavery. Are you with us? Will you be willing to do what's necessary to defeat and depose the Elders?"

The human whispering mingled with the loud noises of the cicadas on the trees. Jaali stood, ill at ease, not sure of what to do with his hands and anxious to leave that place—the same spot where he had once courted his wife and where he had met Mjusi for the first time. When the whispers stopped, his heart almost escaped from his chest. He saw the men and women falling to their knees and lowering their heads until they touched the ground.

"Quickly, leave." Eshu was standing by him again, his arms crossed and a foot tapping impatiently. "The guards are returning, and you've been acknowledged by the populace. Mission accomplished. Time to go."

Still a little shaken by the reaction of the crowd, Jaali swiftly made his exit before anyone would notice. Even though Eshu and Milenda had told him that that's what would happen, he didn't believe them. He was Jaali Asker, an outlander and an ex-slave. He could understand the people worshiping their princess, but him? He was a nobody, a mere speck of dust in the grand scheme of things.

"Milenda would have scolded you already," Eshu said, surprisingly still beside him. "You're not a nobody. The two of you are the hope of a nation."

Jaali brushed a hand over his face, still navigating through the thickness of the jungle. "I'm so tired of hearing that. All the *orisa* say that. Mama Nyeusi says that, but no one is telling us exactly how we are going to accomplish a successful revolution. And stay out of my head."

Eshu raised his hands in front of him. "Well, aren't we a little testy today. It's not so much what you will do as what you've already done."

Another cryptic statement. Tired of the mystery that all the *orisa* seemed to thrive on, Jaali turned to the demigod to tell him just how much he hated being played with like a toy but found only empty space. Eshu had conveniently vanished from sight.

Jaali huffed and, after a moment's hesitation, continued his trek to the campsite. His sister, broken in so many ways, was now safe in the king's palace being cared for by Milenda's *iyalorixá*. They had buried the baby by the river and set a large stone over the grave so the predators wouldn't dig up his tiny body. He could still feel the weight of his nephew in his arms and the pain in his chest as he realized life had left him for good. Swarms of bad memories assailed him, mixed up memories of himself and his sister being kidnapped, raped, beaten again and again, thrown to the side like a bag of trash at the end. His heart felt as if it would implode with the pain each of those memories—the real ones and the ones he guessed at. Jaali pressed a fist against his chest and fell to his knees, dropping his head all the way to the ground, and cried. He couldn't breathe, his whole body shaken by an overwhelming feeling of anger and loss. Both he and Elin had lost more than their families; they had lost their childhood in the hands of monsters.

CHAPTER NINE

Sometime during the night and folded between the layers of restless slumber, she had made the decision. Under the less forgiving light of day, she was not so sure of its value. Milenda struggled with the choice of whether to tell Jaali of her plans or let it slip for now and worry about it once there was no turning back. The whole thing could turn out to be the worst idea she had ever had, and gods knew she'd had plenty of bad ideas in the past. In the end she didn't tell him, afraid he would do everything in his power to stop her.

Guilt left such a bitter taste on her tongue, she was surprised Jaali hadn't tasted it when they made love that morning. As Jaali buried his length inside of her and rocked her until the stars in the sky exploded in her body, she had a moment of vacillation—they didn't keep secrets from each other, one of the strengths of their relationship. From the moment her husband had opened his mind to her and allowed her to peek inside his memories and life experiences, they had vowed never to lie to each other. But was omission a lie?

"You seem distracted today, *msichana*." Jaali, still inside her, held her tightly against him as they lay under the shelter of their makeshift tent. "Have I lost my touch?"

Milenda laughed and kissed one of the many scars on his chest, silent reminders of his past life. "Sorry, *wimbo wa moyo*, I didn't sleep well." She felt him slide out of her and groaned in protest. She loved being connected to him in body as much as they were in spirit. When their bodies were as one, she felt stronger, capable of moving mountains, fearless and invincible. Their love had carried them through thick and thin, and she hoped it would carry them through this as well.

As Jaali washed by the river, she solidified the plan in her mind. It was simple, really—she'd go to the market and reveal herself as the living and breathing Jewel, rightful heiress to the crown of Natale, not just her spirit. The market was not the most guarded place in Natale, probably because it was always so crowded both with people and the merchants' colorful stands, making it nearly impossible to surveil efficiently. But it was however the one place where you could reach more people all in one spot than anywhere else in the nation.

"No, *kidojo moja*, that's not what's going to happen." Yemanjá, imposing and beautiful, appeared in a small poof of air. "Something else must happen at this point."

It was about time the gods actually offered directions on what to do to accomplish the much-needed revolution. "Good morning, Mother. You're looking well." Milenda bent her head in a short, respectful curtsy.

The *orisa* clucked softly while shaking her head. "I told you once, child. Meekness does not become you." She motioned Milenda to stand and then did something incredibly out of character; she raised her hands to Milenda's shoulders and squeezed them gently before bending down to her height and placing a kiss on the princess's *matangazos*.

A shiver went through Milenda, starting at the markings and running through her whole body. It felt as if a current of electricity was lighting up every inch of her body one cell at a time. As ridiculous as it sounded, she could have sworn she was glowing, her veins inside her becoming iridescent.

"Mother, what did you do?" The last time Yemanjá had touched her she'd woken up a dormant gift in her, the one that had allowed her to be with her husband and her daughter even when separated by distance. What had the *orisa* just gifted her with now?

"You're fretting again, Jewel," the beautiful, dark woman said with a small, sad smile on her lips. "You must do something you're not going to like." Not the kind of thing she wanted to hear from the lips of a powerful demigoddess. "You were wise to keep your plans from the Fjorden. He would try to stop you, and this has to be done."

Milenda was trembling, cold shivers replacing the earlier glowing feeling, the sharp claws of fear closing around her stomach. "What do you mean?"

"You will fetch Johari from her guardians and take her with you to the market."

The *orisa*'s words hit Milenda with the power of a well-placed punch. She gasped. "No, I won't do it. It's madness. I can't place my baby in such danger. The Elders want her dead, you know that."

Yemanjá closed her eyes, her long, dark lashes fanning on her perfect upper cheeks. The golden *gele* she was wearing teetered dangerously on the top of her head as the *orisa* lowered her head for a moment. "Do you remember what I said when I promised to help Jaali in the desert?"

Of course she remembered. She had agonized over it for weeks after, not sure of what the demigoddess meant. "That I would owe you and that I'd have to give something in return for your help."

"Right." The *orisa* nodded. "Time has come for you to pay your debt."

Memories of childhood stories flooded her mind, stories where the gods always asked for the firstborn for payment of favors offered. Her heart was beating so fast she thought she'd suffocate if it didn't slow down soon. "You want my daughter in return for what you did for Jaali and me?" She couldn't bring herself to believe that the Mother could be that cruel.

"Johari will be fine, I promise. You and Jaali have already paid in part. This is the final piece—showing Johari in her full Nyota glory to the people of Natale."

The promise calmed her a little, but her mother's heart couldn't stop worrying. "Why is that so important? How is that going to help?"

"You heard the guard—Johari has long been prophesied, a Nyota with white hair coming to save her people.

A *mjumbe*, a messenger to and from the gods, a divine interceptor between the world of the mortals and those who watch over them." Yemanjá raised her hands to the skies to emphasize her words. "When people see her, they'll take that as a signal that the gods are on their side, and they will be more willing to turn against the system. They've been told for generations that they are useless and helpless, only something like that will bring them enough hope to make them believe in themselves again."

Milenda dropped her arms alongside her body. "But Johari is just a baby. She doesn't even have the *matangazos* yet. Do we have to put her in danger?"

"I've promised you she won't be harmed." The *orisa* smoothed the golden fabric of her *kanga*. "When Jaali comes back from his bathing, you tell him you want to see your daughter again and nothing else."

"How can I get her to the market if I don't even know where she is?" Milenda asked, throwing a worried glance at her approaching husband.

"You convince the guards to bring her to you." Another quiet poof of air announced the demigoddess's usual abrupt departure.

Milenda hugged herself. How was she going to convince the guards, who were terrified of being caught by the Elders, to bring Johari to her? Yemanjá made it sound as if it was the easiest thing on earth. She knew better. And how was she going to be able to live with the guilt of hiding all this from Jaali? The guilt that even then clutched at her heart with a fist of iron.

***

Jaali stole a glance in his wife's direction. She'd been acting strangely lately—quiet and absentminded. Quiet both in words and thoughts since he had not been able to reach her that way. He worried, afraid that she was hurting inside and unwilling to share it for fear of upsetting him. Milenda had the tendency to want to protect him even when such protection was not necessary. But this was new. His princess had never totally closed herself to him until now. Something was afoot, and he wanted to know what.

"*Msichana*, what's wrong?" Throwing caution to the wind, Jaali decided to ask instead of tiptoeing around the issue. She lifted her forest eyes to him, and he read fear in them. The same dread she had in her eyes when his people realized for the first time that she was an Afrikan like the Mabaya warriors who took their children. The same fear he'd read in her eyes when he was presented to her as one of the Contenders. "Don't tell me it's nothing, because I can clearly see it's not."

In seconds Milenda crossed the space that separated them and threw herself in his arms, her head tucked against his chest. "Sorry, *wimbo wa moyo*. I can't tell you. I'm so sorry." Her words were muffled and colored with the tears he felt against his bare skin.

Jaali tightened his embrace. "Why can't you tell me? We always tell each other everything." The idea that she was keeping something from him was frustrating and worrisome, but he couldn't be angry at her. She would never do anything like that unless she had a good reason.

"Yemanjá forbade me." Her body stiffened and her shoulders rose. She was angry—at the goddess or herself, he couldn't tell which. "I want to tell you, but I can't. You'll know soon enough."

Cupping her chin with his hand, Jaali lifted her face toward his so he could look deeper into her eyes. "Is it something bad? Is Johari in danger?"

Milenda shook her head, her tight, thick curls bouncing with the movement. He loved her wild hair, the way it grew as an imperfect circle around her head, rebellious like her, out of control. Jaali swept a hand over her soft crown and kissed the tip of her nose.

"No, she's not in danger. Yemanjá promised to keep her safe."

"Then, what is it, *msichana*? What's making you so anxious?" He wanted to wrap his arms around her and kiss her worries away.

"Do you trust me?" Milenda's question shocked him. Had he given her any reason to think he did not trust her? He nodded, too dumbfounded to articulate his surprise. "Then, you will have to place your blind trust on me this time and not ask any more questions. Please." Her eyes overflowed with the need for him to say yes and change the subject. It made him uneasy, but what choice did he have? Milenda had never lied to him.

To get their minds off the uncomfortable feeling of things unsaid and unknown, they bathed together in the river, being careful to stay close to the bank and always protected from the surge of water by large rocks or trees. Jaali lay on a blanket spread over the brush, the sun escaping through the gap between the two river banks, its heat coaxing each of his muscles into total relaxation. As he watched his wife shaking the water off her hair, her small breasts bouncing as she moved, the memory of the first time they had made love caressed his thoughts. He had been so broken then, each small part of his soul shattered into millions of tiny pieces that he never thought could be put together again. And yet, that's exactly what Milenda did that day; her trust in him, her desire for his touch had glued all the pieces together and made him whole.

One day they would be together, Milenda, Johari, and him, living in peace, happy and content with the simple things in life. He had to believe that even when the world seemed to enjoy placing all kinds of obstacles in front of them. They stumbled, they fell a few times, but Jaali knew one day the gods and the universe would allow them a slice of an uncomplicated life.

* * *

Sleep had not come easily that night. Milenda tossed and turned, her mind feverish with what-ifs and fears of failure—failure could mean death after all. In the morning, after a quick wash and a modest breakfast with Jaali, she announced she was going to visit her father and Mama Nyeusi.

"I'll go with you," Jaali said immediately, a look of alarm in his eyes.

"No, remember what happened last time? You can't go

unnoticed, Jaali. Your skin is too white. It's safer if you stay here." A pang of guilt punched her in the stomach, but she reminded herself of the reason why she was lying to him. "I'll be back in no time."

She left the campsite after a long, languid kiss and rushed through the jungle, anxious to get it done. The sooner the better. She had visited her daughter the night before and talked her guards into bringing Johari to her in town. She made her way to the market, tying the usual cloth around her head to hide her identity until it was time to reveal herself. She waited behind one of the *kanga* merchants' tent, tucked between a tree and a bush. Terrified of what may happen, Milenda brought her knees to her chest and hugged them, resting her chin on them.

When she heard the tiny, crystalline voice of her daughter, Milenda felt the usual surge of love rising from her heart into her eyes that were now set on Johari's plump body. Mukami was carrying the child, actively trying to keep her quiet while Naki walked beside them, eyes scanning the area, alert and cautious. Milenda waved them over and stood up, her arms already stretched to receive her baby.

"Thank you, Mukami and Naki. I will never forget you've done this for my daughter," Milenda said, hugging her daughter against her chest.

"Neither will the Elders," Naki replied, her voice heavy with sarcasm. "We are going to be in terrible trouble if something goes wrong."

Milenda ran her fingers over Johari's white hair, still in wonder of how a child of hers could be so much like her and yet so different. "Your job is to keep Johari safe," Milenda said. "She's *mjumbe,* and you must protect her." Both guards nodded and lower their eyes in respect. "As soon as the guards react to our appearance, you must take Johari back to your hiding place and keep her there until we tell you it's safe. When I am queen, I will reward you for your services, I promise."

"Serving the *mjumbe* is reward enough, Jewel." Surprisingly, the comment came from the tall, lanky Naki who always seem to be a reluctant participant in the plot. "You do what you must, and we will do our part."

Milenda removed her covering, kissed her daughter's forehead, stepped into the open space between stalls, and climbed on top of a nearby barrel. Gradually the shoppers began to turn their eyes to them, mouths falling open as they recognized the Jewel and saw Johari's hair. She waited a few more seconds, allowing the cluster of onlookers to grow into a crowd, and then she spoke. "People of Natale, you've heard rumors of my spirit visiting those in the shrine." Whispers filled the air. "It's time you know, I'm not a spirit. Your Jewel never died." A collective intake of breath stopped the whispers. "I'm here in flesh and blood, back to claim my right to the throne. And I bring you my daughter, Johari."

"*Mjumbe.*" The word echoed between bodies in the crowd, exhaled and repeated. One by one the people dropped to their knees and folded to the ground. "*Tunawezaje kukuhudumia wewe, mjumbe? Tuambie na tutakufuata.*" How can we serve you, messenger? Tell us and we'll follow you.

Johari, not impressed by the reverence she inspired, giggled like the baby she was, and Milenda's stomach clenched in guilt. What responsibilities was she bringing upon her daughter? She had hated being a princess with all the obligations, the dos and can't dos, the ceremony, the rituals, the loneliness. Why was she dooming her own child to an even worse future?

An ear-piercing scream interrupted her thoughts. Milenda scanned the crowd, trying to find the origin of the sound and saw the sea of people parting and making room for a squadron of royal guards to pass in her direction. Momentarily paralyzed by fear, Milenda stood, holding Johari and watching the impending attack.

"Call the guards," a voice said, so close to her ear she could feel its warmth. "Call the guards, Jewel. Now."

Milenda didn't have time to dwell on where the voice had come from or who it belonged to. The Elders' men were too close now for her to run. She turned around just long enough to call Mukami and Naki and hand them the baby. "Go. Take her to safety. Protect her."

After a moment of hesitation, the two guards did as they were told and blended into the green and brown of the jungle. Milenda turned to the crowd again as big, rough hands gripped her arms and pushed her to the ground, her sore knee hitting a rock and sending waves of pain up her leg into her thigh. She bit her lip to prevent herself from crying in pain. She wouldn't give them that satisfaction.

The cruel hands of the men who held her against the

dirty and rocky ground pulled her up by the arms, and Milenda felt like a piece of paper, torn and ripped apart as her arms were forced to hold the weight of her body. She struggled to brace her feet on solid ground and relieve her overstretched arms and regain her dignity, but the guards pulled her before she could find her balance and dragged her through the crowd.

An older man stepped in front of the guards, and she took advantage of the sudden pause to straighten and stand on her own two feet. Milenda watched with an equal amount of curiosity and horror as the man stubbornly refused to move to let them go by.

"Get out of the way, old man." One of the guards kicked the dirt in warning. Milenda winced. Why wasn't he moving? Her captors would hurt him. "Get out of the way."

The white-haired man crossed his arms and looked straight into the guard's eyes. "You stupid man. Don't you realize who that is? That's our Jewel who you hold like a rag doll. The gods will not be pleased."

The Elders' men hesitated for only a moment before kicking the defiant old man to the ground. Releasing her arm, one of her captors unsheathed a long *upanga* and severed the man's head from his body. The bloodied head rolled on the ground for a few horrifying moments until it came to a stop right in front of Milenda. The collective sharp breath intake matched her own as she looked at the dead eyes of her defender still staring at her. Bile climbed up her throat into her mouth, and tears flooded her eyes.

Oh, gods. It's happening already. And it's all my fault.

Jaali's nightmare was turning into reality.

Before she could empty her stomach, Milenda was jerked and dragged again, her feet barely missing the severed head. The stench of fear was almost palpable, thick and ominous. She wanted to shout words of comfort, of assurance that things would be all right, but she didn't know that, and she couldn't make herself lie to her own people. Instead, she scanned their faces, many creased by the passage of time and heartaches, eyes dulled by sadness and hopelessness. As their future queen—assuming she'd escape with her life—she had to say something.

Try as she may, she couldn't free herself from the tight grip of her captors, but she collected the courage sprouting from her anger and yelled out with all her might.

"Children of Natale and Isvärld, your day in the sun will come. Keep the faith. The gods are on your side. *Kupigana!* Fight! Don't let the Elders take your right to happiness away. *Kupigana,* people of Natale. Don't let them win."

The guard to her right lifted his hand and hit her over the head with the pommel of his *upanga.* A sharp pain echoed inside her skull, and darkness fell upon her.

CHAPTER TEN

It was not like other times. There were no fine tendrils reaching out and caressing his mind, tying themselves around thoughts and feelings until you couldn't tell them apart. Instead there was a void, a bone-chilling emptiness as if something had sucked every thought from his mind. Jaali knew immediately; something terrible had happened to his wife.

The air around him became thick as mud and just as hard to breathe in. He clenched his hand against his chest, heart running a frenzied race against itself. Where was Milenda? Had she been caught sneaking around the palace? Attacked by bandits on her way home? Why couldn't he feel her presence inside his thoughts?

"She's in trouble, but she's alive." Eshu leaned against a tree, his relaxed pose belying the worry in his voice. "The Elders have her."

Jaali's heart dropped a few inches. "How did this happen? She's been to the palace so many times. Did someone betray her?" As soon as the words were out of his mouth he knew.

The secret, that mysterious thing that had her so unsettled but that she claimed could not share with him. "What did she do? What did Yemanjá have her do?"

"The Jewel presented your daughter to the people." The demigod blinked as if he expected an explosion.

"Whatever for? Are you telling me Johari was captured too?" Jaali stepped closer to the *orisa*, his chest so tight he thought it would explode.

Eshu waved his hand in the air. "The child is safe. Your wife on the other hand is in a heap of elephant dung." He licked his lips and stared at his own nails. "Dung that was expected and necessary."

Jaali clenched his hands into fists, stopping himself from hitting the demigod. "What do you mean necessary? How is it necessary to get Milenda killed?"

"Will you calm down, boy?" Jaali was too worked up to notice the *orisa*'s patronizing tone. "Nobody said anything about her getting killed. She's been captured, that's all."

"The Elders will kill her right away. She's a threat to their power." What was so hard to understand? Was Eshu so shallow that he couldn't grasp the intricacies of the balance of local power?

"The people are aware of Milenda's presence now. The Elders won't kill her for fear of causing a revolution."

"I must go to her. She must be so scared." Jaali covered his face with his hands, despair beginning to cloud his reasoning. "I have to help her."

For the first time, the *orisa* laid his hands on Jaali's shoulders. Startled, Jaali dropped his hands and stared at the demigod. "Don't be stupid. You'll be caught too, and then who is going to take care of your daughter?"

He had a point. "I can't just sit here and hope for the best."

"The Jewel is unconscious right now." Eshu lifted his hand to stop Jaali from interrupting. "She's fine. When she comes to, you can talk to her. Discreetly."

"What am I supposed to do until then?"

"Mama Nyeusi will be coming soon to take you to where your daughter is hidden. Take care of her and wait." The deceptively simple directions didn't fool Jaali. Waiting while his wife was in the hands of the same men responsible for making his trek in the desert a living hell was not simple or easy. But he knew Eshu was right. Milenda would never forgive him if he took after her, leaving Johari behind.

Milenda's *iyalorixá* arrived, her usual white clothing replaced by something that blended with the colors of the jungle. Jaali had packed their few belongings and waited impatiently, pacing along the bank of the river with his wedding *nguba* draped over an arm. The old woman wasted no time with pleasantries. She led him through trees and bushes, weaving around each obstacle in their way until they arrived at a small house tucked in between two angel oak trees, their long, thin branches stretching toward the walls of the house—graceful arms reaching out as if to hug the humble building.

"Johari is inside with the guards who have been protecting her," Mama Nyeusi said, heading toward the small wooden door. "You will stay here until such time as

Milenda and Yemanjá are ready."

Ready for what exactly? What were they waiting for or expecting would happen? "How can I help?"

"You can help by staying out of sight and safe. Your daughter is the hope of a whole nation. She must be protected at all times."

Jaali stopped abruptly as the old woman's words sank in. "What do you mean? How is a baby who can barely speak the hope of a nation?"

"Not *a* nation, young Fjorden," the *iyalorixá* corrected him. "Of two nations, Natale and Isvärld. Once the Elders are out of their power seats, the children of Isvärld will no longer fear waking up as slaves. Milenda is fighting for both."

He wished for a simple life, one where he and his wife had nothing to do with the machinations of power-hungry entities and where they could just be. Guilt at having such selfish thoughts brought a wave of heat to his face. Silently, he lowered his eyes and followed the old woman into the house.

"Pappa!" The familiar, loved voice of his daughter made him look up. The little girl was running as fast as her short legs could in his direction. He crouched and opened his arms in welcome. Johari threw herself into his arms, crossing hers around his neck. "Pappa, you here."

Jaali, arms wrapped around her soft toddler body, covered her cheeks in kisses, his eyes stinging with tears. "*Min lilla kärlek*, Pappa is so happy to see you." Johari giggled and brushed her chubby hand over her father's cheek. "I'm never going to let anyone take you away from me again."

"These are the two angels who saved Johari." Mama Nyeusi's voice brought him back to reality. He rose to his feet, his daughter still in his arms. "Jaali, this is Mukami and Naki. They are willing to stay with you and continue to protect Johari."

A giant of a man stood beside a thin woman, their eyes shadowed by heavy eyelids, the eyes of the weary. "We'll do what it takes to protect the future of our people," the woman said, pointing at Johari who babbled and laughed. "It's been ages since a *mjumbe* came to our rescue. We will protect her with our lives."

Jaali was finding it hard to believe that these two people, who worked under the direct supervision of the Elders, would be willing to lay their lives on the line for his daughter and Milenda. "The Elders will have your heads on a stick if they find out you're doing this."

Naki stole a glance at Mukami who answered, "We both have relatives who have suffered in the hands of the Elders. We're doing this for them and for the future."

Silence fell and lingered for a moment while Jaali made sense of everything that was happening. Their hopes of a bloodless revolution were quickly dissolving like haze. The Elders had Milenda, and if Eshu was right, the people would revolt. Mama Nyeusi told him about the man who was killed at the market for standing up to the guards. In his whole life in Natale, he had never heard of such an event. No one ever dared contradict orders from the mighty Elders in the past. Anger was percolating just beneath the surface, and this time it didn't look like the people were going to take it lying down.

Jaali lowered his head in a sign of respect. "You have my undying gratitude. I'll do whatever I can to help, but for now I was told to stay put and watch over my daughter. I hope you don't mind sharing your lodgings with us."

Both man and woman hastily took their fist to their chests and dipped their heads. "It's an honor, Prince Consort." Jaali flinched, not used to being called that but suddenly aware that he was indeed the husband of a future queen. Not that he had forgotten, but the last few years in his homeland had allowed them to ignore that fact, to pretend they were regular people, just a young couple starting their lives together. The words of the guards drove reality deeper into him, settling itself, heavy and unwanted, inside his chest. The young slave from the Outerlands was indeed the Prince Consort and future king of Natale.

* * *

The sound of the wind in her dream stirred Milenda out from her deep sleep. Her eyes blinked painfully open, and she tried to sit up, but her head pounded so harshly she had to lie down again. The floor beneath her cheek was cold, the same coldness she remembered from the marbled floors of the palace. She wondered where she was being held, whether in the palace or somewhere else, but the dizziness wouldn't let her focus on anything around her. She closed her eyes and touched the back of her head and flinched. Her fingers felt crusted-over hair. *I must have bled.* Or maybe she was still bleeding. Slowly and with no sudden moves, she raised her head again, squinting against the brightness of the room. When she finally managed to open her eyes fully, she was surprised to find there was no light at all, the space barely lit by a candle in a wall sconce. The room was big but had no windows or furnishings of any kind except for a bucket in the corner, she guessed for when she felt the need to relieve herself.

Finally sitting up, she saw the almost dried puddle of her own blood on the floor where her head had lay just a minute ago. Where was she? And more perplexing, why was she not dead yet? She'd been sure that's what the Elders were planning on doing as soon as they had a hold on her. Yet, there she was, battered but alive and mostly all right. When she tried to curl her legs under her, a sharp pain on her knee reminded her of her other injury. Gingerly, she touched her leg from the hip to her foot, trying to get a better idea of the extent of her injury. Milenda's leg was sore, the mere touch of her fingers sending it into spasms of pain, but she was certain it wasn't broken. She'd be able to walk if needed.

"Jaali is mad with worry." The strange female voice frightened her. Milenda's earlier scan of the room had shown no other living being in there with her. With drummers inside her head, Milenda looked around herself again but couldn't find anyone. Maybe she was going crazy or had a concussion. "I'm here if you choose to see me," the soft voice said, coming from nowhere and everywhere at the same time. "Open your mind, child. Open all your senses to what's around you and you'll see me."

Milenda still couldn't see anything. Was this yet another goddess? "Who are you? Show yourself."

Quiet laughter bounced off the walls and echoed in her ears. "I just told you—you hold the power to see me, but you must open up to the possibility."

With her hands cupping the back of her neck, Milenda groaned in frustration. "Why does everyone in my life feel they must speak in riddles? Just say it already. Who in gods' names are you?"

"You get your spirit from your father," the voice continued in a softer, more somber tone. "And your courage too."

Milenda's back stiffened. "What do you know about my father?"

"He was a good man, a great man who sacrificed his life for love." There was a pause and a sound she thought was a soft sob. "He knew that if people found out he had taken the place of the surrogate, he'd be swiftly punished, and yet he did it anyway, such was his love for your mother."

With a gulp, Milenda blinked her eyes a few times until she began to see the outline of a woman. As her form became clearer, it felt familiar. She had seen that woman somewhere before, Milenda was sure of it. "Who are you? Do I know you? What do you know about my mother and father?"

"Whoa, child, that's a lot of questions at one time." The woman, now almost completely visible, waved a hand in front of her and shook her head. "I knew your father very well. Nzinga was an extraordinary leader of the Nyota—those who were left. He had the gift like you, Milenda. Not as strong, but he was able to 'talk' to your mother from a distance. That's how they decided on when and how to meet without anyone knowing."

Despite her doubts, Milenda straightened, fascinated by what the strange woman was telling her. How did this woman know so much about her biological father? A father who she had no memory of and about who she knew close to nothing. Milenda stared at the beautiful woman in front of her, small and much darker in complexion than herself, dressed in a humble but flattering *kanga* dress, the color of a summer sky. Her hair was totally covered by a modest *iqhiya*, the same color as the dress, which emphasized her serene and lovely facial features.

"How do you know all of this? And how did you get here?" The room was obviously locked from the outside, and she couldn't see any other entrances.

"That will wait," the woman said, approaching Milenda and kneeling by her. "How do you feel? You got hit pretty hard on the head." She reached out to touch the back of Milenda's head, but the princess flinched, not sure she trusted this person yet. "Don't be foolish. I won't harm you. Let me check your wound."

Reluctantly, Milenda allowed the other woman to feel her scalp. As gentle as her touch was, it still made Milenda cringe. Her head was sore on the outside and pounding on the inside. "Is it still bleeding?" she asked, worried she was still losing blood she needed.

Her improvised nurse dabbed her head with a white cloth she had conjured out of her clothes. "No, not bleeding anymore, but you have a serious bump, child. You're going to be sore for a long time." Milenda wondered whether her injury would be another obstacle to her plan. "You need to rest and not concern yourself with anything."

Milenda snorted. "Right. In case you haven't noticed, there is trouble stirring in Natale and I'm at the center of it all. No rest for me."

"Yes, just like your father—stubborn as a donkey." The woman sat down with her legs curled under her. "You have nowhere to go, nothing to do right now. Take advantage of this respite and rest your head."

Milenda bristled, her head snapping up a bit too fast and making the world sway in front of her eyes. "I have a revolution to lead and my daughter to take care of—oh, gods! Johari. Is she hurt?" A wave of fear gripped her.

"Johari is safe and sound. Jaali is with her now, and they are both well-hidden from the Elders." The woman smiled, her fine lips stretching to a thin arch. "She's beautiful, Milenda. Your father would have loved her."

Once again, Milenda felt a stab of doubt against her sides. "What do you know about the revolution?"

She sighed, a soft whistle escaping her lips. "I know that your capture was a necessary catalyst for it to start. Being arrested in public not only saved you from being put to death right away but has stirred anger in the hearts of your people. They will uprise now, no doubt. The only question is when."

Milenda digested that information with growing apprehension. The revolution would claim the lives of innocents like in Jaali's dream, the exact thing she so wanted to prevent. She looked up and stared into the other woman's amber brown eyes. "Who are you?"

The woman cupped Milenda's cheek with her cold, soft hand. "Child, jewel of my heart, I'm your mother."

* * *

Johari ran around in circles in her usual infinite race with Gavå, watched complacently by Mjusi. Milenda's dragon friend had curled up in a corner of the room, not too far from where Jaali and Milenda were sitting, their heads close together, and voices hushed so not to alarm their daughter. Milenda had projected herself there not even an hour earlier to Jaali's great relief. He could breathe a bit easier now that he knew she was safe—at least for the moment. The minute he'd felt the long, soft tendrils of her thoughts reaching out to his, it was as if the elephant sitting on his chest had gotten up and left.

Jaali cocooned his wife's small hands in his, their warmth seeping into his thirsty skin and making his heart flutter. He had taken care of her head wound as soon as he realized she was hurt. Ignoring Milenda's protests, he gently cleaned her head and hair and disinfected the broken skin underneath. She had a big bump, the size of a snake egg, in the back of her head, but there was not much he could do about that right then—he had no ice or fresh cold water.

"Where are they keeping you?" Jaali asked her, still holding her hands, afraid she'd vanish if he let go off them.

"I don't know. There are no windows. But it could be

the palace," Milenda said, caressing the palm of his hand with her thumb. "The floors are made of the same marble of those in the palace."

"Have they fed you?" Jaali was being eaten away by all kinds of worries and frustrated he couldn't do anything to help.

Milenda snorted. "If you call that mush they slid through a small slot on the bottom of the door food, then yes, they are feeding me." She pulled on his hand and stared into his eyes. "Don't worry about me. I'm well protected, I think."

Jaali cocked his head, surprised. "What do you mean? Yemanjá?"

"No, someone else." She sounded almost reluctant to share whatever information she had. He pulled on her hand, coaxing her. "You're not going to believe this, but I had a special visitor yesterday before I was strong enough to try and reach to you."

His whole body tensed. "What visitor? One of the Elders?"

She shook her head, her wet curls sending droplets flying all around her. "No, it was my mother."

If she had smacked him over the head with a rock, he wouldn't be as stunned as he was by those words. "Your mother? Your *dead* mother?"

Milenda released a loud, long sigh. "I know, it sounds insane. But it's her." She brought his hands to her lips and kissed them. "Don't ask me how, but she showed herself to me once at the shrine and now in prison. She told me things only my mother would know, and—well, how did she enter and exited the room without ever opening a door?"

Jaali was not sure of what to do with that information. Did that mean her mother had come back in spirit form to support her daughter? Or had Milenda's brains gotten a bit scrambled when she was hit over the head? "A ghost?" he squeaked.

"Not sure what she is yet. She seems solid enough." Milenda had dropped his hand to take hers to her chest, her forest green eyes wandering far. "I even bumped into her at the shrine. I need to talk to Mama Nyeusi, but I can't."

Jaali blinked a few times, still confused by the turn of events and worried about his wife's sanity. If she was hallucinating, her head wound was a lot more serious than he'd thought. She might need medical attention. "I can ask her as soon as I see her," he said, peering intently into his jewel's distant eyes. "She sent word she'd be visiting soon."

A loud screech from Johari snapped Milenda from her trance. She laughed. "You should have seen the people's reaction when they saw her. I never made the connection, Jaali—that she is *mjumbe*. She's our little girl."

Jaali drew her to him, cradling her neck with his hand. "She still is our little girl. Whatever she may be, she will always be our Johari."

Attracted by the sound of her name, Johari approached her parents, a big smile on her face and black fluff from the fur rug stuck to her hair. Milenda scooped her in her arms and kissed her. "Love you, *mtoto wangu tamu*, my sweet baby," she whispered into the little girl's hair. "Mama will be with you again soon."

Jaali smiled, the familiar picture of his wife and daughter in a moment of pure love filling him with joy.

As much as he wished he could hold both his girls in his arms and sleep in the knowledge they were safe and sound under his protection—however weak that may be—he knew she had to leave soon. "You be careful, *msichana*. Promise me." The tone of desperation and fear he heard in his voice was not at all what he wanted to project. When he opened his mouth again, he managed to instill his voice with a more upbeat, more hopeful ring. "Everything will be all right. I know it."

Milenda's face opened in a generous smile and part of him shattered. Why did love, such a joyful feeling, have to be so painful too?

"Yes, we'll be fine." She stretched her hand in comfort. "How's your sister? Any news?"

Elin had been recovering from her terrible ordeal and learning to live with the emotional and physical scars of her life of captivity. Mama Nyeusi had taken her under her wing and sent him regular news of her progress. But his sister still had a long way to go. "She has years of abuse to recover from; it won't be easy." He knew that feeling intimately—of being broken inside and out, not trusting yourself or others, not allowing anyone to get too close. The feeling of hating your own skin and feeling guilt for something that was done to you. It had taken him a long time and the love of his wife to get to a point where he had reconciled with his younger self, and yet, there were still moments when memories came rushing in, uninvited and unwanted.

"*Wimbo wa moyo*, she'll be all right. She has what you didn't have—a family and friends to help her through, to support her while she heals." Milenda cupped his cheek and whispered, "She's loved, and that will carry her."

He hoped she was right. Elin had looked so broken, so fragile the day she had lost her baby by a river who seemed to mock her with the energy and life in its waters. She had been but a baby herself when she was taken and had no good memories to hold her, to keep her sane. But he couldn't stop hoping—Milenda was right, she would pull through victorious. One day.

After their goodbyes, Milenda shimmered for a moment and was gone. Jaali was overtaken by an emptiness so immense it took his breath away. Would they ever be allowed the serenity of a normal life?

* * *

Her days blurred into each other stuck in that dark room with no time reference of any kind. Milenda was not sure she was sleeping at night and awake during the day except for the few times she either visited Jaali or he visited her. She knew it had been more than a week since she'd been captured by the Elders' guards and nothing was happening—good or bad, as far as she could tell. On his side, Jaali was also not seeing any change, any trouble stirring. Mama Nyeusi had visited him a couple times and related news from his recovering sister and the rather unsettling quietness that seemed to have descended upon the city.

"Don't like it a bit," her old *iyalorixá* had told Jaali.

"It's too quiet, like the peace before the storm."

Milenda agreed; something was brewing, and not knowing what that was haunted her. In her mind there was the constant memory of her husband's nightmares when they were still in Isvärld, its threatening fumes hanging over her like a dark, electrified cloud.

"But what can I do? I'm stuck in here." She hmphed like she had done in her teens, her arms crossed over her breasts.

"You are doing something, child." Yemanjá stood before her, bright even in the darkness as if her inner divinity exuded a natural light. Milenda hopped to her feet, ashamed of having been caught in a less-than-mature moment. "Just because you're here and you don't know much about what's happening out there does not mean you're idle."

"How can I be helping while alone and captive?" She cringed at the sound of her own voice, the whining of a child, not the voice of a queen.

Yemanjá's lips twitched as if the demigoddess was fighting the urge to smile. "It is because you're here that things are moving swiftly outside." Always cryptic, the beautiful woman moved her hand to call Milenda closer. "The people of Natale are angry, their anger simmering just below the surface. Their Jewel was captured and treated like a common criminal and their *mjumbe* threatened. The guards did what has not been done in years; they killed a commoner in front of a crowd. A storm of epic proportions is brewing, child. And you're the eye of the storm."

Milenda's stomach dropped a few inches. Not exactly what she wanted to hear. Yes, she knew a revolution was very much needed in order to secure a brighter future for most of the people in Natale and Isvärld, but the thought of anyone getting hurt was disquieting to her. "I don't want any bloodshed, Mother. My people have suffered long enough."

"Unfortunately, the Elders only understand one language—that of violence and death." Milenda cringed. "Blood will be shed, *kidojo moja*. But for a good cause." In Milenda's mind and heart there was no such thing as a good reason for death among the innocent, among those she strove to save from a life of servitude and helplessness. "It will be all right in the end, Jewel. I promise."

It was the first time Milenda had ever heard the goddess utter those words. She had gotten reassurances but never an actual promise. Not sure whether that was a good thing or not, she whispered a thank you and found herself alone in the room again. She felt exhausted all of a sudden, as if the weight of the world had just been dropped on her shoulders and she had no way to avoid it. "A queen's duty can't be denied," she had been told time and time again growing up. Did that still apply if that duty included standing by while the innocent were massacred? How would she be able to live with herself with the blood of her people on her hands? How would she be able to touch her beautiful, pure daughter with bloodstained fingers? Milenda dropped to the ground, curled into a fetal position, closed her eyes, and wept.

CHAPTER ELEVEN

Eshu's pop-up visits had been brief for the past few days. Trouble was brewing in the city, rumors of small pockets of commoners rising up and resisting the push of the Elders. Whispers of sudden deaths in retaliation burned through the populace, leaving a trail of anger and resentment instead of the fear the Elders were hoping it would inspire. Even the Fjorden slaves were voicing their anger despite the fact they'd be swiftly silenced by their owners one way or another. The revolution seemed to be taking momentum, and Jaali both hated and loved the fact he was in hiding—hated the fact he was not actively helping but loved the fact his daughter was safe with him.

When Eshu showed up that morning, barely a day after his last appearance, his visit worried the Fjorden. The demigod had regained some of his cockiness and shallowness overnight, leaning against a wall, studying his well-manicured nails as if reading an engrossing story. Jaali was not sure what to make of it. For the past few days, the *orisa* seemed unusually ruffled and solemn, but something had changed.

"What do you want, Eshu?" Despite the fact he was talking to a god, Jaali couldn't hide the irritation he held for these divine creatures who seemed to play with them as if they were pieces in an elaborate game of Mancala. "Coming to tell me of more death and desolation?"

The lithe, dark *orisa* lifted his intense, kohl-lined eyes to Jaali and clicked his tongue. "Down, pretty one. Is that sarcasm I hear in your voice?" The god's lips stretched into a lazy smile. "Be careful, mortal. I can zap you out of existence with a thought."

To distract himself and disguise his annoyance, Jaali crouched to pet Mjusi's scaly head. The *msuti* growled softly, a subtle warning directed at Eshu. Mjusi was protective of his family, and Jaali didn't doubt he would lash out against anyone who threatened them despite their divinity status.

"Don't worry, *msuti*," Eshu said, an amused twitch on his lips. "I'm not going to hurt Jaali. He's too beautiful, and I would never hurt anything I so enjoy looking at."

A rush of heat climbed up his neck and spread over Jaali's whole face. "What do you want, Eshu? You were here just yesterday." Mjusi growled once more and then eased his heavy head down to the ground. Jaali dropped to the floor next to him and stared at the half-naked *orisa*.

"You are needed, my sweet mortal." Jaali wished the *orisa* didn't talk to him like that. It brought back many bad memories that he'd sooner forget, or at least keep back in the far recesses of his mind. "The *indents* are getting scared after some well-executed public punishments of those who dared speak out."

What else did they expect? He had been in their position not that long ago and remembered well how fear kept him frozen, terrified of uttering even a word. There were days when he hadn't even dared to fix his gaze on anything in particular for fear of poking the *duivel*'s unstable and cruel temper. "That's not surprising, is it? Did you immortal ones expect they would not fear the retaliation from those who hold power over them?" Were the gods really that out of touch with reality?

"Tsk, tsk, watch the tone, sweet one." Jaali swallowed bile, his hands clenching into fists by his sides. "Yemanjá wants you to talk to the slaves again."

That proved it; the divine ones were indeed crazy. They wanted him to go talk to the same people who were undoubtedly by now being watched closely by their owners. How was he to accomplish that without being caught? Or was that the plan? They had done that to Milenda, so why not to him, a much less important pawn in their game?

"We have a plan, mortal." Eshu's voice had turned slightly sour, but his crooked smile still held. "You won't be caught or hurt, I can promise you. After all, I wouldn't want my pretty one to be damaged, would I?"

Jaali heard a frustrated grunt escape his own lips. "Can you please stop calling me that?"

The *orisa*'s eyes rounded, badly disguised amusement dancing in them. "Call you what? Pretty? Well, you are, aren't you? Deliciousness in human form. I'd so love a taste of that were you not the husband of our Jewel. Yemanjá would skin me alive and use me for a doormat."

The Fjorden's stomach churned in disgust, memories of other times he had been addressed like that flooding his mind and the insidious claws of fear and misplaced guilt closing tightly around his heart. "Just don't," he managed to squeak out, fighting the wave of nausea climbing up his throat.

"Oh, poo. You're no fun, mortal." The god went back to his leaning position and the strange fascination with his own nails. "I'll give you that today. But you still have a mission to fulfill."

Jaali sighed deeply, drawing his legs up to his chest and wrapping his arms around them. "What? What is it you want from me now?"

"You need to go rouse the troops, so to speak. You must create enough motivation in the bosom of each slave that they are willing to ignore their fears and fight for what is right." For once, Eshu's voice sounded serious even if he hadn't raised his eyes from his fingertips. "I'll come back with a plan by tonight, but I wanted you to be prepared." Eshu pushed away from the wall and acted as if he was leaving, but then turned to Jaali and added, "I almost forgot, Mama Nyeusi will be stopping by with a weapon. Don't hesitate to use it."

The *orisa* was gone, but his last words lingered. Weapon? What could he possibly be referring to? The *iyalorixá* was not a war monger, and the only weapons she ever carried were her herbs and prayers. Jaali quit speculating about it and went to check on his daughter, who was happily playing with the giant Mukami. The guard seemed totally bewitched by the white-haired little girl and allowed her to climb his impressive mountain of a body, pull on his tightly woven braids, and cover his brown face with spit-full kisses. Hiding around the corner, Jaali watched Johari boss around the man who was at least ten times bigger than she was. He chuckled and then decided to go rescue the poor guard.

Later that afternoon, Naki walked in from her watch outside with news of Mama Nyeusi's arrival. "She's bringing someone with her," the guard said, a question in her eyes.

Jaali blinked. Was this the weapon Eshu spoke of? A human as a weapon? "Who is it?" he asked, but Naki shrugged. "I'll go wait for them outside then."

Whatever he was expecting, that was not it. When Milenda's *iyalorixá* emerged from the thick forest, Jaali's breath caught on his chest. Walking next to her was his sister, Elin—a much healthier looking Elin, pink cheeks and purpose in her walk. He was paralyzed for a moment. The last time he had seen her was when she had lost the baby, destroyed by the loss of the one thing she had of her own, a piece of herself to love and protect the way nobody ever did for her—not that she could probably remember.

Mama Nyeusi smiled as soon as she laid eyes on him, her full, wrinkled face opening in welcome. She placed a hand on the small of Elin's back as if to encourage her to move faster. "Jaali, so good to see you," she said. "I brought you a gift."

Snapping out of his stupor, Jaali ran toward his sister and wrapped her in a tight hug. Elin stiffened at first, unused to a friendly touch, but then relaxed in his arms even if not reciprocating the gesture. "Elin, I'm so happy to see you again," he whispered into her thin, white-blonde hair, aware she couldn't hear him. "And looking well, sister."

Elin pushed gently away and offered him a tentative smile. She lifted her hand and placed it timidly over his heart. It was strange to have a sister who couldn't speak or hear, and he wanted to learn how to communicate with her. The whole process would be complicated by the fact that Elin had never been taught sign language. He would have to teach her once things calmed down—if things ever calmed down.

Jaali turned to Mama Nyeusi with an apologetic smile. "Sorry, Mama. I'm happy to see you too." He led them both to the small wooden bench under the angel oak. "Let's sit and talk for a while." He looked Elin in the eye and pointed at her. "How are you feeling, Elin? You look well."

Mama Nyeusi laughed when his sister glanced at her, confusion in her eyes. "Jaali, use your hands to show her what you mean," she said, her hand pointing at him and then making a circular gesture around her face. "I've been teaching Elin basic signs for communicating. She's a bright girl, your sister." The old woman tapped her middle finger on her forehead and flicked it away, her palm open toward Elin. A smile crinkled her papery brown skin further. "She's learning fast."

"I know sign language, but how much of it does she

know?" Jaali had always had a gift for languages and had taught the Outlandish languages in Natale's prestigious university after freeing himself from his cruel master. He had mastered a couple more languages while teaching there, one of which was the language of the deaf. Turning slightly to his sister, Jaali held a fist by his head, his index finger touching the pad of his thumb before flicking it upward. "Do you understand me, Elin?"

Elin nodded, a measure of relief washing over her transparent eyes, so similar to his own and those of his father. She pointed at herself, placed her closed hand on top of her other palm with the thumb sticking out and moved both hands upward. She wanted to help, he realized with a start. How could she help when she couldn't even talk or hear the sounds around her?

"It's dangerous," Jaali signed, still not sure she fully understood, overenunciating his words in hopes she may be able to read his lips. "Too dangerous, Elin. You could get hurt." He touched his fingertip with the other and shook his head.

The thin, willowy girl shook her head and hit her fist against her chest, grunting.

"They hurt her and her child, Jaali," Mama Nyeusi said. "She wants to defeat the Elders as much as you do. Maybe more. She's been captive most of her life. Allow her that small independence."

Jaali stared at his sister, tears dancing in his eyes. He didn't want Elin mixed up in the upcoming revolution, but he couldn't deny her the right of fighting against those guilty for everything that had happened to her. He signed the word "hurt" again, but with less determination. She shook her head and made a heart-wrenching sound that reverberated all the way to his core. The tears hiding just behind his eyes began pouring out, the sorrow of years of youth and innocence lost mixing with anger. He nodded, and Elin smiled, the hesitant curling of lips of someone who hadn't done it in years.

"That's settled then." Jaali had almost forgotten the *iyalorixá's* presence. "Elin will be helping you talk to the *indents* this time. They need all the motivation they can get."

Mukami had brewed some tea, and Johari couldn't get enough of her newly found aunt. The little princess's rumbustious personality made up for Elin's shyness, and her nonstop chatter balanced her aunt's silence. Jaali watched them, his heart swelling with joy. These moments of peace and familial happiness were rare and far between, but he had to admit they made up for the pain and upheaval that normally enveloped their lives. The only thing missing was his beautiful, brave wife.

"Don't be so sure, *wimbo wa moyo*," a voice echoed inside his head. "I may be far, but I'm always close to your heart." A smile stretched across his lips and he sighed. Now, the moment was truly perfect.

* * *

"*Msichana*, can you hear me?"

Jaali's warm breath blew against the back of her neck,

and her hand automatically stretched behind her to touch him. His body was glued to her back, his legs cradling hers, and his face buried in the crook of her neck. Milenda loved these nightly visits. He didn't come every night but often enough for her to think of it as a routine—one she absolutely adored and didn't want to let go.

"*Wimbo wa moyo*, you're here." She had been half asleep, her dreams a tangle of good and bad memories laced with some frightening what-ifs. His presence made her immediately relax, every muscle in her body softening and yielding to his. "I missed you."

His hand reached around her to starfish on her chest. "I'm here. Yours forever." His soft lips peppered her shoulder, running over her *matangazos* and lighting them with his touch. "I love that you have the stars inside of you, *msichana*. There is no darkness when I'm with you, only light."

Milenda giggled and turned herself around to face him. "Flatterer." The accusation was uttered in jest. She knew her husband truly saw her as the light in his life just as she saw him as her strength. "What news do you bring me?"

Jaali groaned, pretending to be disappointed. "I really just wanted to make love to you, my sweet Jewel."

"If you behave and keep me properly motivated, that may still happen," she teased him, kissing him lightly on the lips. "But first, I must know the news. How's our bundle of energy? Mjusi and Gavå? Mama Nyeusi?"

The Fjorden laughed, tightening his arms around her. "Slow down. For a future queen, you sure are impatient."

Before he could say anything else, her lips had come down on his, and he yielded to her softness and warmth. "See? Now I can't even remember what happened."

Another kiss followed, deeper and more demanding. Milenda knew that soon they would be lost in each other. She wanted to make sure he was lucid enough to convey the latest news from her family and kingdom, so she made herself stop, raising a hand between their lips. "No, news first. Love afterward."

Jaali groaned again, his obvious desire growing against her belly. "All right, you run a hard bargain, Princess." He swept a thick lock of hair from her forehead. "Our daughter and *msutis* are perfectly healthy and happy even though Mjusi really misses you. He's been kind of droopy and constantly puffing out those little clouds of smoke from his nostrils."

She chuckled softly. She missed her friend too. It had been lonely in that dark room, even with all the unauthorized and unexpected visitors she'd had.

"Mama Nyeusi is the same—bossy and outspoken—and Johari has really made two loyal friends and followers in her guards. They love and idolize her. She'll be spoiled rotten by the time this is over." Milenda felt him stiffen slightly, the same thought probably crossing his mind—if this would ever be over. "The only real surprise is that my sister came to visit and she's joining me in a few days when I go address the Fjorden slaves again."

Taken by surprise, Milenda rose her head from the hard floor that served as her bed. "What? Isn't that too dangerous?

They must have heavy surveillance over them right now."

"Mama Nyeusi and Eshu assure me it will be easy." Milenda heard the doubt in his voice. As much as Eshu had proved himself to be a powerful ally, his vain and shallow demeanor didn't inspire much faith in his honesty. "The slaves are getting discouraged. Several have taken severe beatings, and a couple of them were put to death for speaking out. We must do something to bring their morale up and motivate them to fight."

She bit her tongue, wanting to say she didn't want them to fight. She didn't want anyone getting hurt in this fight for justice, but she knew it was futile and juvenile to think that a revolution could happen without any blood being spilled.

"I have no idea what we can say or do to convince them against those who hold all the power over them, but I have to somehow find a way to reach them." Jaali went quiet, his quick breathing the only sound coming from him.

"What will you tell them?" Milenda asked in a tiny voice.

"I don't know. All I'm sure of is I won't lie and tell them it will be easy." Jaali brushed his fingers across her cheek. "I'll tell them the truth; that there will be death and misery before there is joy and freedom. That I can't guarantee their safety. All I can do is fight by their side."

There was silence again, their breaths mixing and mingling. Milenda drew her husband closer, flattening her hand on his back and her ear against his chest. She could hear and feel the beating of his generous and strong heart against her cheek, and she drank it in as a magic elixir that made her stronger and more determined.

"Love will win, *wimbo wa moyo*. Justice and love are our weapons." She believed it, the truth of her words filling her heart with hope, with the exhilaration of victory over evil. Somehow, she knew they would win, but the question remained, how much more loss would it take before they could sing the song of peace and harmony? How many more lives would be taken in the name of hope, in the name of justice? It didn't matter that she knew it was a necessary evil; she would never be able to accept any loss of life as an acceptable price.

***

"They'll be waiting." Eshu succinct statement still rang in Jaali's head. How could the *orisa* be so sure? What had he done to guarantee that the *indents* would be waiting for him free from the watch of their owners?

Elin was by his side, as tall as he was and yet, she seemed childlike in her hesitant step, her constant turning of the head, her slightly wild eyes. Jaali longed to hold her hand and comfort her from her obvious anxiety, but he feared her reaction. Having been abused for as many years as she had, he couldn't be sure she'd accept his brotherly touch. He remembered how he felt even a few years after earning his freedom—unwilling to allow people to touch him in any way, his skin crawling in fear and disgust even when his body accidentally brushed against someone else's. With sorrow, he glanced at his sister and then focused on the path ahead of them, toward where Eshu had promised they would be received with open arms.

As they approached the clearing where the *orisa* had told them the slaves would be gathered, he heard a rumble. Not the rumble of thunder but rather the distant roar of a river, running wild through the jungle, meandering around trees and splashing over rocks in a rush to reach the vastness and limitlessness of the ocean. Jaali strained to listen and thought he could distinguish voices just beneath the sound, the susurration of people scared of being heard. He kept on, hoping that Eshu was right.

When the trees gave way to a meadow, Jaali and Elin were faced with a small crowd of light-skinned people, thin and ragged, their paleness too transparent to be healthy, their eyes those of panicky animals ready to bolt at any moment. He stopped suddenly, and his sister crashed against his back. The whispering stopped, and every eye turned to the two siblings with so much yearning in their gaze that Jaali gasped.

"Don't be afraid," he said, his voice carrying across the clearing. He might have imagined it, but he thought he saw them all taking a collective step backward. He raised his arms, palms facing the crowd. "We're here in peace."

The crowd still retreated, one step at a time. Soon they would be out of the meadow and into the protection of the jungle. Jaali had to find a way to stop them, to convince them he meant them no harm. But before he could do anything, Elin had taken a decisive step forward, her shoulders leveled with his. The crowd paused their progress, their eyes focusing on her willowy figure. She raised her hand up above her head and placed the other over her heart, and the voices ceased completely. His sister had done in silence what he hadn't be able to do with words.

Once the silence had covered everyone and everything, Elin glanced at her brother as if prompting him to address the crowd. Still astonished by her grace and authority, Jaali cleared his throat and readied himself to deliver his speech—the one he was still working on in his head.

He stepped forward and swallowed, his mouth suddenly dried from the tension in everybody's gazes. They were expecting him to be inspiring, for him to offer them an easy way out, hope. Instead, he was ready to tell them freedom would come at a high price—that many would die fighting for it. A question continued to plague him—given the same option when he was still a slave, would he have accepted the challenge, taken the risk? The answer was an emphatic "yes." Anything would have been preferable to what he had to go through on a daily basis as an *indent*. Even death.

"Brothers and sisters, we deserve our lives back." Now that he had been able to answer his own question, the words were flowing freely and decisively. "It won't be easy. Many will die, both Fjorden and Natalian, but ask yourselves what kind of life do you want for yourself and your children? Do you want to spend the rest of your life under the despotic rule of your owners? Even those of you lucky enough to have benevolent masters do not have the right to choose for yourselves, to live the life our ancestors built for us up in the Northern Lands. We are made to bow to those who think of us as objects, as things they can own and do with as they please."

A quick look around told him he had a captive audience now. Some of the slaves had moved forward, no longer cowering in fear. Jaali swallowed the giant knot lodged in his throat as he addressed the one scar he still carried around with him all the time. "Then, there are those of us, like my sister and I, who had the misfortune of being bought by evil men and women. Those of us whose bodies have been used for years as a punching bag, as a sexual tool, as a target for anger and frustration." He paused, his voice catching for a moment. "I thought of death all the time. In fact, I prayed for the peace and release of death to come and take me. Anything would be better than the thought of another hour at the hands of my master and his friends. Elin, my sister, can't talk, but she was used like me, and even though she can't say it, I know she felt the same way—I know that, like me, she prayed to the gods they would have mercy and take her soul."

He looked at his sister, his hand on his heart, and her transparent eyes met his, understanding reflected in them. She knew what he was saying, and he realized with a jolt how he had been grabbing at his shirt, frowning as he uttered the words that stained his past—his body language was all she'd needed to read his words. She smiled, encouraging him to go on.

"I can't promise you that all will be good—I'm not a god, just a man that like you has suffered under the rule of a group of unjust and merciless men. The people of Natale are rising up against the Elders. I'm asking you to join them when the time comes." He took a deep breath and closed his eyes for a moment. A sudden exhaustion overtook him, as if he had aged in the last few minutes. "You can help from within. The day the revolution starts, you can support it by rising up with the rest. Spread the word, gather whatever you can to use as weapons, and more than anything else, keep the faith. We will prevail in the end."

The temptation to lie down on the dirt, curl up into a ball, and fall asleep was so strong he held on to his sister's arm. Elin looked up at him and for the first time covered his hand with hers as she smiled. "You did good, brother," her eyes seemed to say. "I'm proud of you."

The people whispered to each other for a while, and Jaali stood, waiting. His eyes were heavy with sleep, and he felt as if he wouldn't be able to talk again if he tried. He wanted to crawl under the sheets with his wife and daughter and hold on for dear life. Blood would be spilled, and the weight of it fell on his shoulders.

"We will stand with the people of Natale." One woman had stepped forward and away from the others and spoke directly to Jaali and Elin. "We want to be free. At any cost."

Jaali felt woozy, the world wavering in front of him like paint washing off paper. He opened his mouth to reply, but he seemed to have lost control of his body as it slid all the way to the ground, darkness descending upon him quickly. One second was all he had to wonder why his sister and a few of the slaves were running toward him before everything faded into nothing, creating a big, black void of silence.

CHAPTER TWELVE

Drowning

The unfamiliar clanking and clicking woke her up from a fitful sleep. It took her a few seconds to realize what the sound was. Someone was opening her prison's door. She sat up, still half into her disturbing dream where Jaali had taken ill from a mysterious disease. She shook her head. Milenda knew she should be scared, but after days—or had it been weeks?—of isolation inside that dark room, she was numb to external stimulus.

Light flooded the space, blinding her for a moment. She heard heavy footsteps, the sound of hard soles against the marble of the floor. She stiffened. Those steps sounded familiar and didn't inspire confidence. Milenda bounced to her feet, her wounded knee shooting pain up to her thigh and hip as it took on her full weight.

"To what do I owe this unpleasant surprise?" she asked the Elder who had entered the room and stood facing her with his back to the light—undoubtedly a planned stance to create the illusion of a halo around him. "It's been a while."

She strove to maintain a note of haughtiness to her voice, the tone of a royal addressing her lesser subjects.

"Still unwise and childish even after all this time." The comment made her burn inside. "Why did you have to go against tradition? You could have been queen and led a quiet, peaceful life if you had followed the traditional way and picked a husband from the men who survived the Trials."

Milenda loosened a bitter chuckle. "But I did, didn't I? You might have done your best to eliminate him, but Jaali survived." She bit her lip, trying hard not to allow her anger to make her sound like a child. "I didn't break any laws like you did."

The Elder's deep, growling voice echoed ominously throughout the chamber, ricocheting between the empty walls like bullets. "You picked an Outlander, an *indent* for your husband and threatened to soil the royal line."

"That's elephant's dung." Her breathing quickened as the fumes of anger filled her lungs. "You would have killed me eventually no matter what. Having a Nyota for a queen didn't please you a bit."

"True. There would have come a time when we would have to make you disappear like your unwise mother and father, but it wouldn't have been right away." The hooded man spoke the words as if complimenting her. "You'd be allowed to live a few more years. But you chose not to by marrying your slave and questioning our authority."

Milenda strained to see the man's face, but the cover of the black hood and the light from behind him made it impossible. Now that she thought about it, she couldn't remember one single instance when she had actually seen any of their faces—the council of twelve men who ruled the nation with an iron and unfair fist.

"To prove to us all how immature and foolish you are, you decided to return to Natale and start stirring waves of discontent where before there were none." The Elder tilted his head up enough she could distinguish a strip of brown skin in the shade. "Did you really think you could go against us and win?"

"I already won," Milenda spat the words, the urge to cross the space between them and strangle him strong and hard to resist. "I may be stuck in here, but Jaali is out there, canvasing for what's right and motivating the populace to rebel against you."

A low cackling sound emerged from below the hood. The Elder was laughing at her. "Jaali won't be doing much of anything anymore. And your daughter, the little white-haired freak, will soon be in our custody too."

Milenda forgot to act royal or mature. The anger inside her boiled to the surface at the mention of her baby, and she threw herself at the Elder, aiming for his neck. She was small, but he was not very tall either. Except, he anticipated her move and dodged her attack as easily as if swatting a fly. In the momentum, Milenda lost her balance and fell to the ground, her knees hitting the hard marble with a sickening cracking sound. Trying to stop her head from hitting the floor as well, she braced herself on her hand. A scream of pain rose to her mouth, but she managed to squelch it. No matter how much she hurt, she wouldn't give the Elder the satisfaction of seeing her cry.

The Elder slid his hands through the wide sleeves of his robes and clapped. "Bravo, Jewel. You are nothing but entertaining, my princess. I would take care of that knee if I were you. Not that you'll need it much where you're going."

He turned around and walked leisurely to the open door, stopping before reaching it to turn halfway around and look at Milenda, still sprawled on the floor. "I hope you said your goodbyes to your beloved slave, because you won't be seeing him ever again. Take care. Or not. It doesn't really matter." Darkness fell as he closed the door behind him.

What did he mean by that? Why had he said that Jaali wouldn't be doing much of anything anymore? In a sudden panic, Milenda reached out to her husband, fear gripping her. Nothing. There was only a void, a void that uncomfortably reminded her of the time Jaali had been shot just outside the desert. Her blood went cold; something terrible had happened.

* * *

Waves of nausea made his stomach clench and press against his ribs, squeezing it until he felt it may explode. Try as he may, Jaali couldn't open his eyes since their lids had changed into small curtains of lead, too heavy for him to lift. The identity of those who carried him out of the clearing and back to the hideout was a mystery to him, but then again much of what was happening and all that he was feeling were unknowns. His body convulsed in pain, shivers defying the sweat that covered his skin. Once in a while, the coolness of a wet towel relieved his discomfort for a moment or two before the pain, the dizziness, and the confusion came back with a vengeance.

Voices reached his ears, undistinguished and anonymous. "What's wrong with him? Is he going to make it? What should we do?"

The soaked towel someone had placed against his lips was not enough to quench his gargantuan thirst, but he sucked on it with all the energy he had left. In a far corner of his mind, panic was taking shape. Was this another trick from the Elders? The same kind they had played on him during the Trials? *Oh, gods. Don't let the hallucinations come back.* The mere thought of reliving his slavery days was scarier than anything else. Even scarier that death.

"*Wimbo wa moyo*, what have they done to you?" The loved voice of his wife blew in his ear and, even though blinded by whatever that strange fever was, he could feel her hands on his cheeks, on his arms. "The Elders did this. But what is *this*?"

He wanted to tell her he was all right, to appease her worry and fears, but his lips wouldn't form the words. He was conscious of his surroundings, but somehow separated from it. How was that possible?

"I'll take care of him for a while," he heard Milenda say.

"But your knee is bleeding again." Was that Mama Nyeusi's voice? "And your wrist is swollen and bruised."

"Don't worry about me," Milenda whispered as if she didn't want him to hear it. "I'll be fine. We need to find out what those bastards did to my husband."

"I have someone inside the Elders' quarters," the same female voice said. "They'll find out what's going on and report it to me."

"Mama, will you watch Johari? I don't want her to see her father like this. Give me a few moments with Jaali alone, please."

There was silence for a while, and Jaali thought he may be losing a handle on his consciousness. But then he heard his wife's sweet voice by his ear again. "I'm here for you, *wimbo wa moyo*. We'll fix it. We won't let them win." She started to sob, and he convulsed again, from the fever and frustration. "I love you."

Jaali knew his struggle to stay conscious was a losing battle for he felt himself slip into darkness quicker and quicker, but he still fought against it. He wouldn't let the Elders win. Never again.

His last thought before oblivion took him under went to his wife, his love, the woman who had saved him many times over. A woman he knew would do anything in her power to keep him safe just as he would do for her. His jewel.

* * *

The throbbing hadn't stopped. Milenda's knee had swollen to double its size, and an angry redness was spreading from the wound up and down her leg. For once she was grateful for the lack of light in her prison that made it easier for her to ignore the alarming stain. She had left Jaali, still racked by a high fever and convulsions, in the care of Mama Nyeusi who watched over him like a mother hen, clucking as she went on with the business of cleaning him up, cooling him down, and keeping him hydrated. Her old *iyalorixá* told her Jaali was having seizures, but she still couldn't identify the cause.

"They've poisoned him." The woman who claimed to be her mother stood beside her, her inner glow illuminating the chamber. "The Elders poisoned him."

No longer surprised by the unexpected appearances of gods and spirits, Milenda straightened her back, a hand cupping her knee. "But how? They didn't know where Jaali was. How could they have poisoned him?"

The ethereal body of her mom seemed to shimmer as she kneeled beside her daughter. "My guess is it's something from before." Milenda's eyebrows rose. "From when he was participating in the Trials. The Elders have technology only available to them. I heard about a time-bomb poison they used in people they wanted to get rid of but didn't want to make it too obvious. Rumors in the palace said that they had got rid of a few foreign diplomats that way."

"A time bomb?" Milenda's heart beat against her chest bone. "Will it explode?"

"No, not that kind of bomb," her mother said. "They named it that because it can lay dormant and harmless for years until the Elders decide to trigger it. When they do, the tiny capsule that holds the poison bursts inside the human carrier and floods his body with a deadly substance. It may take weeks for its full effect. Those diplomats died long after they had left Natale, and no one could blame the Elders for it."

Bile climbed up her throat, anger mixing with fear. "But why now? Why didn't they do it while we were in Isvärld?"

"They thought he was dead. Why bother then?" Her mother covered her hand with hers, prying her fingers away from the knee. "You're hurt, child. Let me take care of you."

Years of wishful thinking and sadness for an absent mother made the Jewel jerk her fingers away from the woman's. "I can take care of myself. I've done it my whole life."

There was sadness in the former queen's eyes. "I know, and I'm so proud of the way you turned out. I missed all your firsts—the mother-daughter talks, the pilgrimages to the ocean to pay Yemanjá's our respects. But it was not my choice, daughter. It was taken away from me just like they're trying to take everything you love away from you now." She wiped what looked suspiciously like a tear from her cheek. "Let me take care of you. You're hurt, and if that wound doesn't receive some attention, you'll end up making the Elders' job a lot easier."

Reluctantly, Milenda allowed her mom to gently probe her knee injury and examine it carefully. Milenda watched the woman who had chosen love over an easy life, not unlike herself. Would she end up like her mother? Dead and forgotten?

"I don't even know your name," Milenda said in a small voice.

Anytime her father mentioned his wife, he always

referred to her as "your mother" or "the queen," never by her given name. Was the simple mention of her name too much of a hard reminder of her betrayal and later her death? Her father, the king, had loved his wife just as strongly as Milenda loved Jaali, but their love had been doomed as soon as the Elders insisted that her mother find a surrogate father to continue the royal line.

"Mirembe. My name is Mirembe." Not raising her face to her daughter's, she continued to checking the wound. "Your father called me Mire. Melchior, I mean. I used to love it when he whispered that in the privacy of our chambers."

"Did you ever love him, Mother? Or were you just doing what you'd been told to do?" Milenda was surprised by her own question. She had never consciously asked herself that question for fear of what the answer might be. But she needed to know. It was yet one more mystery in her puzzling life that she wanted solved.

Mirembe looked up at her then, her sparkling green eyes wet with tears. "I did love him once. It was not hard to love your father back then; he was a good man, kind and patient, loving. I didn't love him enough though. And when I was told to let a strange man inseminate me, whatever love I had for him turned into dislike. I guess I thought of him as the cause of my predicament even though he was as much of a victim as I was."

Silence fell around them, and her mother lowered her gaze to her knee again. Milenda understood. How would she have reacted in the same position? Probably like her mother had—not that she could even imagine not loving Jaali.

"May I kiss your knee?" The abrupt strange question tore Milenda from her thoughts.

"Kiss my knee? Whatever for?"

Green eyes met Milenda's again. "To heal it."

Not sure she had heard it correctly, Milenda blinked. "What?"

"The gods gave me a gift too, my daughter." When Milenda didn't reply, Mirembe asked again, "May I?"

Milenda nodded and watched mesmerized as her mother bent down over her legs and placed a kiss over the wound. Her lips were soft but cold, and as soon as they touched her skin, a icy wave ran through her leg all the way down to her toes and up to her belly and higher still. It lodged in the center of her chest, cold at first but warming up with each passing second. When the coldness had all but been replaced by heat, the wave retraced its steps from the heart down to the knee and below.

"What did you do?" Her leg, warm and tingly, seemed to glow like her mother's body.

"It will heal now, Milenda," was all the answer she got. "Tell Melchior I'm so sorry I didn't love him like he deserved and that he has been a good father and will be a great monarch once the Elders are defeated. I'll be watching from the other realm. I love you."

"What other realm?" Milenda made a move to hold her, but she had already disappeared, a soft residual glow the only thing left behind. Her eyes filled with tears, longing in her heart—the same feeling she had so many times as a child for the mother she never had. A whisper escaped her tremulous lips, "What other realm, Mother? Where are you going and where have you been?"

***

The weight around his ankles held him as he struggled to move forward toward the door. Surrounded by red, thick fog, Jaali treaded forth in vain. He hadn't moved an inch, and the door, the opening that promised sunshine and peace, was as far from him then as before. His chest hurt from simply breathing, each intake of air burning in his lungs as if laced with fire. Even in this miasma of mixed-up thoughts he knew his mind was fighting for his life. He recognized the usual nightmare, the haunting of times past.

"I won't give up," he yelled, his voice echoing from the bloody haze. "You won't take me away from Milenda and my daughter."

Laughter met his words. "We told you you'd regret disobeying us." The Elders, their voice something he would never forget, speaking inside his head. "You dared to challenge us, now you'll pay for it."

"No, I won't go." But even as the words left his lips, he felt it—the emptying feeling of his soul leaving his body. "No, I won't let go…"

***

Mirembe had come to her again in her dream, wrapping her arms around Milenda's shoulders and holding her while she sang a lullaby. "Mama, I missed you. I've missed you forever."

A loud noise woke her up. She automatically jumped to her feet, pausing only to notice how her knee was not sore anymore. A ray of light spread on the marble floor, stretching and widening until it reached her bare feet.

The door was open.

She expected the Elders or one of their minions to cross the threshold with bad news, but no one ever came. Cautiously, Milenda tiptoed to the door, sure that someone would walk in at any time. However, no one did, not even when she stuck her head out the door to look outside. The corridors were empty and silent. Like she suspected, she was in the palace, a room in the recesses of the Elders' chambers.

After waiting for a moment, Milenda took a step out, and when no one came to stop her, she took off running quietly, the pads of her feet barely touching the cold marble, and her ears and eyes on high alert. She had no idea who had opened the door, but now wasn't the time to ponder about it. Once she was away from the palace and her captors, she would give it a thought, but for now escape was first and foremost in her mind.

As quietly as she could, Milenda navigated through the familiar halls of her childhood home, cautiously peeking around corners and hiding behind doors every time she overheard voices coming her way. As soon as she was in the less sophisticated—and much less populated—corridors of the wing she had used to sneak in the palace a few times before, she sped up. Thankfully, whatever her mother— or her mother's spirit—had done seemed to have almost completely healed her knee, and she could weave through hallways and doorways much faster. The door that Mama Nyeusi had left unlocked so many times for her suddenly stood before her, and she allowed herself to breathe out the air she had been holding.

"Run, child. The guards are coming." She was not sure if it was her mother's voice or Yemanjá's, but she didn't linger to find out. She ran as fast as her legs could carry her, out of the palace and into the relative safety of the jungle. Milenda ran blindly among the trees, remotely aware that she was being guided by something or someone she couldn't hear or see toward the house where her husband and daughter were hidden. She wasn't sure where the energy to sprint that far had come from, but again she didn't care. Her heart was flying ahead of her into the arms of her loved ones.

A screeching sound made her pause for a moment or two. It was a familiar sound that warmed her inside and out. "Mjusi!" The *msuti* landed before her with a big thud of wings, breaking branches and shrubbery and raising a cloud of dust. Milenda crossed the space between them in a couple long steps and threw her arms around the flying lizard's thick neck. "I missed you, my friend. How did you know I was coming?"

Mjusi clicked his tongue and shook his head, greeting her. Milenda stood up, her hand still gently patting the *msuti*'s scaly head, and looked around her.

"Can you take me to where Jaali and Johari are?" She didn't have to ask twice. The small dragon swung around and walked away, stopping to turn and look at her as if saying, "Well, are you coming?" His long tail almost whipped Milenda's legs. "I'll follow."

They weren't far. In less than ten minutes, they had reached a small clearing, dominated by a small house and an old angel oak tree that reminded Milenda of an old woman with wild thick hair sticking out in all directions. She took off, outrunning Mjusi who clicked his tongue when she passed him.

As she crossed the threshold, Mukami lifted his *upanga* in a defensive move but relaxed shortly after he recognized her. "Exalted Jewel, please forgive me." He went to his knees and bowed his head deeply. "You honor us with your presence."

Milenda shook her head and waved her hand, motioning for him to stand up. "No, no, Mukami. I'm not exalted, and you're the one who honors me with your service." Her formal tone surprised her. She hadn't used it in so long, she could hardly recognize her own voice. "Please, stand up and take me to my husband."

Mukami did as he was asked, leading her to the other room where Naki cradled a sleeping Johari in her arms. Mama Nyeusi sat on the edge of a cot holding Jaali's hand. The old woman turned her brown eyes to Milenda, dropped his hand, and smiled sadly. "Child, you're here."

Jaali looked more like a ghost than her mother had, his pale skin even paler, practically transparent, and his beautiful blue eyes closed. The skin on his face and bare chest was covered in a sheen of sweat even though his whole body was shaken by tremors. "Mama, how is he?"

Mama Nyeusi shook her head. "I don't know, Milenda. He hasn't regained consciousness yet." The *iyalorixá*'s voice was strangely subdued, and that scared Milenda more than anything else. "I don't know what's wrong with him."

The princess dropped to her knees by the cot and held Jaali's hand. "I know what's wrong, Mama. I know what the Elders did to him." For the next hour or so, both women, young and old, leaned their heads together and spoke in whispers about the monster the Elders had placed inside of Jaali and made plans on how to save him. There were no easy answers for Mama Nyeusi had never heard of such a weapon, poison, or whatever you chose to call it. Finding an antidote without knowing what was killing him was an almost impossible mission.

Tears flowed abundantly over Milenda's cheeks, but she was unaware of them. In her grief, her senses were overwhelmed by love and despair and oblivious to physical sensations. A nudge on her back made her turn around to find Mjusi, his green body blurred by her tear-rimmed eyes. He nudged her again, as if trying to tell her something. "What, my friend? What can I do to save my love?" The dragon let out a soft screech and bumped Milenda's back again, more forcefully this time, propelling her against the bed. "What are you trying to tell me?"

Surprisingly, it was the *iyalorixá* who answered. "Reach out to your husband, child. Ask him what you can do to help him. Let him know how much you want him back—how much you need him back."

Milenda stared at the old woman and then at Mjusi, a

glint of hope in her heart… and fear. What if she reached out and Jaali wasn't there anymore? The one thing that made him human, his soul. She knew she had to give it a try. There were not many choices left.

Closing her eyes, she sent her thoughts to Jaali, searching for his conscience, any thread of brain activity that she could latch on to and communicate with. "Jaali," she called, her soul separating from her body in search of his. "*Wimbo wa moyo*, please say something."

At first there was nothing, but a black void, but as she probed further, a flutter of scrambled thoughts touched her—a tentative, confused feathery touch that she welcomed as water to her parched soul. These threads were not well-formed or even recognizable as complete thoughts, but they were signs of life and they filled her with hope.

"Jaali, I need you. Johari needs her father. I grew up with an absentee father, and I don't want our daughter to endure the same." Milenda was not sure what to say, but she kept on talking, engaging him in a one-sided conversation in hopes she'd awaken his senses. "I don't know how to help you, *wimbo wa moyo*. Please help me—tell me how I can help you come back to us."

It was strange to project herself to the same place where she was. She had never done that, always reaching to Jaali or Johari from afar, but now her husband was lying not even two feet from her. The blur that resulted from such close proximity made her dizzy, so she closed her eyes, trying to settle her stomach. Nothing happened; her head still filled with a thousand butterflies, flapping their wings against the back of her eyes, sending the world into a spin.

"Jaali, I love you more than anything in the world. I don't want to live without you—to be a queen without you. My people and yours need you too." Her mouth was working independently from her now, stuck in instinct mode. As long as she kept talking, maybe he would hang on to life. "Please, Jaali, say something. Tell me what to do."

Her eyes snapped open as a different kind of stirring touched her thoughts—firmer, more decisive and definitely more cohesive. Milenda held her breath, not wanting to hope in vain. There it was again, a more distinct poke, a tendril of thought trying to grab hold of her own. Then, the hold loosened into a familiar caress. Jaali was conscious of her presence, of her voice.

"Love you," the words reached her like a whisper from a distance, but clear as crystal. "Help me."

A sob climbed to Milenda's lips, and she held on to his hand again, ignoring the dizziness that such movement caused her. "I want to but don't know how. Tell me how." Bending down over the bed, she touched his lips with hers, and she almost fell to her knees again. Her mouth and his were connected by a flow of some electrifying current, a mighty river of energy and strength. Despite her surprise, she knew it was a life-giving breath. Was that what Yemanjá had gifted her a few weeks back? Had she given her some new and unknown power to heal those she loved?

"Child, you think too much." The *orisa*'s voice echoed in her already crowded mind, soft and caring. "These are abilities you've always had. I didn't give you anything but maybe directed you into discovering your own strengths. Heal your man, Jewel, and start the revolution."

* * *

Jaali spun in the whirlwind of his own thoughts and feelings, fully expecting to either crash or find out he was only dreaming. Milenda's voice still rang in his ears as a song he couldn't get enough of. Her sweet, familiar voice pulled him away from whatever hole he was in and led him closer to her loving arms. He wasn't in pain, not physical pain anyway. Being well-acquainted with it, Jaali knew that wasn't what held him down. Confusion and fear were the anchors around his ankles, keeping him from floating up and breaking the surface.

"Sweet Jaali, I need you," his wife's soft voice, pregnant with tears, caressed him and cajoled him into fighting harder against the weight pinning him down. "Please, *wimbo wa moyo*, we need you by our side."

Something inside him was struggling to get out. He could feel it, pushing against his chest bone, the pressure swelling with each word Milenda uttered. Would he eventually explode? His innards spilling out like the contents of a shattered gourd, leaving him empty and lifeless? *No, no, I can't let that happen.* Milenda was waiting for him, expecting him to stand by her side during the revolution, expecting him to be with her, raising their child together.

"You have to fight, Jaali. Fight as if the hordes of hell are after you." He was not sure Milenda had actually said it or he had told himself that in a moment of clarity.

Moments like that were coming more frequently now. Was that a good sign or the opposite? Was he recovering or simply dying? His mind wandered, lost for a moment or maybe days at a time—he couldn't tell. But then a ray of brightness, of pure unadulterated understanding would flash through his mind and he would see clearly; he could see the lines and nuances of what happened to him and what he must do to go back to reality. At moments like that, he swam with all the strength he had left, not losing sight of the light above, the sparkling of sunlight just out of the blurry ocean of confusion he was drowning in.

"Fight, Jaali. Fight for me, for Johari. Fight for yourself. Don't let the bad guys win again."

He took a deep breath, the first he was aware of, and held it in his lungs for a moment before exhaling all the pain, the confusion, the frustration. The muddy waters parted, and he felt himself propelled upward, straight into the warmth of the sun. Jaali gasped and coughed, the mire that had been inside him releasing with his breath. Slowly the world cleared—he saw the rough ceiling of the hideout, the worried and wrinkled face of Mama Nyeusi, the beautiful green eyes he loved so much.

But the voice he heard came from somewhere within, a familiar cocky voice he never thought he'd miss. "It's about time you snapped out of this," Eshu said. "We don't have a lifetime, you know. The revolution awaits."

CHAPTER THIRTEEN

Planting the Seeds

The seed was planted. Now it was a mere question of feeding and watching it grow. Milenda couldn't help feeling an exhilaration that bellied the paralyzing fear in her heart. Change was coming; the revolution was underway even if the Elders hadn't quite realized it yet. Yes, things could go very wrong, but her optimistic soul chose to believe a brighter future awaited her and Jaali's people. If she was to do one extraordinary thing in her life, let that be freeing her nation from tyranny and giving the Fjordens a chance to sleep without fear of being enslaved.

"Mukami, how many guards do you think you and Naki could turn to our side?" Jaali asked the burly man. Mukami was standing by the small table, Joahri propped on one of his hips, a contradictory sight—raw strength and tenderness.

"I know there are a lot of us who are not happy with what's been happening lately," Mukami's booming voice echoed in the hideout. "The Elders lost quite a few followers when they captured the Jewel and her *mjumbe* daughter."

The big man smiled sheepishly at Milenda. "You mean a lot to our people, my Jewel, and the guards are no exception."

"But there are those who are still loyal to the Elders, right?" Jaali was scribbling on a piece of paper. Milenda stole a glance at it but couldn't see what he was writing.

Naki answered this time. "Yes, a segment of our soldiers are faithful to the oppressors. But the majority will be easy to persuade onto our cause."

Johari laughed, her baby giggle popping in the air and making everyone smile. No one could resist her daughter's laughter. *Mjumbe* for sure. No regular child could have that power. It was wonderful and yet frightening. Johari was an easy target for the Elders and their minions, untold power in the body of a helpless toddler.

"I want you and Naki to contact those you believe will follow us and start planning a coup from inside the palace," Milenda said, brushing a hand over Johari's crazy white curls. "Make sure everyone understands the royal family is on our side and shouldn't be hurt." The last thing she wanted to do was lose the father she so recently had recovered or his new wife who was firmly on their side.

"Anything you ask, my Jewel," Mukami said, bowing his head. "First thing tomorrow morning we'll head to meet with some of our friends in a safe place. They'll do the rest."

"What about the *indents, msichana*? What can they do?" Jaali asked, his gauntness reflecting his recent encounter with the Elders' venom.

Milenda smiled and leaned against him, tethering on two of the chair's legs. "Your sister took over that job after what happened to you." Jaali looked at her, his eyes rounding in surprise. "With Mama Nyeusi's help, she's been visiting several pockets of *indents* who are freer to move around and spreading the message that a revolution is coming, alerting them they are needed to make the system explode from the inside out."

"How does she do that when she can't speak?" Naki asked.

"The day I got sick, Elin was with me, and she was far more efficient at reaching the crowd in silence than I was with speech," Jaali said, a smile curling his lips. "The *indents* know who she is, how she was treated and, more importantly, how she was rescued from the hands of her cruel owners. She's a hero to them, and they will follow her wherever she asks them to."

"She's talking to them as we speak." The unexpected voice startled all of them into defensive stances. Mukami took a few steps backward and sheltered the little girl with his massive arms, and Naki slid her *upanga* out of its sheath and propped it in front of her, ready to strike. Both Mjusi and Gavå hissed and whipped their tails in warning just as Jaali and Milenda jumped out of their seats and braced themselves for the attack that never came. "Relax, people. It's just me."

Milenda's muscles softened at the sight of her stepmother, Amare, standing by the front door. Her long, attractive body was wrapped in a blood-red *kanga* cloth, her hair hidden inside a tall yellow *gele*. "Amare, are you sure you weren't followed here?" Milenda worried that her brightly colored clothing stuck out like a sore thumb among the dark greens of the jungle.

Amare waved her hand in the air. "No one followed me," she said, her eyes rolling like those of a teenager. "I created a diversion. Everyone was too busy running to put out a fire in the far end of the palace."

Surprised and impressed, Milenda exclaimed, "You set fire to the Elders' wing?" The urge to laugh hysterically almost choked her.

"Not me. Mama Nyeusi." Amare brushed an imaginary speck of dust from her *kanga*. "That old woman is devious. I'm so glad she's on our side." Milenda felt a pang of guilt, knowing too well that her *iyalorixá* had been feeding Amare a contraceptive for the past three years so she wouldn't conceive before the Jewel's returned to power.

Jaali offered her a chair and a refreshing drink that she graciously accepted. "Why are you here?"

"My husband." She looked at Milenda. "Your father sent me with a message. He wants you to know that everything is ready in the palace."

"Will he retire to a safe place once the rioting begins?" Milenda wanted her father tucked safely away somewhere while all the violence and turmoil took place.

Amare chuckled. "Neither he or I will be going into hiding. We're a part of this, and we will stand by your side." She raised a hand to stop her stepdaughter from saying anything else. "You can't deny your father the privilege of doing what's right for his nation. He feels that he has let down Natale for too long. He's more than willing to risk his life to make things right."

Milenda's lips turned into a frown. "No, he must go somewhere safe. It's no good to have a revolution if our leader dies in the process." It had taken her so long to connect with her father, she was not about to lose him. "Amare, you're his wife. You can convince him. Threaten him with certain death if you have to."

The tall, elegant woman laughed, her head thrown backward. "You don't know your father very well, do you?" That was an understatement. "He is determined to make amends for his long apathy."

Defeated, Milenda plopped down on a nearby chair and grunted. "Why do I have to be surrounded by stubborn people? Why can't you be sensible for once?"

Jaali laid a hand on her shoulder, its warmth immediately soothing her. "King Melchior is within his rights to make this decision, *msichana*. He is the reigning monarch, after all." Milenda looked up at him, the expression on her face speaking volumes. "He is, my love. You have to give him this."

Milenda was not ready to give up. "What if he dies without an heir?" As soon as she said it, she knew how silly she sounded. Of course, he already had an heir, a reluctant princess maybe, but an heiress all the same. "Amara hasn't even conceived yet." The statement was a last, weak protest against what she was seeing as a potentially suicide mission.

"I have refused to take a surrogate—with your father's permission, of course." Amara's admission hit Milenda with the force of a *dibeke* ball. How did Mama Nyeusi not know that? "We don't need an heir since you and your daughter are in line for the crown, so there was no reason for me to be unfaithful to your father just to become pregnant. I knew fully well that Melchior was infertile."

"Then, why did you marry him?"

Jaali squeezed her shoulder, obviously not approving the rather personal question.

Amare lowered her eyes to her folded hands. "He's a kind man, who has lived most of his life alone, and he was generous with my family some years ago when we were in need of financial help. I was a child back then, but I still remember thinking 'this is the man I want to marry'."

Milenda had the sudden urge to jump off her chair and hug her stepmother. She had never imagined, not even in her wildest dreams, that this woman had married her father for love. "You love him?" It was a whisper laced with the saltiness of tears, emotion overwhelming her.

"Of course I do." Amare sounded outraged. "Why else would I have married him? To be a queen?" She laughed out loud. "Who would want to be queen of a nation ruled by men like the Elders?"

Shame ignited Milenda's *matangazos,* and the heat climbed up her neck into her face. She silently thanked Yemanjá for the dark skin that hid her embarrassment at assuming the worst about her stepmother.

"Well, it's settled then." Jaali broke up the awkward silence. "Now, it's our turn to set things in motion on this side of things. May the *orisa* protect and help us in our war against tyranny."

As if on cue, Johari let out a high-pitched wail immediately followed by Gavå's own. The toddler stretched and wiggled in Mukami's arms, her white hair aglow in the semi-crepuscule of the house. The baby dragon whipped her tail around as she skittered around the big man's legs under the watchful and tolerant eye of Mjusi.

Milenda got up and gently removed her daughter from the guard's arms. "It's all right, *min lilla kärlek.* Everything will be all right. The *orisa* will keep you safe."

The little girl stopped crying, opened her bright green eyes, and placed a chubby hand on her mother's cheek. "I know, Mama. I know."

The room went quiet. Johari's words were not those of a toddler, but before they could recover from their surprise, Johari reverted to her childish prattle, begging to be set down by her pet dragon. While she chased Gavå around the room, Milenda sought Jaali's hand for comfort. What kind of destiny was reserved to their daughter, the *mjumbe*? Would she ever be allowed a real and full childhood? Somehow Milenda doubted it.

* * *

Milenda's head was firmly tucked under his chin, and he could hear the soft purring of her breathing as she was transported to the world of dreams. Jaali couldn't sleep. His body was still alive from their lovemaking, and his mind was too wired to let him relax. Prominent in his thoughts was the knowledge that this was possibly the last peaceful night they would have together for a while—maybe forever.

As much as he tried to stay away from such thoughts, the truth was that they both knew there was a real chance of either of them dying in the process of liberating Natale from its oppressors.

"You keep forgetting the gods are on your side." Eshu, dressed as immodestly as he possibly could be short of being naked, stood by their bed, his well-muscled arms crossed and an annoyed expression on his face. "Why do mortals have to be so pessimistic all the time?"

"Because the gods enjoy messing with us, Eshu." It was an honest answer, delivered with just a smidgen of sarcasm. Jaali stole a glance at Milenda to check if they had wakened her, but the princess slept peacefully, her left arm draped over his chest. "If you divinities stopped messing with us, we wouldn't always assume the worst."

Eshu snorted and sat on the edge of the bed, smoothing out the wrinkles in the linen with his hand. "Oh, stop. What's life without a little sport?"

Jaali tried to stop the usual frustration mixed with anger he always felt around the *orisa*. "So that's all we are for you, a sport, a plaything?"

"Keep your pants on, pretty one—oh, wait! You are not wearing any pants." Amused by his own joke, the *orisa* burst out laughing. Jaali looked at Milenda, fully expecting her to wake up. "She can't hear me unless I decide otherwise."

There was no point in fighting the capricious demigod. Jaali sighed. "What do you want now, Eshu?"

"I'll be there." Eshu's voice had turned somber, which made Jaali nervous. The *orisa* was not known for being too serious. "And so will Yemanjá and even your biggest fan, Freya."

Jaali's eyes opened wide. "Freya? Why is she here?"

"She wants to free her children as much as you," Eshu said, his voice only slightly louder than a whisper. "She insisted on being part of the revolution."

Again, Jaali was reminded that Freya's superficial appearance was not necessarily her true nature. Inside the flirty, often inappropriate demigoddess there was someone who truly cared about her people. "Tell her I'm grateful for her help. We can use all the help we can get."

"As divinities we can't interfere too much, but that doesn't mean we won't give events a slight shove in the right direction when needed." Eshu wide, toothy smile illuminated his face, some of his usual playfulness and cockiness restored. "Yemanjá wants the Jewel to know her mother, Mirembe, will also be fighting by her side, even if she can't see her. Just like her name suggests, Mirembe is the bringer of peace—she birthed the Jewel, who in turn gave birth to the *mjumbe* who will connect the mortals with their gods."

His head suddenly pounding, Jaali brushed a hand over his eyes. "I'm not even going to ask what that means," he said. "It's hard enough to understand that my own daughter is some kind of divinity herself."

Eshu chuckled. "Not a divinity, a *mjumbe*—a messenger." Jaali sighed again. What did that mean anyway? "Someone with special gifts who will be the bridge between her people and the world of the gods, someone capable of carrying out certain tasks that normally only the *orisa* could."

Still not totally comprehending what his daughter's role in this whole revolution was, Jaali asked, "Then why can't the *orisa* do it themselves? Why do you need a go-between?"

"Do you know how many hours we work every day to watch over you silly mortals?" Eshu took a hand to his chest and assumed an air of outrage. "There are a lot of you and only a few of us. It will be nice to have someone who can help us watch over this part of Afrika. Maybe we will even be able to sleep once in a while."

It was Jaali's turn to snort. "I thought gods didn't sleep."

"We don't," Eshu replied, sliding off the bed and onto his feet. "That doesn't mean we wouldn't enjoy the occasional nap."

Without goodbyes, the demigod vanished. Jaali stared at the empty spot where Eshu once was, as if expecting the *orisa* to come back. Were gods all equally rude?

Milenda stirred in his arms, her bare legs rubbing against his. His body immediately responded to her touch, a reaction that still surprised him even after these many years. After living in hell for so long, incapable of feeling the physical excitement of love, the pleasure and thrill his wife could always conjure was a welcomed but still shocking revelation.

"Jaali?" Her sleepy voice added another layer of pleasure to that moment. "Who were you talking to?"

"Eshu came to visit, *msichana*. He came to tell us the heavens will be on our side." The earlier doubt about how beneficial to them the help from the *orisa* would be was gone. Eshu had sounded pretty thrilled about having a *mjumbe* around, which could only mean he would do anything to make sure nothing bad would befall Johari.

Milenda lifted her head just enough to look at him. "Really? Do you think he really meant it?"

Jaali answered with a kiss that ignited a fire inside of him. "They will do whatever they must to protect our little girl. I'm sure of it." Milenda's breath caressed his lips, and he swelled against her. "Can I show you how much I love you, *msichana*?"

The princess smiled against his mouth and ran her tongue between his lips. "I would be very upset if you didn't, *wimbo wa moyo*."

Tomorrow his nightmare could come to pass, but right then they still had each other. Husband and wife spent the rest of the night making sure neither would ever forget how much they meant to each other. That memory would help carry them and support them through the trying times ahead.

* * *

Mayhem reigned in the streets. The cacophony of voices in various states of alarm reached Milenda's ears before the scene came together in her mind. The wheel was set in motion, and there was no going back.

Milenda leaned against Jaali, her heart beating faster than seemed possible, and watched the scene from some distance away. Mama Nyeusi had shown up at the house with news that the palace was under lockdown. The guards had revolted like Mukami had promised, but it wasn't clear who was in control. The old woman had escaped unnoticed among the confusion to run to their hideout and watch Johari while they took care of what was quickly turning into a giant of a rebellion.

"Must we go in separate ways?" She knew the answer to that question, but she felt she must voice her reluctance to be apart from her husband at a moment like this. "I could go with you to the slave exchange and help you."

Jaali pulled her closer and kissed her forehead. "We have to do this, *msichana*. There's no other way. You're needed at the market to incite the populace, and I'm needed beside my brothers and sisters." He swept her wild curls away from her face. "We'll be fine. The gods are protecting us."

Knowing that didn't make her feel any better. There was no telling what the *orisa* would do. Milenda looked deep into Jaali's bottomless eyes and smiled sadly. "I know. I'm just scared, *wimbo wa moyo*. I love you and don't want to lose you."

"I don't want to lose you either, but this is the moment we've been preparing for for years." He drew her closer and wrapped his arms tightly around her. "Things are going to be all right. I know it." He bent down and kissed her, her anxieties turning into heat as their lips touched. "We'll be together again soon."

Milenda watched as he strode away from her, across the main street, and disappeared around the corner. The sting of tears burned in her eyes, but she couldn't allow the flood of emotions to delay her. It was bad enough she had to leave her baby daughter behind, closely guarded by her *iyalorixá* and a fierce baby dragon. Her friend Mjusi had faithfully chosen to follow her into battle—not that she was expecting to actually have to fight, not physically anyway. She was wanted by the Elders though, and her earlier escape had not endeared her to the powerful men—this time she was sure they would not let her live.

"Let's head to the marketplace, my friend." Mjusi growled beside her, exuding the funny puffs of smoke he released anytime he was upset and wanted to look threatening—which he did, now that he had grown to a considerable size, still smaller than his family in Isvärld but a lot bigger than he had been when they crossed the sea over three years ago. "I'm not sure if your smoke will scare the guards, but I thank you for trying anyway."

The flying lizard followed her on foot until they arrived at the edge of the market, just behind a row of stalls. Milenda could hear the murmur of many voices, words whispered in fear, and she hoped she was not going to be the cause for more pain. She signaled Mjusi to fly over to hide in the trees until he was needed and stepped into view of the crowd gathered there.

Startled by her sudden appearance, the men and women huddled in the center of the market straightened and prepared to flee. Milenda raised her hand and yelled, "Don't run. This is your Jewel, and I mean no harm to any of my people."

Their bodies visibly relaxed, shoulders dropping and breaths released. Milenda saw that they were carrying makeshift weapons: farming tools, large tree branches, even some household items. They were ready to fight, however humbly. Her heart went out to them. She only hoped she was worthy of their faith in her.

"I don't have much to offer you in terms of support, my friends, but what I have is yours," she said in a steady voice that belied her shaking insides. "The *orisa* are on our side, but I can't promise you there won't be casualties, so I won't blame you if you give up the fight." She raised her arms toward them. "But I do hope you don't."

A slight commotion distracted her and her people. A couple of guards advanced in their direction, their *upangas* drawn in from of them. It didn't take long to realize they were not friendly, and Milenda's stomach plummeted. Was she going to die even before the battle began?

Milenda closed her eyes for a moment, bracing herself for the attack, but instead she heard a loud, collective gasp. Confused, she opened her eyes to see Mjusi bearing down on the guards, the impressive span of his wings making him look a lot bigger than he was. After the initial paralysis of surprise, the guards regrouped and pointed their weapons at the flying creature. She was not sure what she had expected, but Mjusi took her by surprise. With a loud roar, the *msuti* opened his mighty jaws, revealing two rows of large, blade-sharp teeth, and breathed fire on the approaching soldiers. Mouth agape, Milenda watched as her best friend swooped down and nearly hit the small crowd with his wings, pursuing the frightened guards down the streets. When had he learned how to do that? Was that what the smoke puffs were all about?

"Friends," she addressed the people again, "the king and his consort are trapped in the royal compound. We need to gather more men and storm the palace to capture and disable the Elders. Once we do, we will have restored the power to our monarch, my father, who wants to change things for his nation, for you all."

With the roaring sound of Mjusi still hanging in the air, the people looked at her with a glint of hope in their eyes. "We will do whatever it takes to help you, my Jewel," a young man said. "We want to protect your daughter, the *mjumbe*. She's our future, the future of our children."

Inside of her, Milenda's heart danced with joy, immediately followed by fear. What was she leading these innocents into? She swallowed her apprehension and said, "Are you with me, then?"

The men and women looked at each other as if conferring, and then all eyes turned to her. The young man spoke again. "We are with you. Let's storm the palace and rescue the king."

And so it started.

CHAPTER FOURTEEN

Jaali was trying to keep positive, but every time he looked around to his ragtag army of slaves, a sense of impending doom descended upon him. How was he going to make a dent in the Elders' regime with a group of emaciated and starved into weakness people? They had no weapons other than their fists, and even though there were a few of them whose muscled bodies would definitely be up for the challenge, they were too small of a group to make any difference. The other slaves, those who dwelled in darkness, hidden away by their owners like his sister had been, could not leave the compounds where they were kept under lock and key, much less fight beside them.

"Still the complainer, I see." The eerily familiar voice made him turn so quickly, the bones in his neck creaked like an old door. Freya, in all her glory, was walking just behind him. "Why is that, pretty boy? Why can't you learn to be positive?"

Freya wore close to nothing, and a wave of heat climbed

up his neck to his face as his eyes met the demigoddess's voluptuous body. She hadn't lost her knack at making him blush and bring back those feelings of helplessness and shame he would sooner forget. The others, walking just behind him, seemed oblivious to her presence, so he whispered under his breath, "What are you doing here, Freya?"

"Well, that's a stupid question if I ever heard one—and I have. You humans are delightful in bed but not very smart, are you?" Jaali's blood boiled in his veins, but Eshu had told him she was coming to help, so he tried to keep calm. "I'm here to help free my children, of course." Her voice had gone from teasing and sarcastic to somber in seconds.

Jaali wanted to say he didn't need any help from her, but he knew too well he did. Only the hand of a god would succeed in making this pitiful army effective. "How are you going to do that?" Bitterness crept into his voice despite his best effort to keep civil. Freya always rubbed him the wrong way.

"Don't concern your pretty head with details." Freya threw a long blonde-white braid over her shoulder, her generous breasts almost popping out from the thin cover of her shirt. "I will do what I need to do, so that you and my other children walk free in the end."

"What about Eshu?" Jaali stole a quick glance at the men and women following him, and his heart swelled with pride and concern for those courageous individuals, who were so willing to risk their lives to save the rest. "He said he'd be helping too."

The demigoddess chuckled softly. "He will. Eshu likes to keep his secrets from the lesser gods." Jaali was confused by her words but didn't interrupt her. "He will strike when he decides it's the right time."

Jaali sighed and looked down so the others couldn't see him talking. "What do we do once we get to the first slave compound? We have no weapons, and our numbers are no match for the Elders' guards."

"A great number of the guards have defected. When you get there, those who are now on your side will turn against those loyal to the Elders and help you release the slaves." He knew about the defecting guards, but he had assumed there were only a handful of them. Freya made it sound as if there were enough to turn the odds to their side. "Once you have things under control, take their weapons and march to the next compound. Enlist, repeat."

"Some of the slaves will be too feeble to help," Jaali said, remembering his sister's state when they had rescued her. "What do we do with them?"

Freya moistened her lips before replying, "Give them a few weapons and leave them to guard the guards." She burst out laughing. "Funny, right? To guard the guards. Get it?"

Jaali was in no mood to laugh. Many of them would surely die in this battle against the Elders, and it didn't seem like the right time or place for jokes. "What do we do once we have collected all the *indents*?" Providing that they would make it through all the compounds in one piece.

Freya stopped suddenly, her usual expression of boredom clouding her beautiful face. "You storm the palace, of course.

Do you have any imagination at all? You tire me." And she vanished in her trademark cloud of mist.

Despite his general dislike for the shallow divinity, he was grateful she was there to help them and wished he was comfortable enough around her to thank her. There was no time to delay though. They were almost to the first plantation, a large coffee estate that used over one hundred *indents*, most of whom were locked in large, stuffy buildings after their chores were done. It was too early in the morning for them to have finished their work, but word about the palace lockdown had already run through Natale, a bush fire that spread faster than the wind. Jaali was certain the slavers had locked up the *indents* and had them heavily guarded while the owner's family hid somewhere safe.

Sure enough, the estate was empty, devoid of any sign of life other than animals. They hid behind the trees for a moment, studying the compound. Jaali could see a couple of guards stationed in front of the large door of one of the buildings. That's where the slaves would be. After a short discussion with the others, Jaali led the way toward the building. There was no point in hiding, so they all walked in plain sight until they were standing just a few feet away from the armed men.

"Leave now," one of them yelled. "You're not welcome here."

"Free our people," Jaali ordered, his voice surprisingly firm. "Let them go, and we won't hurt you."

The two guards burst out laughing. "You're a funny one," the other guard said. "What are you going to do?

Attack us with your skinny selves and impale yourselves onto our *upangas*? Don't see any other way out for you all."

The noise of a great door sliding open distracted them all for a few seconds. Five or six other guards stood under the doorway, right behind the first two. Jaali gulped. There were too many of them, and they all carried fierce-looking *upangas*.

"I see things differently," one of the newly arrived men said. "Brothers, lay down your weapons. We don't want to hurt you but will if we have to."

To everyone's surprise, the commands were not directed at the band of slaves but at the two other guards instead. The two men dropped their weapons and raised their hands over their heads, shock and confusion plastered on their faces.

The defectors took their weapons, and the one that seemed to be the leader turned to Jaali, handing him one of the *upangas*. "We'll follow you to the next compound." He gave orders for a couple of them to stay and guard the prisoners and then twisted around to yell inside the building. "Come on out. It's safe."

A long chain of Fjorden people walked from the shadow of their prison into the burning sun outside, blinking eyes shaded by their hands, some too weak to walk without the support of their fellow *indents*. Jaali's heart quivered at the sight. At least half of them were children, and the others all young adults—the life expectancy of a slave normally not extending further than the early twenties. He knew he would have died young had he not escaped slavery when he did. Some accepted weapons from the defecting guards and joined Jaali's small army, others sat under the protection of the trees to watch them march away.

"Protect them, please," Jaali told the two soldiers who were staying, pointing at those too weak to follow them. "They've suffered enough."

The next coffee plantation was only a few miles away, and the swelling in numbers seemed to have added fuel to their fire. They all quickened their step and straightened their backs, determination and hope in their every move. The band of outcasts still had a long way to go, but Jaali's hope glowed brighter. Maybe, just maybe, they could actually win this war.

* * *

"We'll have to go in from the back," Milenda said, crouching under the greenery in the shadow of the palace's walls. Whoever had taken over the palace, friend or foe, had done a good job at blocking all the entrances. Of course, they didn't know the palace as well as the Jewel did. Growing up without a mother and friendless, Milenda spent a lot of her days wandering the hallways and exploring all the nooks and crannies of the large royal home. She was aware of a couple forgotten entryways nobody else would likely know of.

Her small army had grown as they made their way to the palace grounds, but they were still few in number. What they lacked in size, they made up with enthusiasm and willingness to make this work. While most of them rested in the shade of the trees, Milenda and a couple of leaders met to discuss their strategy.

"We don't know what's going on inside the palace. Are you sure there are some defectors among the palace guards?" she asked Mukami, who was crouching beside her, his enormous height towering over her even when not standing. He nodded. "Well, then as soon as we are all rested and night falls, we will enter the palace through one of my childhood secret paths, just behind the building. It's a tight passage, but we can cross it one by one."

While they waited, they shared a meager meal, salvaged from the villagers' homes, and Milenda's thoughts wandered to Jaali and Johari. Her daughter was safe enough, she knew, but Jaali was right in the center of danger. Once in a while, she would reach out to him just to make sure he was still all right, and he seemed as anxious to check on her often. The last time she had reached to him, he had told her his band of escaped *indents* were not far from the palace. She hoped they would arrive before she had to storm the royal home, so they could be together. She also wondered about her father and stepmother inside the fortress. Were they safe or were their lives at risk? The Elders were still in the palace as far as she knew, a less-than-comforting thought considering they would be willing to do anything to stay in power—even killing the king.

Milenda reached out to her daughter and found her cuddled against Gavå on a rug. The sight of Johari's chubby cheeks and plump pink lips always brought a smile to Milenda's face and a song of love to her heart. There was the product of Jaali and her love, a perfect little creature made up of Natalian, Nyota, and Fjorden genes—a mixture so perfect, the gods had made her their messenger. That thought brought worry back to her mind. She broke the connection and shook her head, not wanting to bring negative feelings into an already stressful situation.

There were still a couple hours before sundown. A few of the men and women were napping, curled between trees and bushes and looked so at peace, Milenda decided to join them for a while. "Mjusi, wake me up in an hour," she asked, laying her head on the dragon's body. The *msuti* wrapped his long tail around her as if protecting her and growled softly. "Me too, my friend, me too."

A clamor of voices woke her up later. She jumped to her feet instinctively, her hands flying to Jaali's *buugeng*, its sharp edges cutting into her fingers. Warm blood dripped down her hands, but she didn't feel any pain. Running toward her was her man, the one person who made her forget every woe. "Jaali." She dropped the weapon and ran to meet him, her body slamming into his in a tight embrace. "*Wimbo wa moyo*, I'm so happy you're here."

Jaali held her hands still locked behind his neck and brought them together between them. "What's this?" Blood still dripped from the cuts in Milenda's hands. "How did you hurt yourself?"

"It's nothing, just a shallow cut," she replied, unwilling to switch her attention from her husband. "I held your *buugeng* wrong. It will heal soon enough."

He looked at her, blue eyes reflecting her face and the shades of the trees, searching. "Let me wrap them." He took her hands to his lips and kissed them. "I have some gauze in my bag. Mama Nyeusi wouldn't let me leave without it." He chuckled softly and opened his satchel to remove the promised thin cloth.

Milenda watched him as he wrapped her hands in two pieces of gauze, gently so not to hurt her, his fingers sending shivers up her spine and lighting up her *matangazos*. "If you don't stop that soon, they will be able to see me from the palace." She was only half joking, for her marks were glowing fiercely in the twilight of the evening, her usual reaction to his touch.

Jaali laughed and covered her shoulders with the piece of *kanga* cloth he had wrapped around his head to protect him from the blazing sun. Then he bent down to cover her lips with his, the heat of his touch burning through her like a wildfire. She moaned against his mouth and tucked her head in the crook of his neck. "We'll be all right, won't we?"

He didn't say anything, but the movement of his chin against the top of her head told her he was nodding. "I love you, *msichana*. Always."

The time had come. The sun had said its last goodbyes, and the moon, round and pale, shone its dim light on the earth. Stars studded the cloudless sky, millions of shiny eyes looking down on them, watching the mortals' struggles with interest. Blending with the night, the assorted group of slaves, guards, and villagers followed their future monarchs to the back of the palace where they hoped to find a way in. None could predict what awaited them once between the walls of the royal house, but they all knew the risk they were taking.

The hidden doorway was indeed still there, half buried in greenery that the soldiers had to cut through with their *upangas*. Like Milenda had told them, the passageway was narrow and low, allowing only one person at a time to enter it. Jaali wanted to go first, but Mukami refused to let him go and led the way himself, closely followed by the Fjorden and the princess right behind him. Mjusi had stayed outside, not able to fit through the tunnels, but he would fly to meet them inside once he was called. Milenda's bare heels sank into the soft, muddy soil as they made their trek through the tunnel. Her still glowing *matangazos* lit up the dark tunnel, allowing them all to see enough—not that there was much to see: beaten earth walls and low ceiling, wet dirt floor and the strong, earthy smell of moisture tickling their noses. Even Milenda had to bend down a little to fit in the small space. Mukami and Jaali were practically crawling through the tunnel, their hands braced against both sides of the walls.

A sense of panic grew inside her. Milenda was not sure whether it was because of the claustrophobic closure of the walls or if something in her was sensing danger ahead. The anxiety became so strong, it was hard for her to breathe. She reached out for Jaali and stopped him. "Something's wrong." Jaali turned his head to look at her. "I don't know what, but something is very wrong."

They couldn't go back now, so they continued their trek forward, Milenda's heart becoming heavier and heavier with each step they took. Was it danger or grief? Suddenly afraid something terrible had happened to Johari, she reached out to her daughter, but the little girl was happily playing with her pet dragon. What were her senses telling her? This was a new thing for her, unfamiliar and unsettling. She whispered a prayer to Yemanjá and went on, not sure of what they would find at the end of the tunnel.

Surprisingly, there was nothing at the end. As they emerged from the tunnel into the artificial light of the palace hallways, they found only empty space. No one was around. Mukami scouted ahead but couldn't find a soul wandering the corridors of that side of the palace. Strange indeed, this time of day when the Elders demanded their meals and the palace was normally boiling with activity. Maybe her father had been the one shutting down his household and had the Elders under custody. But that pressure in her chest, that weight that left her breathless, what was that all about then?

As they turned around another corner, a different reality began to emerge—lifeless bodies peppered the halls, their spilled blood still running fresh from *upanga*-inflicted wounds. Milenda recognized some as servants she had known when she still lived there, servants loyal to her and her father who would never lift a hand against them.

Suddenly she knew. "My father is in danger." The Elders were in control.

* * *

Milenda had taken off running, oblivious to the danger lurking at every corner. Jaali had tried to stop her, but the fear that her father may be in grave danger drove her faster into the bowels of the under-sieged palace. Jaali trailed her, the heavy footsteps behind him telling him the others had followed suit. The bloodied bodies piled up along the walls more frequently as they went deeper into the building.

"No, no!" Milenda stopped suddenly and dropped to her knees by the body of a young woman whose face was half hidden by a scarf. "No, not Asha. She's just a child."

Recognizing the name as that of his wife's young servant, Jaali dropped beside Milenda and held her by the shoulders as she bent down to the girl's body and cried. "Sorry, *msichana*, so sorry." What else could he say? They knew there would be deaths, but there was no preparing to watch someone you cared about lying in a puddle of her own blood.

The princess sobbed, her forehead touching the girl's chest and her hands caressing the youthful, thin amber arms. "She was such a good girl. So patient, so sweet. Why would they kill such a wonderful creature?"

Jaali, still holding her by the shoulders, tugged her away from the body. "I hate to do this, Milenda, but we're in danger if we stay here," he said. "We have to go, *msichana*. We have to keep going."

Still sobbing softly, Milenda allowed her husband to coax her to her feet. "The Elders will pay for this."

Jaali's body stiffened—he had never heard Milenda sound so angry.

Mukami had doubled back once he noticed he was not being followed anymore. "Jewel, we must go. The king's quarters are not far now."

The princess slumped against her husband and resumed her way along the hallway. The earlier spunk in her step, almost frantic, had been replaced by the weight of sorrow. Jaali could feel the heaviness of her heart as clearly as if it were his own. One more turn and they were standing in front of the royal quarters, a place that brought both good and bad memories to him. The first time he had been brought there, he had been close to death after the long, torturous trek through the desert. But it was here also that he reunited with his jewel and where they married in front of a crowd of thousands. In their lives, the good and the bad seemed so indelibly connected, it was sometimes hard to tell them apart.

Milenda stepped forth, but Mukami stopped her. "No, Jewel, I'll go first." He wrapped his big hand around the door handle and turned it. Cautiously he stepped inside and then waved them in. Only Milenda and Jaali entered the room. The others would stand guard outside while they spoke to Melchior and his wife.

As soon as they closed the door behind them, Jaali knew something was not right. The royal couple were sitting at the far end of the room, next to the big window, but they were not moving. Like two statues, they sat beside each other, silent and still. He reached out to stop Milenda, but she had already crossed the space toward her father. "No, *msichana*, something's not—"

Two large men appeared from the shadows and grabbed the princess. "Let me go," she yelled. "What's this? Father?"

Mukami drew his *upanga,* but it was obvious there was

nothing they could do—the Jewel was in the custody of the Elders' men, and any gesture of aggression toward them would put the princess's life at risk.

Belatedly, Jaali noticed the cloth wrapped over the king's mouth. Both he and Amare had been gagged. Jaali studied the situation and inched toward the couple, hoping to reach them safely and set them free. But before he could do it, the tall, dark figures of two Elders emerged from a small door behind the king. "So, we meet again." The voice that he had become used to hearing from inside his head was now in the room, echoing against the stone walls of the palace. "You're a slippery one, Jewel."

Milenda squirmed in the guards' arms. "Let my father go. Let us all go, and I will be merciful."

Rolls of laughter ricocheted from one wall to another. "We are so glad to know you'll be willing to forgive us for our treachery."

"I said merciful, not forgiving." Milenda's voice was a growl low in her throat. Jaali could see her *matangazos* shining an angry red. "You *will* be punished."

"Sweet, innocent Milenda," said one of the Elders, his face obscured by the hood, as he walked forward to stand next to her. "You were always a fiery little thing, weren't you? Like a wild cat—small but fierce. Unfortunately, you are not in a position to make threats. We have you and your father in custody, and we will soon have your daughter too."

Jaali couldn't decide what to do. Should he yell for help? Those outside the door would storm into the room only to meet with certain death. If he fought his way to his wife, he would be dead in no time. His life was of no value to the powerful men who had put him through hell in the desert. Once dead, he would be of no help to Milenda.

He watched in a mixture of fascination and horror as his wife kicked and bit her way from the guards that held her and threw herself at the closest Elder. The man, almost double her size, buckled under the surprise attack and fell to his knees. The guards didn't waste any time, and Milenda was once again in custody.

The Elder stood up, shook off his robes and adjusted the hood, which had miraculously stayed put. "You shouldn't have done that, little Nyota mutt."

"Don't you dare be disrespectful to the future queen." So focused on what was happening between his wife and the Elder, Jaali hadn't noticed the king had been freed from his gag and ties. He was now on his feet, still unable to move much as yet another man stood behind him, ready to pounce should he try anything. "Bow to your queen, traitor."

The Elder laughed and bowed mockingly to Milenda. "I beg your forgiveness, my Jewel. I meant no disrespect, Exalted One." The bite of sarcasm was not lost on anyone in the room.

Milenda, regal and beautiful, glowered at the hooded man. "You may mock me now, but you'll regret it in time." His wife spoke in a muted tone that could only mean she was about to do something crazy. Jaali's heart did a flip. Milenda's bravery didn't always translate into safety. He bit his tongue so he wouldn't yell out a word of caution, but he hoped she could hear him anyway. Her voice came loud and clear inside his head. *"I'm going to reach out to you, Jaali. Stay away from the Elders."*

Panic filled his heart as he heard her say, "I'm warning you. My magic is strong, and the gods are on my side. Bow down to me now." The Elders looked at each other and laughed while the guards tightened their hold on Milenda's arms. "Well, you can't say that I didn't warn you."

One minute she was standing firmly in front of her two captors, the next her body had gone flaccid and slipped through the men's hands to the floor. Jaali didn't have to look to know what had happened. The blow of warm air told him Milenda was now standing by his side, one hand wrapped around his upper arm. A gasp rolled through the room. Everyone was shocked at what they were seeing, their gazes bouncing between the two Milendas—the one lying on the floor and the other hanging on to her husband's arm.

"What's this sorcery?" one of the guards exclaimed, staring at the still body on the floor and then at his masters.

The Elders were paralyzed for a moment, but it didn't last long. The one furthest away from them pulled a dagger from a hidden pocket in his robes and threw it at the standing Milenda.

"No." The scream came from the king, who threw himself between the flying dagger and his daughter. In horror, Jaali watched as the monarch dropped to the floor in slow motion, a hand grasping the handle of the knife protruding from his chest and eyes wide in surprise.

Milenda returned to her body and quickly ran to throw

herself by her father's body at the same time as Amare. In the momentary confusion, Mukami had somehow gotten control over the guards, and Jaali held his *upanga* up to one of the Elders' throat. The second one wasted no time and departed the same way he had arrived. Jaali screamed for help then, and the small army outside the room poured in, taking in the situation and quickly getting into action. Relieved from his task of holding on to the Elder, Jaali dropped next to Milenda and Amare, who were both crying and trying to stop the life from spilling out of Melchior.

"Father, why did you do that? Please, don't die on me now. Please, Father." The inconsolable cries coming from both his wife and Amare stung. He felt helpless, not knowing what to do—what was there to do?

Jaali was just about to pry Milenda away from her father's lifeless body when she threw her arms up in the air and yelled, hiccupping between words and sobs, "Mother, please help. Mother, you have the gift of healing. You can help him."

A woman who looked a lot like Milenda suddenly appeared amid the small crowd. She wore a simple *kanga* dress and a drab *iqhiya*, tears rolling down her beautiful face. "Child, there is nothing I can do."

"You owe him this," Milenda yelled, looking up at the woman who could be no one else but her mother. "You didn't love him enough. You owe him."

The woman, a slight shimmering around her whole body, got down on her knees by them. "I do owe him, child, but there is nothing I can do. There is no life left in him. He's gone, *kidojo moja.*"

"No, no, it can't be," Milenda's cries pierced his ears and his heart. He did the only thing he could; he wrapped his arms around her and pulled her to him. His wife sobbed into his chest, the young woman she had been when they first met reappearing. "No, I can't lose another parent. Not him too."

Jaali brushed a hand over her head, pressing a kiss on her forehead. "I'm so sorry, *msichana*, so sorry."

The room was silent, the type that came with such grief there were no words that could express it. Only Amare's and Milenda's sobs pierced the silence. No one dared say a word. After a while, Milenda stopped crying and pushed away from Jaali's embrace to stand before the others. Tears streaked her face and a visceral red glow emitted from her *matangazos*.

Her words chilled Jaali to the bone. That didn't sound at all like the Milenda he knew, and it scared him. Had the Elders finally managed to turn her into one of them? Ruthless and full of hate?

"Get your weapons and hunt those bastards down. No mercy."

* * *

"Nobody touches them." The order came from somewhere within Milenda's being. She had never hated anyone or anything, but now her heart was filled with the toxic gases of anger and pure hatred. "They're mine. The Elders are mine."

The hooded man they had in custody was kneeling on the floor, his hands bound behind his back and his face still obstructed by the large hood. Jaali had helped Mukami tie him up, and now he stood beside him while she wiped her tears and took control of the room. Amare, her eyes reddened and bloated by the tears, stood beside her. A part of Milenda recognized how much her stepmother needed the comfort of a hug and a kind word, but the rest of her was intent on making sure the Elders would never hurt another living creature.

"We'll spread through the palace and secure all rooms. Mukami, I leave you in charge of that." Milenda looked at her husband without seeing. She needed to catch every single Elder and all their minions. "Jaali, you're with me."

Jaali moved to stand beside her and was quickly followed by Amare, her face still streaked by rivulets of pain. "I'm coming too."

Milenda snapped her head in the direction of her stepmother. "No, it's not safe. You stay with them here."

Amare shook her head emphatically. "You can't stop me. I have as much right to make sure justice is exacted as you do." A sob interrupted her speech. "They killed my husband."

For the first time since her father had died in her arms, Milenda turned to Jaali for advice—an exchange of glances, a silent conversation. Jaali nodded. Amare would be coming with them in search of the escaped Elders.

They couldn't be very far. The palace was still on lockdown, and they had left people stationed close to the exits to make sure no one escaped. "They must still be in the palace," Milenda said, trying to recall what she knew about the Elders' side of the royal mansion. They had quite an array of rooms available to them, many places and corners to hide. This was one side of the house she had never been particularly familiar with. The Elders had always scared her with their mysterious hoods that never revealed their faces, their deep voices, and obvious authority. Even as a child she had known to stay well away from them. Her skin and *matangazos* always prickled uncomfortably when in their presence, no doubt detecting the cruelty and darkness in their souls.

"The Elder escaped through a secret door in the closet," she said, more to herself than anyone else. "Which means they've used the secret passages that run within the walls of the palace." Common lore had it that they had been built so that the monarchs of Natale could sneak their lovers in without being noticed by the palace staff. Milenda had run through them many times, enjoying the fact that she couldn't be seen and pretending she was invisible. She led the small party to a door camouflaged by a wooden sculpture. Inside it was dark, and a musty scent saturated the air. Her *matangazos* had finally faded into their normal brown, matte color and didn't provide any light.

She turned around to return to the room and look for a source of light they'd be able to use, but her way was blocked by Yemanjá, resplendent in gold and looking every inch the demigoddess that she was. "Where are you going, child?"

"Mother, we need light." Her words were barely out of her mouth when the corridor filled with a bright glow. Milenda looked around and gasped. The narrow space meandered in curves and corners, broken here and there by door like the one they'd come through. "Thank you, Mother."

The *orisa* took a step closer to her protege and cupped her graceful hand on Milenda's cheek, releasing a wave of the tingling warmth the princess had gotten used to. "I'm sorry your father lost his life, *kidojo moja*. I wish there could have been a different outcome, but sometimes bad things must happen in order to open the doors to the good."

"Who else are you going to take away from me, Mother?" Milenda's voice sounded like that of a child even to her own ears. "I don't know how much more I can take."

Yemanjá sighed, her hand still on the princess's face. "The gods give you nothing more than what you can handle, child. Your father loved you, but now it's your turn to make things right. It's always been your destiny, your fate."

Milenda opened her mouth to retort, but the goddess had vanished, the heat of her hand lingering in her cheek, oddly comforting and soothing. "I loved my father," she whispered into the air where the *orisa* had stood just seconds before. But Yemanjá was right, crying wouldn't bring him back, and there was his kingdom to think about—a nation of people who had largely been taken advantage of by the Elders, the same men who had almost killed her husband and had now taken her father away.

"Let's go," she said, swallowing the tears that had emerged in her eyes. "They have to be here somewhere."

Jaali squeezed her arm gently as if to make sure she was all right. She managed a smile and a mind message telling him not to worry about her. The party of three resumed their trek through the passage, wiping cobwebs out of the way and checking every door along the way. For a while all they found inside those rooms was emptiness—an odd, incongruous silence and peace that belied whatever else was going on inside those walls. Milenda's mind slipped a few times toward her girl servant, Asha, dead in a pool of her own blood, and that of her father, eyes closed and body still with death. She shook her head and kept going, the memories fanning the flames of her anger.

Around another corner they came upon another door, half hidden by moss. Amare was the first one to see it. Milenda's stomach lurched—somehow she knew that was where they would find them. She tightened her hold on the *upanga* hilt and took a deep breath. "They're here."

Neither Jaali or Amare questioned her statement. They both held their weapons higher and more firmly, ready to face whatever was behind the door. Milenda didn't wait long. Her hand flew to the handle, and she threw the door open to reveal a group of Elders huddled in the center of the room, so immersed in conversation they missed the visitors.

A veil of red blurred Milenda's vision as anger boiled inside of her. Before she could even think, she propelled herself toward the group, *upanga* raised above her head, a wild cry escaping her lips. The hooded men turned around, but it was too late—the irate princess came down on them, slashing and slicing everything in her way. Blinded by hate,

Milenda was only vaguely aware of the blood spurting from the wounds she inflicted or the screams of pain and terror— she would take no prisoners today.

CHAPTER FIFTEEN

The Queen

"Stop, *msichana*, stop!" Jaali stopped her arm from striking another blow to the bloodied bodies of the Elders. One of them was crawling away, leaving a trail of blood in his wake. Milenda grunted and pulled her arm away, fighting him for control. "No, Milenda, it's enough. Enough."

Still growling, Milenda pulled one more time before dropping her arms along her body, her eyes clouded with anger and her face, neck, and arms speckled in reddish stains.

"Give me the *upanga*," Jaali demanded, taking hold of her hand. "They are not going anywhere." Of all six men, only two were still moving. Jaali could only hope, for Milenda's sake, that most were still alive. His wife had attacked them with the fury of the gods. He didn't blame her, but he knew she would, once the adrenaline stirred up by pain and hate faded. His jewel had never hurt a living creature before.

Reluctantly, Milenda let go of the weapon, her fingers

detaching from the hilt one at a time. Jaali threw the *upanga* into a corner of the room, away from the wounded men. From the corner of his eye, he saw Amare, her hand over her mouth stifling a scream of horror in the face of the carnage her stepdaughter had caused.

"*Msichana*, it's all right. It's over now," Jaali said in a soft voice he hoped was soothing. Once he was sure she was no longer in a state of rage, he drew her into his arms and hugged her tightly. "It's going to be all right." He wanted to take her away from the sight of the mangled men before she came to her senses, but he couldn't leave without making sure none of the Elders would escape. So he held her instead, her face buried in the fabric of his shirt, eerily quiet for someone who just seconds before had gone berserk.

"What can I do?" The shaken voice of Amare reached him from behind. He glanced over at the royal widow and a wave of overwhelming sympathy rolled through him. Jaali wished he could do or say something that would lighten her burden, her grief. She had just lost her husband, the one man she loved enough to give up on ever having children, and no comforting words would make it better.

"Can you take Milenda to her room? She needs to rest." So did Amare, but maybe it was better to keep her busy, not giving her time to think too much about what had just happened. "I will go talk to the others and tie up any loose ends, but she needs to sleep."

Amare nodded and gently freed Milenda from the arms of her husband and allowed the princess to lean on her. "I'll take her to her old room."

Jaali watched the two women walk away, before checking for vital signs among the felled Elders. After tying up the survivors so they couldn't escape, he left the room in search of the others.

"We have all the Elders.," he said as soon as he found a group of his own people. Pointing at a few members of their small army, he said, "You, collect the dead. Bring the bodies here. We'll have to take care of their burials later."

Followed by some of the slaves and more than a few of the defectors, Jaali checked each room that side of the building to make sure no loyalists were hiding. Once in a while they'd come by a man or woman cowered in a corner of a storage room, too scared for their lives to do them any harm. The loyalists were collected and gathered into the room that had served as the Elders' holding cells. Eventually Milenda would have to decide what to do with them, but for now that would do. The Elders themselves, the four who had survived, were being held in another room. Jaali stopped by once he had done a full sweep of the palace and spoken to some of his men newly arrived from town. He wanted to see the faces of the men who had tried to destroy him and his wife.

The reviled individuals were lying on the floor with various injuries, some more serious than others, a couple of their loyal servants tending to their wounds. Their heads were still covered by the hoods—no doubt with a little help from the attending servants. Jaali strode to one of them and, bending down, forcefully removed his hood, exposing his face, and then he moved on to do the same to another one.

When he was done with all four, Jaali studied them. He was not sure what he expected, but this was not it. There was nothing noteworthy about the Elders—their brown skins discolored by the lack of sunshine, their hair short and sparse. They were regular people who would have gone totally unnoticed in a crowd. And yet, they were anything but regular. These were the cruel and power-hungry men who had spread misery to the people of two nations. These old, unremarkable men had forced terrible memories on him and others. For a long time they had held the power over the people of Natale, but their reign of terror was over.

With a sigh, Jaali turned on his heels and left. He strode toward Milenda's room, beginning to feel the exhaustion that came in the aftermath of violence. He wanted to lay down next to his wife and cocoon her in his arms, reassuring himself she was still there.

Amare was dozing on an armchair by Milenda's bed. He told her to go next door and sleep. Mama Nyeusi would take care of her once she arrived with Johari. He had sent a scout to make sure things were safe and quiet in town before sending out for them. For now, all he cared about was his princess, his jewel, who had killed several men today. Jaali took off his shoes, dropped the *upanga* on top of the bedside table, and climbed on the bed. Milenda was fast asleep, her *kanga* dress still bloodstained but her skin clean. Amare must have washed it off. He stretched beside her, his arm draped over her waist, and fell immediately asleep.

A rustling beneath his arm woke Jaali. Milenda was awake, tears streaking her lovely amber face and shining in her green eyes. "*Msichana*, it's over." He was not sure why he felt he needed to tell her that. She smiled sadly and then brushed her hand across his cheek, a whimper escaping her lips. "Don't cry. It's going to be all right."

Milenda stared down at her dress, and her eyes opened wide. "There's blood all over my dress." She sat up on the bed, frantically wiping her dress with both hands. "I killed the Elders. Oh gods, I killed another human being."

Jaali wanted to say they were hardly human, but instead he sat up and slid an arm over her shoulders. "You were very brave, and your people thank you for it, *msichana*."

"What kind of queen will I be if I take justice into my own hands?" The sobs made her hiccup with every other word. "I'm a murderer."

"You are no such thing, Milenda. You're my life and the hope of a nation." Jaali drew her closer to him. "You must be strong now and move on. We both have to move on."

Milenda dropped her head on his shoulders, her *matangazos* glowing in a sad, almost purplish color. They stayed still, holding each other, their body heat a small but welcomed comfort.

A rumbling of voices grew in a crescendo outside the window. "What's that?" Milenda asked, distracted for a moment.

Jaali slid off the bed, pulling his wife gently after him, and they both walked to the window, their bare feet barely making a sound on the hard, cold stone. Jaali grabbed a throw from the bottom of the bed and threw it over Milenda's shoulders, whose body hadn't yet stopped trembling.

Outside the walls of the palace and stretched as far as the eye could see was a sea of people, many holding torches against the impending dark. Jaali opened the window, and the thunder of their voices subsided as they both stepped out into the balcony. Instead, a silence descended upon the crowd, the feeling of expectation hanging in the air as solid as the palace walls. Jaali pressed Milenda against his side.

"You have to say something," Jaali whispered, kissing her forehead.

Milenda hesitated, her shudders vibrating against him. "I can't. I'm not worthy of being their queen."

As if on cue, a great flapping sound made them all look up in time to see Mjusi hovering just feet above the balcony, his majestic wings stirring up the air around them. Milenda smiled and whispered his name, her best friend and companion, and they both made room for the *msuti* to land beside them. The flying lizard had grown quite a bit in the last year and could barely fit in the balcony now, so he perched on it instead, growling and clicking his tongue at the princess.

Milenda wrapped her hands around his thick, scaly neck and cried. "Sweet Mjusi. I'm so glad you're all right."

"He was a great help against the guards in town who were killing those who were against them," Jaali explained, repeating what his men had told him earlier and stretching his hand to pet the dragon. "He chased the guards with his fiery breath and scared them so much, they all surrendered eventually. Because of him, there weren't as many casualties in town as we thought there would be."

"Thank you, Mjusi," Milenda whispered. The creature seemed to impart some kind of energy with his human because Milenda finally stepped forward to the edge of the balcony and addressed the populace. "People of Natale. Your willingness to sacrifice yourselves and those you love to fight for a better future hasn't gone unnoticed." She took a deep breath and continued, her hand seeking Jaali's. "It's with a heavy heart that I tell you my father, King Melchior, has passed. He was killed trying to protect me." The collective gasp rose from the streets into their balcony. Jaali squeezed her hand in his, hoping to share some of his strength with her. "I am now your queen. Even though I'm not worthy of such a position of power and responsibility, I promise to do my best to always put you first in all my decisions."

There was a clamor from the people and, at first, Jaali thought it was a protest. Milenda glanced at him in panic. The voices rose until the words were clear. "Long live Queen Milenda," they roared. "We love our Jewel."

Milenda and Jaali kept silence for a while as the people of the nation yelled out their support and faith in the royal Jewel. Tears danced in Milenda's eyes, and Jaali could see the soft glow of her *matangazos* through the fabric of the blanket. He pulled her closer to him and whispered, "I love you, *msichana*. Everything will be all right."

The Jewel lifted her face to him and smiled, a sad, hesitant curling of her lips. "There is something I must do right now," she said.

Jaali let go of her and, letting the blanket slip all the way to the floor, the Jewel stepped closer to the ledge and waved a silent request for silence. The people immediately ceased talking and trained their eyes on their new queen.

"My first act as the Queen of Natale is to declare slavery illegal and free all *indents* in the country. We will not be a nation that enslaves other human beings for our own glorification and profit. From now on, we shall be known as a nation of free people, not one of slavers. Fjordens will no longer be slaves but our brothers and sisters. The Jewel of Natale so declares."

Another sound wave rippled through the crowd. "The Jewel has so declared," they said. "Let it be so."

* * *

Memories of that day so very long ago—or so it seemed—when she woke up to the knowledge that it was the day she would choose the Contenders to her hand filled her mind. She was but a girl then, barely eighteen years old and spoiled by a life of material wealth but also lonely and starved for the one thing she had never known. Love had been missing back then. Love was the one thing she had an abundance of now. This morning she was waking up to the day of her coronation, something as irksome as the choice of Contenders but necessary for the good of her nation. But unlike then, she was waking up entangled in her husband's legs and arms, their naked bodies curved to accommodate each other's. Jaali's breath caressed the back of her neck, his lips brushing against the curve of her spine, sending tiny bursts of pleasure through her body. Reluctant to move and acknowledge the dawn of the last day she was only a princess, Milenda kept still, enjoying the feeling of warmth and safety her husband's presence always provided.

"*Msichana*, are you awake?" His lips moved against her skin, and she sighed. Maybe if she pretended to still be asleep, Jaali would not move. "We have to get up. You have a coronation to attend."

Milenda groaned and, giving in to the pressing reality, turned around to face her husband. "You do realize you're being crowned alongside me, right?" She knew he was as reluctant to be the royal consort as she was of being queen. "You'll be known as His Royal Highness Prince Jaali of Natale." She giggled at his expression of dismay. "I will still love you the same though."

Jaali wiggled closer until she could feel his desire for her. She moaned softly. "Sorry, my Jewel, we don't have time for fun right now," Jaali said with a sideways smile. "We have to pretty you up for the ceremony."

With another groan, Milenda threw her hands around his neck and kissed him. "Why, do you think I'm not pretty enough for you?"

It was his turn to sigh. "No one in the world even comes close to your beauty, my wife." And he proved it with his lips.

As the second royal declaration, Milenda eradicated the tradition that required a royal bride to be groomed to an inch of her life. She remembered the day of the Choice as one of the most grueling days of scrubbing, makeup, fittings, braiding, and whatever else came with the ceremonial rite of coming of age. She was not going to have to go through the same thing the day of her coronation. Mama Nyeusi had a word or two to say about her decision to simplify the ceremony, but for once she had stood firm, winning Jaali's approval.

Before dressing up, Milenda wanted to visit their daughter who was staying next door in a room fitted for her small self. At first, they had asked Naki to take care of her and Gavå, but the tall guard was a soldier and had requested to be exempted from the post. Amare had stepped up and volunteered to take her place. Since the day they had both lost a father and a husband, Milenda's stepmother had taken to following Mama Nyeusi around, wanting to learn the ways of the *iyalorixá*. Milenda was glad she had found something to keep her busy and distracted from the fact she had just lost her loving husband, and even happier that she was going to be watching over her daughter.

Johari was sitting up on her bed, her white hair in total disarray, and her green eyes glittering like the stars they were. As soon as she saw her mother, she screeched and Gavå raised her head, curious to what had caused her human companion to make such sound. "Mama!"

Milenda held the little girl and kissed her nose. "*Min lilla kärlek*. You're looking well." The young dragon stood up and clumsily pounced a few times in their direction to come and rub her head on Milenda's legs. "You're looking good too, little *msuti*."

"They've been angels, the two of them," Amare said from where she sat by the wall. Milenda knew that was a lie—a gentle one, but still a fib. She knew Johari and the dragon were anything but angelic. Johari was a bundle of energy, and so was her pet dragon. "Should I bring her over when everything is ready for the ceremony?"

Milenda set her daughter down, and she was off faster than lightening, running around in circles behind Gavå, making it hard to tell who was chasing who.

"She will be part of the ceremony." This was another break from tradition. No children had ever been allowed to stand by their royal parents during coronation. But Milenda wouldn't hear of it. Johari would be right there with both Jaali and her, sharing the limelight. After all, their little girl was *mjumbe* and would one day carry heavy responsibilities on her shoulders, so she should share the coronation as well. "Bring her as soon as everything is ready. I don't want to tire her needlessly."

Amare stood up and chuckled at the twirling child. "She has a lot of energy, doesn't she?"

Milenda stepped closer to her stepmother and laid her hands on her shoulders. "Amare, I want you to know that you'll always be part of this family, and I hope you'll want to stick around for a long time."

"I'm not going anywhere soon," Amare said with a smile. "You can count on me. Mama Nyeusi has accepted me as her apprentice. Gods permitting, I will be Johari's *iyalorixá.*"

Milenda squealed in delight. "I'm so happy, Amare. Johari will need someone by her side. Thank you."

With a wave of the hand, Amare shooed her

stepdaughter away. "You've got to go, Milenda. Go get ready. I will take good care of your girl."

Despite her plans for a simpler ceremony, the day was still spent in a flurry of preparations. Mama Nyeusi fussed over her hair as in the past, combing and braiding until Milenda's head hurt. The royal clothiers came carrying a beautiful golden *kanga* that they wrapped carefully and artistically around her body, and the milliner propped a tall golden *gele* on her head. Jaali was being seen to next door, and she could hear him regularly grunt in frustration. She had given orders to let him pick his own clothes, but he was not used to being served hand and foot by an army of servants all too eager to do a great job.

Hours later they were finally deemed ready and escorted to the waiting room where they were to sit—or stand—in wait of the moment when they would appear on the same balcony where they'd been married in front of the whole city and quite a few foreign guests. The one big difference was that the people of Natale were now mixed with the *indents* who had chosen to stay in Afrika and build a new life. Milenda and Jaali peeked through the curtains and smiled.

"Isn't it amazing, *wimbo wa moyo*? To see your people standing side by side in harmony and freedom with mine?" Jaali pulled her closer to him. "I dreamed of this day— except I was not about to be crowned queen."

Jaali turned her around to face him. "You will be the best queen this land has seen in centuries," he said, serious. "You've already made the best changes in ages, even before you were crowned."

Milenda sighed. "But I never wanted to be queen. All I wanted was to be a regular girl, living in your small *hema*, happy and free."

Jaali pulled her to him, careful not to dislodge the *gele*. "You could never be regular, *msichana*. You're too exceptional, too special. You're the woman I love, and I wouldn't want you any other way."

"So, you're saying you wouldn't love me if I was just a girl." She raised an innocent face toward him.

Jaali laughed. "I would love you no matter what, my jewel."

The sound of drums erupted from outside, rising in a crescendo that matched the beating of their hearts. They both glanced beyond the curtains and the windows into the sea of people outside chanting their names.

"It's time, Your Highness." Amara and Mama Nyeusi were standing by the door, Johari on hand and Gavå scampering behind. "Your kingdom awaits."

Swallowing the knot in her throat, Milenda offered a hand to her daughter who ran to hold it. "Johari, be a sweetie and behave, all right?"

The little girl nodded, and Jaali held her other hand. Together, they opened the glass doors and walked onto the balcony. The hot sun greeted them, along with an abrupt silence from the crowd. Milenda felt as if an invisible hand had wrapped itself around her neck and squeezed. No escaping your own destiny, she figured. But then again, hadn't she? Hadn't Jaali? Both would have been dead had they not taken control over their own fate.

A blast of wind announced the arrival of Mjusi who landed by their side, thrust his head back, and blew fire up in the air with a mighty growl. The people gasped and then burst into applause. The *msuti* seemed pleased with himself as he settled beside them, little Gavå cuddling against him ready for a nap.

Milenda watched the waves of humans stretching before them and swallowed, clearing her throat for the speech she was expected to give before the coronation. To her right, half hidden around a corner, Mama Nyeusi stood with Amare, the royal crown in her hands, a dainty silvery ringlet she had commissioned for herself. Amare held Jaali's crown, a plain silver ring with no adornments of any kind. She turned her eyes back to the crowd and raised her hand to silence the low rumbling Mjusi's appearance had stirred.

"People of Natale. Friends. We're here today to promise you a new era—an age of fairness, tolerance, and justice. As your new monarch, I'm also here to declare my husband, Jaali Asker, Prince of Natale to rule next to me and bestow upon you all his generosity and loving heart." She paused to glance briefly at Jaali who seemed serene on the outside but was shaking inside as she met his thoughts with her own. She took another deep breath, turned, and signaled the *iyalorixá* to approach.

The old woman and Milenda's stepmother walked across the balcony, Mama Nyeusi's wide skirts swaying like the bell in the University tower as they came to stand before them.

"Do you, Milenda Nwosu, swear to serve Natale and all its people, to protect them and support them in good and bad times, with fairness and justice? And with love?" Mama Nyeusi's voice projected across the lawn like hers had, thanks to the tiny microphone hidden in her shirt. The importance of the occasion certainly justified the use of some of the olden and protected technology.

"I do. With all my heart." Milenda removed her *gele* and bowed her head to accept the crown her *iyalorixá* artfully placed on her head.

Amare stepped forward, and Milenda took Jaali's ring crown from her hands and turned to her husband who was still holding on to their daughter. "Jaali Asker, *wimbo wa moyo*, my love and companion, will you accept the heavy burden of ruling Natale along with me? Do you promise to be fair and just, and love my people with all your heart?"

Jaali fell to one knee and bowed his head. "I do, Jewel. I do." And then in a whisper for her ears only, he added, "I love you, *msichana*."

A great roar rose from the crowd when Milenda placed the simple ring on her husband's head and, as he stood up to face the people of Natale as their Prince Consort, a sudden communal whisper ran through the waves of Natalians and Fjorden. "Yemanjá!"

Both Milenda and Jaali turned around and gasped. Behind them, standing magnificent in her usual golden *kanga* dress and *gele* was the Mother. Standing to one side of her was Eshu, half naked as always, and on her other side, the terrifyingly beautiful Freya. In unison, people went down to their knees and bowed their heads. Voices rose in a chant praising the beloved demigoddess. Despite the somberness of the occasion, Milenda smiled—the Mother had become so much more than a distant and untouchable deity to her family. As strange as it sounded, she now thought of the three demigods as family.

"Rise, good people of Natale," the goddess commanded, lifting her hands to the skies. "We're here to bless the new queen of this nation and her beloved royal husband."

Slowly, the sea of people stood up, a colorful pattern of hills and valleys, spread as far as the eye could see. Yemanjá signaled Milenda and her family to move next to them and addressed the populace again. "The gods are with these rulers and their daughter, Johari, our *mjumbe*. You must be too. Natale is in good hands and under our protection."

Mama Nyeusi and Amare had respectfully stepped away and now watched from a distance, their heads bowed and eyes wet with tears. Next to them, Milenda thought she could see her mother, a transparent figure that wavered like a mirage.

"My northern sister, Freya, is here to wish the couple and her children, the Fjorden amongst you, all the happiness and prosperity." Yemanjá turned to her other side and looked at Eshu. "And my brother, Eshu, here also to accept and bless the new royals."

"*Heri kuwa miungu yote*," the crowd chanted. *Blessed be all the gods*.

Yemanjá stepped forward and, surprising the new queen, took Johari into her arms. For the first time ever, the demigoddess truly looked like a mother, cooing and allowing the child to play with the giant hoops in her ears. She played with the little girl for a few minutes, seemingly oblivious to everyone's eyes on her, waiting to see what she did next.

"This white-haired child will be your queen someday," she said finally, balancing Johari on her hip. "Like her mother, she's a half-Nyota, gifted by the gods and charged with being our messenger to you here in the world of the mortals. Treat her well and love her for she is now your Jewel, a new star in our constellation."

The crowd roared, but Milenda's chest tightened. It was a mixture of happiness and fear for her daughter, so small and already so burdened. Johari didn't seem to mind, giggling and pulling on the goddess's earrings like any other regular child would do. Milenda made a promise to herself right then: Johari might be far from a normal child, but she would do everything in her power to see to it that her daughter would lead a happy childhood, loved and surrounded by friends and family.

The young Jewel would not be lonely like her mother. Milenda would make sure of that.

* * *

Strange how some places stirred both good and bad memories. Jaali was standing in the very same spot where he had been taken by a terrible fever after his fall from Mjusi's back during the Trials. He had never expected to want to go back there, but there he was, sitting on the exact place he had that night, watching his beautiful queen wade naked in the bubbling water of the life-giving brook. Like then, the moon shone upon her amber skin and the darker spots on her shoulder and neck, creating the illusion of a full-body halo.

Desire stirred in him, and he had to fight the urge to get on his feet, undress, and run into the water to join her. He wanted to savor this moment. Gods only knew when they would have another private moment like this, now that they were in charge of running a kingdom in desperate need of so many changes. He leaned back on his elbows and watched Milenda move like an angel under the moonlight, splashing water over herself. Gods, he loved her so much it physically hurt sometimes. His *malaika* of a wife who had saved him from a lonely and loveless life. His jewel who had made him believe he was worthy.

She turned around, her small breasts bouncing and the kinks in her hair jettisoning water around her. He swelled at the sight. "Come join me, *wimbo wa moyo*. The water is lovely." *You are lovely*, he thought. *Lovelier than the moon and the stars.* "Please."

Slowly he peeled his clothes onto the sandy ground and walked to the edge of the water, wanting to run all the while. "You look like a goddess, *msichana*."

Milenda giggled and shushed him. "Don't jinx it. Next thing you know, Eshu or Freya will show up to ruin the moment." He held her outstretched hands, letting her pull him closer until their bodies touched. Milenda moaned quietly. "That night, three years ago, was the happiest moment of my life."

Jaali bent and kissed her *matangazos,* getting an instant reaction—the uneven brown spots firing up like stars in the night. "Even if I was lame and still delusional from the fever?"

She laughed and flattened her hands against his back, pulling him closer still. "I would have you in any shape or form—lame, broken, or whole. I love you."

He ran his hand along her side, brushing over her breast, sliding over her waist, and settling on her hip. He would never get enough of his wife. Every single time he touched her, the love and passion for her reignited, each time brighter and hotter. Jaali continued the track of his hand to her behind, cupping the perfect round mounds and pressing her to him. "When we make love, I always wonder how you see me. How you feel when I touch you, when I'm inside you," he whispered, his lips stroking her earlobe.

Milenda's hands mimicked his, curving around his bottom and pulling him tightly against her. "Maybe you can," she whispered with a sigh.

Before he could ask what she meant, he felt it—the unmistakable touch of her thoughts inside his mind, a caress of another kind. She was reaching out to him, linking their minds, so he could feel what she was feeling. He moaned, aroused by the intimacy of what she was doing. They couldn't be closer, melded together as they were, mind and body.

Every caress, every kiss he bestowed on her caused waves of sensual pleasure that overflowed into him, overwhelming his senses and making him tremble in delight. Their connection allowed him to feel exactly what she felt when he took her breast in his mouth and suckled it until her body was on fire and begging for more. When his fingers slipped inside her, he almost lost control.

"Is that how it always feels for you?" he asked, breathless and having trouble holding back the imminent explosion within him.

Milenda wrapped her hand around Jaali's arousal and whimpered, rolling her eyes and throwing her head back. "Yes. And is this how it always feels for you?"

Jaali couldn't answer. Slipping both his hands under her buttocks, he lifted her and walked out of the brook, her legs tied around his hips and her lips glued to his. As soon as he reached the sand on the edge of the water, Jaali dropped to the ground, stretching his legs in front of him and delighting at her heat against his. He needed to be inside her and so did she. It was a primal urge and yet so very complex in all its layers.

When they came together, he thought he had burst into a million supernovas that lit up the skies and announced his ecstasy to the world. The amplified climax had taken him where he had never been, and he knew the same applied to Milenda who now lay next to him, her head on his chest and leg draped over his. Breathless, they lingered still and quiet, afraid of dispelling the magic of their lovemaking.

"Why haven't we ever done that?" Milenda asked softly, her breath warm on his skin.

Jaali chuckled. "You're the one with the gift. I had no

idea that was even possible."

Milenda raised herself on an elbow and looked at him, her green eyes twinkling with mischief. "I didn't know either. The idea just came to me in the moment." Then she burst out laughing. "Yemanjá had told me there were other gifts I was yet to discover, but I never thought this would be one of them."

The stars and the moon looked down upon them, and Jaali remembered Milenda once telling him she thought those were the eyes of the gods watching them. He pointed at the sky above them. "We sure gave them something to talk about, didn't we?"

Milenda burst out laughing, and he laughed with her. Life was about to become very different for them. No more *hema* in the jungle, no more running naked along the great Miungu river or playing with their daughter under the shade of the Marula tree. They would be living in the palace surrounded by servants and government officials with little time to themselves, attending to matters of state as they attempted to fix their broken society. The large number of Fjordens who had chosen to return to their Northern homelands had to be taken across the waters, this time with the respect and comfort they deserved. There were so many duties and responsibilities hanging over their heads, they often wondered whether they would have time to be a family again.

"We always will, *wimbo wa moya*," Milenda said, their connection still intact. "We love each other and our daughter, we have people and gods watching over us, not to mention two *msutis*." Jaali kissed her forehead. "Look where we are. Here we lived through both the worst and the best time of our lives. We've always been able to turn the bad into something wonderful. We will always do that."

Jaali tugged at her, bringing her closer to him. "The day I met you in that downpour, I knew you were something special and someone who would turn my miserable life into something amazing. I may not have known at the time, but I loved you from the moment I looked into your beautiful green eyes. You're my angel, *msichana*."

"Let's never forget how we felt the first time we met," she said, a touch of sadness in her voice. "I don't ever want to forget it."

Jaali kissed her, the stars igniting inside of him again. "I will never forget the way you made me feel then or now, *msichana*. You are and always will be my one and only jewel—my rebel jewel."

He looked up at the sky again and could have sworn he saw the eyes of the gods winking at them. Jaali winked back and smiled, layering the *nguba* over him and Milenda, and drifting off to sleep, safe in the knowledge that tomorrow a brighter new day would dawn.

Thanks for reading *Rebel jewel*. I do hope you enjoyed the conclusion to The Jewel Chronicles. I appreciate your help in spreading the word, including telling a friend. Before you go, it would mean so much to me if you would take a few minutes to write a review and share how you feel about my story so others may find my work. Reviews really do help readers find books. Please leave a review on your favorite book site.

Don't miss out on New Releases, Exclusive Giveaways and much more!

JOIN MY NEWSLETTER:
BIT.LY/REISNEWSLETTER

LIKE ME ON FACEBOOK:
BIT.LY/FBNATALINA

JOIN MY READER GROUP:
BIT.LY/REBELSOUTCASTS

FOLLOW ME ON BOOKBUB:
WWW.BOOKBUB.COM/AUTHORS/NATALINA-REIS

Follow me on Twitter:
twitter.com/TichaB

Follow me on Pinterest:
www.pinterest.com/lisboeta62/

Follow me on Goodreads:
bit.ly/GRNatalina

Follow me on Instagram:
bit.ly/IGNatalina

Visit my website for my current booklist:
bit.ly/WebNatalina

I'd love to hear from you directly, too. Please feel free to email me at catarinadeobidos1@gmail.com or check out my website bit.ly/WebNatalina for updates.

ACKNOWLEDGEMENTS

As always, my first thank you goes to Africa, the continent that inspired me to write this series and the languages that inspired the Natalian and Fjorden dialects—two languages that found their inspiration in Swahili, Swedish, and Norwegian. Apologies for the liberties I took with all of them.

Thank you to all of those who cheered me on when I thought I couldn't finish Rebel Jewel. Amazing people like David Holloway, Lisa Meyer, and all the writers in the Writing Room.

A heartfelt thank you to my publisher who believed in me and the Jewel Chronicles when no one else would.

Hugs to my editors, Virginia Cantrell and Olivia Ventura, for fixing my mistakes and gently prodding me in the right direction. I don't know where I'd be without you.

Thank you to the lovely Kim Deister who made my day with her kind comments and all other my beta readers, Tina Moran, Kolleen Fraser, and Andrea Robinson for all their invaluable insights.

To all the amazing fantasy writers who have inspired me such as Sheri Tepper, Guy Gavriel Kay, David Eddings, Mary E. Pearson, Suzanne Collins, Holly Black, and Cassandra Clare to name only a few, thank you for creating worlds of wonder for this introvert dreamer to get lost in.

To my parents and sister, who never stopped believing in me, a million thanks and all my love.

Thanks go to my husband and my sons who have to put up with me and my writing madness. I love you, guys.

And finally to all the beautiful readers out there, thank you from the bottom of my heart. I hope my stories will help you escape from reality and give you as much pleasure as they have given me.

Never stop dreaming.

ABOUT THE PUBLISHER

Hot Tree Publishing opened its doors in 2015 with an aspiration to bring quality fiction to the world of readers. With the initial focus on romance and a wide spread of romance subgenres, Hot Tree Publishing have since opened their first imprint, Tangled Tree Publishing, specializing in crime, mystery, suspense, and thriller.

Firmly seated in the industry as a leading editing provider to independent authors and small publishing houses, Hot Tree Publishing is the sister company to Hot Tree Editing, founded in 2012. Having established in-house editing and promotions, plus having a well-respected market presence, Hot Tree Publishing endeavors to be a leader in bringing quality stories to the world of readers.

Interested in discovering more amazing reads brought to you by Hot Tree Publishing? Head over to the website for information:

WWW.HOTTREEPUBLISHING.COM